HELL FOR THE HOLIDAYS

For my brothers and incredible sisters-in-law.

HELL FOR THE HOLIDAYS
A Christopher Miller Holiday Thriller

Carroll & Graf Publishers
11 Cambridge Center
Cambridge, MA 02142

AVALON
publishing group incorporated

First Carroll & Graf edition 2007

Library of Congress Cataloging-in-Publication Data is available.

HC: ISBN-13: 978-0-7867-2060-6; ISBN-10: 0-7867-2060-3
PB: ISBN-13: 978-0-7867-2061-3; ISBN-10: 0-7867-2061-1

9 8 7 6 5 4 3 2 1

Interior design by Maria E. Torres

Printed in the United States of America

PROLOGUE

Christopher Miller's daughter still had the nightmares.

She wouldn't wake up screaming. She'd sleepwalk down the hall, drift into her parents' room, and stand frozen at the foot of their bed while her eyes went wide with terror.

In her dark dreams, the seven-year-old could still see the bad man dressed like Santa Claus. She could feel the gun muzzle pressed hard against her head and hear him laugh and tell her all the horrible things he was going to do to her.

She remembered the gun most of all.

Remembered how it felt—a cold circle tight against her skin.

"It's okay, Angel," her mother would wake and tell her. "The bad man can't hurt you anymore. The bad man is gone."

Christopher Miller would rouse himself and remember: *Yeah. The bad man's gone. All gone. Daddy shot him.* He'd rest his big hand on her tiny shoulder and lead his sleepwalking daughter back toward the door.

"How about an official FBI escort up the hall?" he'd whisper. "You're safe, Angel. Daddy's on duty. Nobody can hurt us ever again. I promise."

He'd say it even though he knew it wasn't true.
No place is safe.
Not this country.
Not this house.
Not this family.

1

"I'm not a gypsy, Mrs. Melo," Angela said politely. "I'm Princess Jasmine. From the movie!"

Halloween night.

Christopher Miller had escorted his daughter across the street to trick-or-treat at their neighbor's house—a brick split-level just like his, just like all the homes up and down the block in this part of Jersey City. Natalie, his wife, was handing out miniature Baby Ruths to all the trick-or-treaters back at their house, no doubt pretending not to recognize all the neighborhood kids in their costumes.

His daughter wasn't into scary outfits, no Vampira or crazy chainsaw killer. Angela wanted to be pretty Princess Jasmine from Disney's *Aladdin*.

Miller, of course, had suggested she be a Motown singer, like she'd been last year. He even promised he'd be her backup singer, her very own Pip. But his daughter wanted to be a princess, so Natalie found the Jasmine costume at the Party Store out near the mall. Deciding that the two-piece outfit was far too gauzy for a crisp autumn night, she'd insisted Angela drape her winter coat over it.

So now, as they stood on Mrs. Melo's stoop, Miller couldn't help but smile at his beautiful little girl. She had a very serious, very regal expression on her face but, truth be told, she looked kind of comical: an African-American harem girl in a sparkling tiara and puffy white cape, her North Face parka draped across her shoulders.

"Have you seen *Aladdin?*" Angela asked the grandmotherly Mrs. Melo.

"Sí, sí, sí! Princesa Jasmine!" Mrs. Melo was holding a plastic jack-o'-lantern filled with miniature candy bars. "Such royalty deserves a special treat." Looking as if she'd been waiting for this just this moment, Mrs. Melo headed off to her kitchen.

"That's very kind of you!" Miller called after her, switching off his toy flashlight. It was molded to look like Dracula. Or maybe that Count Chocula guy from the cereal box. He was fifty-one years old and he remembered when Halloween meant going door-to-door in this same Jersey City neighborhood with a pillowcase your mother let you have because it was ready for the ragbag. Now you could get official trick-or-treat sacks at McDonald's or in the morning paper—basically a showy plastic billboard for this year's holiday blockbuster, usually another computerized cartoon.

Mrs. Melo now returned to the front door.

"Here we go!"

She held a cellophane bag tied with orange and black curling ribbon, stuffed with what looked like two pounds of Halloween candy. In her other hand, she held a foil-wrapped loaf. Miller sniffed. Fresh-baked banana bread.

"Hey, you don't have to—"

"*Sí*, I do! Is Halloween. If I do not give to you the treat, you give to me the trick, no?"

"That's right," said Angela. "Those are the rules."

Two years back, close to Christmas, Christopher Miller had done a favor for Mrs. Melo, and the widowed Dominican grandmother had been baking him banana bread ever since. He'd also wound up in a little trouble with his bosses at the FBI for doing that favor.

Actually, a lot of trouble.

"Thank you."

"You're welcome, King Christopher."

"He's not a king," Angela corrected her.

"No? But he is the *princesa*'s father, *sí?*"

"He's supposed to be a football player."

For his costume, Miller had put on his old Notre Dame football jersey. Number 45. The one he wore in the USC game when he'd made that open-field run some people still remembered. Some people.

Thirty-some years later, it still fit. More or less. Miller was 6'2", weighed in at 205 pounds, most of it solid muscle except for a slight paunch—what his wife called his banana-bread basket.

"Happy Halloween, Mrs. Melo," he said. "I'll come over on Saturday and fix that gutter."

He had seen the dangling downspout when they first climbed her stoop to ring the doorbell. Most weekends, he hauled his ladder or toolbox or caulk gun across the street, fixed whatever needed fixing.

"Thank you, my friend. Bless you. Happy Halloween."

"You, too. C'mon, Angela."

"Thank you! Thank you!" Angela chanted as she tottered down the short set of steps.

Miller was pleased. His daughter never forgot to say thank you. She was a good kid. Too good to be knocked off track by one monster, even a bad guy dressed up like Santa. Of course, the therapy helped. Natalie was a forensic psychologist. Used to work at the field office in Newark with him. Natalie had friends. Good people. Smart professionals who knew how to listen to children talk about their nightmares.

"Where to next?" he asked when they reached the sidewalk.

Angela stopped. Stood for a second. Swung her head up and down the street. Studied the houses. Considered her options.

"The haunted house," she whispered.

"You sure?"

Angela nodded.

The haunted house wasn't really haunted—it just looked extremely spooky every Halloween, decorated that way by an imaginative Italian family that went all out for every holiday. Glowing nativity scene at Christmas. Twelve-foot-tall inflatable bunny for Easter. Tonight, cobwebs were draped across the living room windows, skeleton hands dangled out of the mailbox, and scary moans echoed out of a boom box hidden somewhere in the shrubs.

The total effect was pretty terrifying, especially if you were seven years old.

Especially if you'd spent time with a real monster and were prone to nightmares.

"You're sure, Angel?"

"You asked me where I wanted to go next."

"I know, but—"

"Besides, that house isn't really haunted. It's only make-believe."

"Why don't we work our way up the block?" Miller suggested. "Make it our last stop."

Princess Angela put her hands on her hips. "Daddy— *I am not afraid.*"

He reached for her hand.

"Okay. Come on. But let's just go see what the Fosters are giving out. Remember last year? They had those Snickers bars. The big ones."

Angela flung her bag down to the ground.

"I am *not* scared!"

To prove it, she bolted up the sidewalk.

"Angela!"

She raced toward the haunted house, arms flailing, legs whirling. Miller took off after her. He still ran three or four miles most mornings. Still had his legs, his wind.

But, man, his daughter could fly, puffy jacket and all. Plus, she had a head start.

"Angela!"

He'd never catch her.

"Angela! Stop running! You stop this instant!"

She wouldn't listen.

She dashed into the street. Didn't look both ways. Didn't slow down.

Didn't see the car.

2

.

Alexander Schmitz sat slumped on the couch at his father's house, thumbing the remote.

He surfed through the cable channels, hundreds of them, pausing only for a flash before moving on to the next half-second clip of garbage. Buffalo, New York, had lousy cable. Alexander blamed the government. The FCC. They were the ones who forced the television networks to run this pabulum. Garbage about gay men decorating normal men's apartments, pawing through their underwear drawers, making fun of their cowboy boots.

He was twenty-seven years old and had been living at his father's home in Eggertsville, a suburb of Buffalo, for two years—ever since he left the army. These days he worked part-time at Loblaws. The grocery store. Stocking shelves was okay. The cans didn't talk back. Didn't ride his ass all day long like those bastards in the army.

He didn't miss the army. It had been only a steppingstone. A vocational-technical school. Other than that, it basically sucked. It was no longer an armed militia of true patriots. They let anybody in.

His father worked at the nearby State University of New York at Buffalo. He was a janitor—a floor mopper when he should have been something better, maybe even a professor, but the government had their quotas and handed out all the good jobs to the worst people they could find. Lazy people. People of color. People who called in sick or went home early.

Alexander didn't know where his mother worked or if she even had a job. Probably not. Twenty-six years ago, when he was a baby, she'd left home and never come back.

He clicked the remote.

Nothing. Garbage.

The doorbell rang.

His father wasn't home. He had gone to a meeting. That meant Alexander was in charge of dishing out candy to any little beggars who appeared at their doorstep, even though he had a very low opinion of Halloween. Teaching children to beg. To expect something for nothing.

But Alexander was a good soldier. He would do as his father and Dr. John Tilley commanded. He would blend in. Play along. Wait.

The doorbell rang again.

He rose from the couch and found the bag of lollipops. Cheap ones with ropey loop handles instead of a single hard stick.

Now the doorbell rang in double time: da-dong, da-dong. Somebody was rocking the button, in and out, in and out.

"Hang on."

Da-dong, da-dong.

Jesus. Greedy little creeps.

"Trick or treat!" The voices on the other side of the door sounded male, older. Too old to be out trick-or-treating.

Alexander peered through the peephole.

College kids. Five of them. All boys. None in costumes. Just hooded sweatshirts. He couldn't make out their faces because the porch light wasn't illuminated. He had purposely left it off.

Even in the shadows, however, he could see that each boy held a lumpy pillowcase stuffed with candy.

"Come on, man!" hollered one of them. A frat-boy type. "We know you're in there!"

Another kid kept jabbing at the doorbell.

"Trick or treat, smell my feet, give us something good to eat!"

One of them was about to pound his fist on the front door when Alexander swung it open.

"May I help you?"

"Yeah. Trick or treat, dude!"

Alexander touched the double bar bridge of his aviator frames with his right forefinger, slid the sunglasses up his nose about a quarter inch. It was dark out, but he always wore protection. The tinted lenses hid his eyes as he sized up his visitors.

"Aren't you fellows a little old to be out tonight?" he asked.

"Damn, is that all you got?" Another of the youths, who up to this point had remained hidden behind his cohorts, stepped forward.

A black boy.

"Little baby lollipops? Damn, son. That's lame."

His friends laughed.

Ah. So this one was the class clown. SUNY Buffalo's very own Cedric "The Entertainer."

Smart-mouthed. Uppity. Just like all the coloreds on television.

Exercise restraint. Sublimate your natural instincts. You're a soldier. Use your training, your discipline.

Alexander pulled lollipops out of the plastic bag. One for each boy.

"Here you are," he said.

The black boy made a grab for the entire thing.

"This shit's so lame, you gotta give us all of them!"

Alexander smiled. Touched the bridge of his sunglasses again.

"Fine," he said pleasantly. "Enjoy."

"You blind or something?" the black boy asked sarcastically.

"No."

"That your costume?"

"Enjoy the rest of your evening, gentlemen."

"Who you supposed to be?" The black boy rocked his head from side to side, twinkling keys on an imaginary piano. "Stevie Wonder?"

His friends whooped a keg-party laugh and bounded off the porch, tossing the lollipop sack back and forth, littering the lawn with candy that shook free. Alexander heard the boys laughing about what a loser he was.

Then they were gone. Up the street. Out of range.

Too bad.

There were weapons in the house. Several, in fact. The army had taught him how to use them all. They'd even given him medals. Gold stars and colorful ribbons for being such a fast learner, such an excellent shot.

However, there would be no retaliatory strike against smart-mouthed college kids tonight.

Dr. Tilley was saving Alexander Schmitz for bigger things. More important things.

Much more important.

3

The car screeched to a stop.

Angela was okay. Standing on the far side of the street—two feet away from where the car had jumped the curb and taken down a few rubber garbage cans.

Miller ran to his daughter.

"You okay, Angel?"

"I'm sorry, Daddy."

"Are you hurt?"

"No. I'm sorry I ran like that. I didn't want you to think I was scared."

"Is anything bleeding, honey?"

"Daddy, I told you—I'm fine."

"Promise?"

Angela raised her right hand. "Promise."

He kissed her forehead. Caught his breath. Fussed with her Halloween costume.

"Don't ever do that again, sweetheart," he said sternly.

"I won't. I promise. Did all my candy get smooshed?"

Miller smiled. "We'll inspect it later."

"Okay. But you don't get to eat it all like last year when you inspected it."

"Christopher?"

It was Natalie. His wife. She was out on their front porch, cradling a witch's cauldron full of candy bars. She must have heard the car skidding off the road, heard it slam with a hollow thunk-crunch into the plastic trashcans.

"No one's hurt," Miller shouted over his shoulder. Then he looked again at the car straddling the curb.

Not yet anyway.

"I'm okay, Mommy," he heard Angela holler. "Don't worry."

"Stay right there. Don't move, baby."

"I won't, Mommy."

Okay. Natalie would take care of Angela. Miller would now take care of the driver who shouldn't've been driving so recklessly fast down a residential street. He stormed down the asphalt toward the car. He could hear its dead engine ticking. Hissing. Cooling off. Something Miller had no intention of doing—not just yet, anyway.

The car door swung open.

The driver stumbled out.

It was Fernando Acevedo. Miller knew him. He lived up the block. Everybody called him Freddy. Acevedo was only about twenty-eight but he and his wife already had three children: two girls and a boy. His youngest was Angela's age. His oldest, the boy, was almost ten.

Acevedo lurched into the middle of the street, twirled around, looked dazed. He was an agent with the U.S. Customs Bureau and had the pumped-up build of a middle linebacker who hits the weight room twice a day.

He was wearing his uniform. Had his gun belt strapped on. His legs, thick as tree trunks, wobbled under his knees.

"Freddy? You okay?"

Freddy looked over to the sidewalk. Saw Natalie hugging Angela.

He stumbled sideways. Miller braced him under the arm.

"Take it easy, Freddy."

"Did I—?"

"She's fine. What's going on?"

There were tears in Freddy's eyes.

"They took Carlos!"

4

It had been an excellent day.

Dr. John Tilley stood in the great room of his remote hunting lodge. Split logs roared in the fieldstone fireplace. Its stacked stone chimney rose forty feet to the rough-hewn beams and knotty pine paneling of the cathedral ceiling. The wall of massive, mortared stones served as a rugged backdrop for an impressive display of proud whitetail deer, elk, and antelope. Nine muscular necks and heads in all, their antlers curling up and jutting out like spiky hands.

Tilley filled his chest with the rich, smoke-and-pine–scented air.

Damn, he loved Wyoming.

He owned fifty thousand acres, including a grand slice of a mountain range. His so-called "hunting shack" was a thirty-thousand-square-foot log castle. Eight bedrooms. Seven full baths. Outbuildings for guests and the staff.

The Hate business had been very, very good to him.

Tilley glanced at the Rolex wrapped around his wrist. Still early.

The phone call would come. Soon.

He settled into an overstuffed leather chair. Felt it cradle his lanky frame. Beside the chair, there was a large end table fashioned out of bent tree limbs and lacquered cedar planks. Tilley's high-tech satellite phone looked incongruous resting on top of it.

Relax, he told himself.

The call will come when it comes. He rocked his wrist, rechecked the time.

Eight o'clock. October 31. Halloween night.

He kept his Rolex set to the Eastern Time zone. Where all the action was taking place.

Once the call came, he would give each cell its coded orders. He was the only one who knew everything, and he kept the carefully orchestrated sequence of events detailed on a laminated document similar to what a football coach might use to call plays on the sidelines. He studied it. Looked for flaws. Found none.

The phone chirruped.

Tilley raised it to his ear.

"Yes?"

"I got him!"

"Mr. Pettus?"

"Yes, sir?"

Tilley knew the connection was secure. He had invested a great deal of money in the technology to link his chain of scattered cells. He also believed in being cautious. "Tell me again. Properly."

"I, uh, you know. I got the package. In storage. Right here. Tied up."

Tilley noted the man's name on his laminated game plan.

Red Pettus. The kind of name that always seemed to accompany the muscle. But it didn't matter what they were called as long as they followed instructions.

"You want me to dispose of the, uh, package now?"

"No," Tilley replied. "You are to hold it in storage. Wait there."

"Wait?"

"You will be contacted. Hold your position."

"Yes, sir."

"Did anybody see you pick up the package?"

"Maybe. Maybe not. But afterward, I switched vehicles just like I was told."

"Good." Tilley was getting bored. Phase One was in motion. It was all he needed to know.

"Sir?"

"Yes?"

"Is it okay if I take the candy? I'm hungry."

"Candy?"

"The kid. He was out trick-or-treating. He has a bag full of—"

"This communication is terminated. Hold your position."

Tilley switched off the satellite phone with his thumb. Shook his head.

It had been an excellent day. He wouldn't allow abject stupidity to ruin it.

There were now calls to make.

And too many loose ends.

Including Mr. Red Pettus.

5

Christopher Miller drove his friend and neighbor, Freddy Acevedo, up two blocks and over one.

Freddy pointed toward a cluster of people huddled beneath a street lamp. Adults and children. The kids were all wearing their costumes.

"That's Carmelita! This is where they grabbed Carlos! Pull over!"

The headlights cut across the crowd. Miller read the panic reflected back in every eye. Two women were propping up Freddy's wife, Carmelita.

"*Ay, mi dios!*" she cried as they jumped out of the car.

"Carmelita!" Freddy ran to her.

"*Tomaron* Carlos! *Tomaron* Carlos!"

Miller understood enough Spanish to know what the young mother was screaming: "They took Carlos!"

"Did anybody see anything?" Miller asked the crowd. "Were any of you with Carlos when this happened?"

"A bad man took him!" screamed one of the children. He was dressed as Batman.

"How many bad men were there, son?"

But the boy couldn't answer. He started crying, turned away, and tried to hide behind his mother's legs.

"*Señor?*" said one of the men.

"Yes, sir?" said Miller. "Did you see something?"

"Yes. I saw it all."

Miller caught his first break: the man spoke English. He had seen something.

"I am Carlos's uncle." He held a flashlight in one hand, his daughter's tiny fist in the other. She was obviously another princess from some Disney movie. "We were all out trick-or-treating. I took Carlos because Freddy had to work tonight and Carmelita needed to be at home with the baby."

"Go on. What happened?"

"He had been driving slowly behind us up the street. Following us. Suddenly, he stopped. Rolled down his window. Yelled, 'Which one of you is Carlos Acevedo?' We were startled."

"Then what happened?"

"Carlos is a good boy. Very well mannered. So, he answered the man. Told him his name."

"And the guy grabbed him? He was alone?"

"*Sí.* He jumped out and took hold of Carlos by the front of his shirt. I tried to stop him, tried to pull Carlos free. But the man kicked at me. Sideways. He hit my ribs. Knocked me down. Kicked me between the legs. Next, he picked Carlos up by the belt and threw him into the back of the van and drove off."

"Can you describe this vehicle?"

"*Sí.* White. Like a van for a plumber or an electrician, you know?"

"Sure. Probably an Econoline."

"*Sí.*"

"Okay. This is helpful. Did you get a good look at the abductor?"

"No. He had on a mask. A Halloween mask."

"Okay, but was he short, tall, fat, skinny?"

"Skinny but with strong arms and an undershirt without sleeves. He looked like someone from a gymnasium. Muscular. And his arms were covered with blue tattoos, all the way up and down. No other colors. Just blue. Also—I could see he had a red beard. It stuck out below the mask."

"Excellent. Do you remember anything else? About the abductor? About the vehicle?"

"The van was old. It rattled when he drove away." The man pointed up the street. North. "He was driving very fast and the muffler was scraping against the ground. It made sparks."

Miller pulled out his cell. He speed-dialed the Jersey City PD. Gave dispatch the description.

"Male. Slender but muscular. Red hair. Beard. Or goatee. Wearing a mask when last seen. Has blue tattoos running up and down both arms. Driving a white van, possibly a Ford Econoline, with a loose muffler. Suspect possibly traveling north, maybe headed for the turnpike."

The Jersey City PD dispatcher thanked Miller, told him the description would go out in a revised Amber Alert. She also needed details about the missing child.

"Hang on," said Miller. He now handed the phone to Freddy. "They need a description of Carlos."

Freddy nodded. Switched into cop mode. Tried to forget he was a dad for the two minutes it would take to provide the necessary information.

"Ten years old. Four feet tall. Brown eyes. Black hair. Buzz cut. Kind of chubby, you know? Wearing a Halloween costume. What? A cop. He dressed up like a cop."

Just like his dad.

Miller knew these folks needed him. Needed somebody to be in charge. He'd stick with them. Quarterback this thing. Bring Carlos home. Kidnappings had long been his area of expertise at the Bureau. He'd phone his boss, Charlie Lofgren, later. Get retroactive approval. Lofgren was a good guy. Wouldn't bust his hump about getting involved, unlike that other boss—the one in D.C. who, two years earlier, had tried to ruin Miller's life because he helped out a neighbor.

"Mister?"

Miller felt a tug at his sleeve.

"Mister?"

It was the princess.

"What is it, honey?"

"The car was from Kentucky."

"Really?"

"Yes, sir. I read the license plate while my father was fighting with the man."

"Kentucky—"

"That's a state," the girl said. "I memorized all fifty."

"Is that so?" Miller needed his cell phone back from Freddy. He had to give the cops this new information.

"Mister?"

He felt another tug.

"Yes, honey?"

"K-R-S. Oh-five-oh. That was written on the license plate, too."

Miller was stunned.

"You sure?"

"Positive. I learned letters and numbers a long time ago. Letters and numbers are baby stuff."

6

Alexander Schmitz sat on the sofa sucking one of the lollipops he had retrieved from the bag before opening the front door to the trick-or-treating thugs.

It was red. Should've tasted like cherry but it didn't. It tasted like red corn syrup. He took it out of his mouth and rewrapped it in its crumpled cellophane sheath.

His cell phone rang. The special one his father had given him last week. He muted the television and flipped open the phone.

"This is Schmitz."

"Alexander Schmitz? This is Dr. John Tilley."

Instinctively, Alexander stood and assumed the stance he always took when in the presence of superior officers.

"Yes, sir."

"We need you. Immediately."

"Yes, sir."

"Can you be in New York City tomorrow?"

"Of course, sir."

"Good. Your driver will meet you in baggage claim."

"Yes, sir."

"And, Mr. Schmitz? Pack a bag. You won't be coming home for quite some time. Make the necessary arrangements. Do you have a lady friend?"

"No, sir."

"Good. Excellent. Quit your job."

"Yes, sir."

"Don't bring any equipment. Everything will be provided."

"Yes, sir."

"I'm told you're the best."

"God gave me a gift, sir. The army helped me hone it."

"I know. I've seen your file. Your father must be very proud of you."

"Yes, sir."

"Soon, he'll be even prouder."

Alexander didn't respond. He didn't want to appear presumptuous. Not to Dr. John Tilley.

"Mr. Schmitz?"

"Yes, sir?"

"We built this nation."

Alexander knew what to say in response: "We will take it back."

"Safe travels, son."

He heard Tilley hang up. He closed his phone.

Then Alexander Schmitz went into the bathroom to shave his head.

7

"You touch any of these Snickers bars, boy?"

Red Pettus sat on the edge of the king-sized bed in the hotel room and thumbed the controller for the Xbox rigged up to the television set. The Xbox cost extra, just like the ten-dollar can of honey-roasted cashews or the six-dollar Pepsi, but Pettus didn't care. This was all on somebody else's tab. He went where they told him. He waited like they said.

An alien exploded green guts all over the screen.

"Got him! Got him with my ray gun."

"That's a plasma pistol," muttered Carlos Acevedo.

Pettus turned around. Looked at the chubby little boy behind him on the big bed. He let the mayhem continue on the TV screen without him.

"Well, aren't you the bright little beaner?"

Carlos just looked at him and said nothing.

"You scared of me, boy?"

Carlos pushed back against the pillows.

"You better be scared, boy. Hell, I'd slit your throat with a rusty butter knife if my bosses tell me to. Wouldn't think nothin' of it, neither."

Pettus moved around the bed. Reached out and flicked the plastic badge pinned to the front of the kid's Halloween costume.

"A spic cop. Jesus. What the fuck do you people think this is? The United States of Mexico?"

Pettus moved toward the window where he could see the whole skyline of Manhattan. The Empire State Building was the tallest building in New York City—on account of what those other brown bastards had done to the World Trade Center. The top of the skyscraper was pumpkin-orange tonight. Lit up that way for Halloween. Pettus slid the thick vinyl curtains shut. Blocked out the view across the Hudson River.

"You touch any of this good shit?" He pawed his way through the pile of candy he had dumped out onto the work desk near the window. He found a long cellophane tube of miniature malted milk balls. Let the nine little balls tumble out into his mouth and crunched happily.

The room phone rang.

"You Catholic, boy?"

Carlos hesitated. The phone rang again. Carlos nodded his head.

"Them fag priests teach you any prayers?"

Carlos nodded again. The phone sounded a third time.

"Well, if I was you, I'd start sayin' 'em." Pettus sliced his finger across his throat.

The phone continued to ring.

He swiped chocolate off his lips with the back of his wrist. Snatched up the receiver.

"Yeah?"

He listened. Nodded.

"We will take it back," he said to his caller. "What about the kid? Okay. Okay. I got it. Hey—do me a favor. Order me a brew. Coors if they got it. Thanks, bro."

Pettus set the phone's receiver back into its base. Finding the cord, he jerked it hard. He heard the line rip out of the wall behind the headboard. The room had only the one phone; Pettus had made sure when he checked in yesterday.

He quickly glanced at the windows. Closed the curtains tight. They were.

He pulled a roll of packing tape out of the small gym bag he'd brought with him.

"Turn around, boy."

The fat kid moved too slowly.

"Turn the fuck around!"

Pettus bound up Carlos's hands and feet.

"Just like ropin' a calf. A dumb animal, by the way, that smells a whole lot better than you do."

He wrapped tape around the boy's head. Sealed up his mouth.

Then he went to the door, hung the DO NOT DISTURB sign over the outside knob, and pulled the door shut behind him.

Carlos heard the lock click.

On the TV screen, the Xbox version of *Halo II* still raged. The Master Chief, the robotic warrior from the future, kept slaying aliens with his rapid-fire plasma rifle.

He killed them all.

8

Miller made sure Freddy and Carmelita Acevedo got home safely.

But he had a secondary motive in escorting them. As a precaution, he had taken Freddy's sidearm. A Sig Sauer P-226, the semiautomatic handgun issued by the Department of Homeland Security to uniformed Customs agents. Miller knew what he'd be tempted to do with his service weapon if somebody snatched his daughter off the street.

"Let me hold it for you," Miller had said. "Just for tonight."

"I need my weapon!"

"No, you don't. Not tonight. Let the rest of us take care of finding Carlos. You take care of Carmelita and the baby."

Freddy had reluctantly agreed to do as his friend instructed.

So now Miller was cruising the side streets of Jersey City with his neighbor's sidearm riding shotgun in the glove compartment.

Might be a good thing.

He had gone home to pick up his own vehicle but hadn't taken the time to run inside and slip on his Glock

M22, the same gun he'd been carrying since he went through the FBI Academy at Quantico. He hadn't gone inside because he didn't want to scare Angela.

"Daddy's going out to help find a boy that was kidnapped by a bad man just like you were, honey. Don't eat all the Halloween candy before I get back."

Wouldn't have been a wise move.

Instead, he had telephoned Natalie, told her what was going down. She understood—her neighbors needed Saint Christopher out on the streets tonight, and she was cool with it.

He turned the corner at Washington and Grand for the umpteenth time. He needed a plan but didn't have one. Instead, he cruised the streets, hoping he might bump into a van from Kentucky.

Miller had gone to school in this neighborhood. Saint Peter's Prep. The Jesuit high school had been "educating men of conscience, competence, and compassion" since 1872. The tough teachers didn't care whether you were black, white, brown, or green, whether you lived two blocks from the Holland Tunnel or had a suburban backyard that bordered the Watchung Mountains. They only cared whether you did your homework, scored well on your SATs, and treated other people with respect.

Miller did all three.

He flicked on the radio. 1010 WINS. The all-news station out of New York City.

"Repeating this hour's top story: An Amber Alert has been issued for Carlos Acevedo. Age ten. He was last seen—"

Miller snapped the radio off. He'd already heard the alert ten times. Still didn't get him any closer to his goal.

He circled the block.

He hated this. By now, he should have been racing up the field, following a lead. He wanted to bring Carlos Acevedo home. The police scanner in his car squawked with pointless chatter. The logistics of deployment. Nothing meatier.

"A body in motion remains in motion," he mumbled, his high school physics class coming back to him. "A body at rest remains at rest."

Miller was a man of action. A crazy fullback thrashing with reckless abandon through any obstacles in his path, hoping to find daylight, relentlessly chasing after criminals, usually kidnappers—a specialization that started back in 1984 on what everybody else still called "The St. Christopher Case."

It had earned him a very special medal.

Seems this woman showed up at a private school, identifying herself as an employee of Kathryn G. Johnson's mother. She said she needed to take the young girl home immediately because both parents had been unexpectedly called out of town. Death in the family. Fortunately, there had been no death. Unfortunately, the woman wasn't employed by Kathryn's mother. She was a member of a gang hoping to extort a million dollars from Kathryn's father.

Mr. Johnson paid the ransom, met all the kidnappers' demands. The gang, however, did not play fair. They skipped town without returning his daughter.

Miller was the one who figured out Kathryn was being held in a tobacco barn near an overgrown hay field in rural West Virginia. Intense ball carrier that he was, he was also the one who had stormed in, grabbed her, and carried Kathryn out before anyone could hurt her.

He'd taken two slugs in his left hamstring on that little touchdown run. Fortunately, his Kevlar vest took the other bullets that smacked into his back as he raced for the tree line.

The story of Miller's "Run to Daylight" was splashed all over the media. He had played football for the University of Notre Dame, so it was a great angle. But he didn't get too worked up by all the publicity. He was, however, seriously moved when young Kathryn G. Johnson presented him with a medal, a very simple stainless steel medallion.

"Saint Christopher Protect Us," it read. The nickname stuck.

Miller still slipped the chain over his head every morning. Still tried to live up to its inscription.

Saint Christopher Protect Us.

"Okay," he said out loud, "who'd want to kidnap Carlos Acevedo?"

He had to focus on this being a kidnapping. That way he might be able to help. That way he wouldn't have to think about what else it might be.

"You think Freddy is still betting on the Jets?" he asked himself.

That might make sense. Miller knew his neighbor had an unhealthy weakness for the Big Green Machine. A blind devotion the football team did not often return with things like touchdowns or victories.

Might make sense.

Maybe Freddy had run up some heavy betting debts this fall. Maybe his bookie was sending him a message: pay up or we'll hurt your family.

It was definitely a possibility.

Miller turned left. He'd go talk to Freddy. Why hadn't he thought to ask the man if he had any enemies before hopping into his car and cruising the streets hoping for a lucky break?

An urgent voice crackled out of the scanner.

"All available units. White van with Kentucky license plate number K-R-S oh-five-oh has been located in a parking lot at the Newport Centre Mall. Officers at the scene report finding a Halloween mask in the front seat."

Miller pressed down hard on the accelerator.

He'd talk to Freddy later.

This was better.

Plastic Halloween masks made you sweat. Sweat was loaded with DNA. Masks also usually had some sort of elastic strap around the back. The thin string was typically anchored into the sides with small metal clasps the size of staples. The clasps always seemed to rip out hair when the wearer put on or took off the mask. More forensic evidence for the crime lab to examine.

There might be other information in the car. Maybe a map or a rental agreement. Maybe a stub from a parking garage.

Miller was now a body in motion and would not rest until Carlos was safe at home with his mother and father.

No. After that, he still wouldn't rest.

He'd go hunt down the masked bastard who did this.

9

Red Pettus was working on his third Coors.

"It don't make no sense," he said to his new friend. "I grab this spic kid just so he can spend Halloween in a fancy hotel room at the Hyatt Regency? Shit, man. No fucking sense at all."

The man across from him shrugged.

"Yeah, yeah. Well, leastways I'm going to get me another goddamn beer." He raised his hand to signal the waitress. "Damn nigger acts like she don't see me."

"Careful," his companion advised. "That guy at the bar?" He gave a slight sideways tilt of his head.

Pettus turned around.

"The one with the buzz cut."

Pettus saw the guy. Built. Razor burn up to the tips of his ears. Sipping what looked like orange juice.

"Probably off duty."

"Yeah." Pettus swiveled around in his seat.

The two men were seated in plush white chairs in the hotel's Vu Lounge. Through the floor-to-ceiling windows in front of them, they looked out on New York Harbor.

"Statue of Liberty's got a flat ass," Pettus cracked, shaking a fistful of mixed nuts, admiring the view.

"Guess people in Jersey get used to looking up her skirt, checking it out."

"I guess."

"You want another beer?"

"No thanks."

Pettus smoothed out his jeans. Tugged at the armholes of his sleeveless T-shirt. Everyone else in the bar was wearing a business suit or a polo shirt and khakis. They were mostly men. A few women—but they dressed like men. Businesspeople. Rich assholes and cold bitches.

"So, how come we never met up before?" Pettus asked.

Again, the man shrugged. "Different cells. Works better that way."

"I reckon. What about my van? Do I get it back?"

"You'll be reimbursed."

"Shit, I better be."

The cocktail waitress came over to their chairs.

"Can I get you gentlemen another round?"

She was African-American.

"Where's that other waitress?" Pettus asked. "The blonde?"

"Her shift ended."

"Shit," said Pettus.

His contact shot him a glance.

"Would you like another round, gentlemen?" the waitress asked patiently.

"He'll have another Coors," said the man across from Pettus. "I'm good."

"I'll be right back."

Pettus watched her walk away. Made a face. Then he drained the last drops out of the bottle he had going. The other man checked his watch.

"You gotta be somewhere else?" Pettus asked.

"Yes. In a little while."

"Another mission?"

"Yes."

"Am I supposed to go with you?"

"No. You are to remain here until midnight."

"Here? In the bar?"

The man nodded. "Therefore, I suggest you treat the waitress a little more politely."

"Alright, alright. Shit." He dug around in the nut bowl. "Too many damn walnuts. Last night I come down here and they had these shiny-looking little crackers in the bowl. I asked the waitress what the fuck they were and she said they was Chinese rice crackers and wasabi peas or some shit. I told her to haul that Chink shit away and bring me some goddamn peanuts."

He looked up to see if his new friend was enjoying his tale.

The chair was empty.

Pettus twisted around. Saw the guy standing near the bar. If he needed a drink, why didn't he just tell the waitress to bring him one?

Pettus waved.

The guy ignored him. Stared up at the plasma-screen TV hanging behind the bar.

"His name is Carlos Acevedo," Pettus heard the television say. *"He was abducted earlier this evening while trick-or-treating near his home in Jersey City. Police are*

*looking for a white man driving a van with Kentucky
license plate number K-R-S oh-five-oh—"*

The guy who'd been sitting with him was now
pointing at the TV screen.

"Hey!" Pettus heard him say. "That's him!"

He was looking straight at Pettus.

"That guy over there! I saw him with a young boy!
Saw them upstairs!"

10

There were at least a dozen sets of police lights swirling around the van when Miller arrived at the Newport Centre Mall.

He flashed his ID to the first Jersey City cop who tried to block his access to the vehicle.

"Special Agent Miller. FBI."

The cop nodded. Let him pass.

The van was parked near a lamppost at the edge of the lot. The parking slots around it were vacant—except, of course, for all the police cars and ambulances and fire department vehicles. Inside it, he could see the forensics team. Picking things up with forceps. Placing them carefully into evidence bags.

"What've we got?" Miller called out to nobody in particular. "I'm FBI. What've we got?"

"Yo! Saint Chris!"

It was Lieutenant Tony Cimino. A buddy on the Jersey City force.

"Tony—the kid. The one who got snatched. He's a neighbor."

Cimino nodded. Understood.

"Your bosses know you're helping us out this time, Chris?"

"Yeah. I called Lofgren. Told him what was going down. He's cool with it."

Cimino gestured toward the van. "So far, we know our guy likes peanuts. The crime scene team found crushed shells all over the floor underneath the steering wheel. Looks like he worked his way through half a pound while he waited to nab the kid. We found a piece of the boy's Halloween costume in the backseat. Cute little cop hat. Had a plastic star up front and everything."

"Damn."

"Yeah. Anyway, we figure our guy dumped the van here because he knew he'd been spotted when he made the grab."

"Then what?"

Cimino shrugged. "Not certain. Maybe an accomplice with another vehicle, waiting for him."

"We need more. Fast."

"We're all over it, Chris. Got guys checking for reports of stolen vehicles, working the rental companies."

"What about the mask?"

"It's been swabbed for DNA. The lab's got it now."

"You find any hair?"

"Red. Just like the beard that the witness said she might've seen poking out under the guy's chin."

"He."

"Come again?"

"The witness was a male."

Cimino nodded. "Another neighbor?"

"The boy's uncle. But, hear me. Switching vehicles? That takes planning. You think we're dealing with a pro?"

"The thought definitely crossed my mind," said Cimino. "This Acevedo. Does he have any enemies? Could he owe anybody enough so they might want to hold his kid as collateral?"

"He's a cop. U.S. Customs."

"Okay. Fine. He's on the job. But, like I said—"

"I'll talk to him."

"Good. Not for nothing, Chris, but that's where we need you the most. Acevedo knows you. Let's hope he trusts you. Find out if he's got any dirty little secrets he's hiding from his wife and the rest of the world."

Miller took one last look inside the van. When he got to Freddy's house, he'd ask him about his fondness for the New York Jets, a team that played all their home games in New Jersey but didn't have the courage to change their name.

"Lieutenant Cimino?" a young cop called out. She had a radio mike gripped in her hand. "Sir?"

"What?"

"An off-duty cop just got him."

"The boy?"

"No. The kidnapper. Took him down on the loading dock out back behind the Hyatt Regency."

"Is he talking?"

"No, sir. He's dead."

11

Donny Oglethorpe piloted his eighteen-wheeler into the Toyota auto facility at Port Newark.

It was nine thirty at night but Donny could make out the towering skeletons of the giant cargo cranes off in the distance. Their steel frames were dotted with blinking safety beacons.

So airplanes don't bump into them, Donny figured. They're so damn tall, one of those jets dropping down into Newark Airport might just catch a tire on a crane hook or something. He knew the cranes were used to unload containers off ships: big steel boxes jammed with cargo from Korea or China or Japan. Each container the size of Donny's truck. Heavy suckers. That's why the cranes had to be so huge.

Donny's rig cleared the chain-link gates and rumbled into the Toyota terminal. The Japanese carmaker had what amounted to a huge parking lot near the docks so cars could roll right off the boat and wait to be transported to dealerships up and down the eastern seaboard. Donny had heard that Toyota's patch of asphalt spread out over close to ninety acres. Hundreds of shiny new cars all lined up in tidy rows like some neat freak's Hot Wheels collection.

Donny eased on the brakes. Heard them hiss and huff.

A man with a clipboard came over to the side of his rig. He had on a Toyota jacket, like something a baseball coach might wear.

"Howdy," Donny called down. "Guess this is the place, hunh?"

The guy nodded but didn't look up. His eyes were focused on the sheets of paper clipped to his clear plastic board.

"I'm here to pick up that load for Mr. Hancock? Hancock Toyota down in Knoxville? Tennessee?" Donny had lived in east Tennessee most of his life. His statements always sounded like questions.

The man with the clipboard ticked something with his pen.

"Slot fifteen," the man said, pointing to where Donny should maneuver the back end of his empty car carrier.

Donny worked the wheel with one hand and expertly slid the ninety-six-foot-long double-decker into the assigned loading slot. The cab rattled when the engine rumbled to a stop.

"Looks like you're going out full," the clipboard guy said after consulting a pink slip of paper. "Both decks. Four up. Four down."

Donny swung open his door, clambered down, found the ground, and hiked up his jeans. Pulled his undershorts out of his crack.

"Been pushing this thing since six this morning. Only stopped couple times to tank up. Miracle I ain't got hemorrhoids."

Mr. Clipboard nodded. He didn't seem all that interested in the state of Donny's sore butt. The guy didn't want to talk, fine. Meant Donny would be loaded up and out of here all the sooner.

Donny watched him make a few more marks on the pink paper.

"Sign here. Initial there."

Donny marked where the man pointed. "So, which eight are mine?"

The man pointed. "Front of the row. Camry, Camry Solaris, 4 Runner, Rav 4, Sequoia, Sienna, a Camry, and another Camry."

"Dang. Them Camrys is popular, ain't they?"

"I suppose."

Man, Donny thought, *this guy probably doesn't even talk to his wife or his dog.* Fine. Cut the chitchat. In and out. That's what tonight was all about. Roll in, roll out. Pick up the merchandise and deliver it by Friday.

Clipboard Man signaled to two longshoremen in navy blue jumpsuits. Car jockeys. High-paid valet parking attendants who'd maneuver the cars off the asphalt, up the ramp, and onto the back of Donny's rig. They were union guys, not management. Didn't get to wear the nifty baseball jacket.

"This'll take about twenty minutes."

Donny nodded. It always did.

"You got any coffee?"

"In the hut."

"Mind if I steal a cup?"

"Help yourself."

"They doin' them damn random inspections again tonight?"

"Don't think so."

"Good. Last time I come up this way, Customs crawled in and out of every damn car on my rack. Took an hour. Hour and a half. When them Homeland Security assholes finally finished, I ended up in the middle of rush hour on the Turnpike. I'll tell you what—my butt was sore that day. My hemorrhoids had hemorrhoids!"

Mr. Clipboard didn't smile. He just ticked more boxes on his papers. He tore off the top sheet, handed it to Donny.

"Customs is short-staffed tonight," he said.

"Really? Somebody call in sick so they could go trick-or-treating with their kids?"

Mr. Clipboard shrugged.

"Maybe."

Damn. Mr. Hancock had been right. "Donny," he'd said, "you make that pickup on Halloween night, I guaran-damn-tee no one will hassle you."

12

"He's fine, Freddy. I was just up in the room."

Miller met the Acevedos in the lobby of the hotel. They walked while they talked, headed for the elevators.

"Did he hurt my boy?"

"No, Freddy."

"You sure?"

"The paramedics already checked him out. He's good to go. A little shaken up but nothing serious."

Miller pressed the button for the elevators.

Freddy moved in closer. Whispered so Carmelita couldn't hear his next question.

"Did this guy … did he … ?"

Miller shook his head. "No, Freddy. He did not."

Freddy blinked hard. "Good," he said. "Good."

The elevator doors slid open. "He's in room four-oh-six," said Miller. "The cops asked him a couple questions. Now he's playing on the Xbox."

"Xbox?"

"Yeah," said Miller.

And, according to what Carlos told the JCPD, that's all the bad guy did, too. Played Xbox. Then, he went downstairs to grab a beer and got riddled with bullets.

Miller had seen the body before the medical examiner zipped it up and hauled it away. There were eight bullet holes in the dead man's back. Standing in the circle around the corpse with the Jersey City cops, detectives, and ambulance crew, Miller couldn't help but stare at the red-haired man's blue tattoos. There were a dozen on each arm. One in particular had caught Miller's eye and he had leaned down to examine it: some sort of goddess in a winged helmet astride a stallion, thrusting a spear toward heaven.

"Video games?" asked Freddy as he stared up at the digital floor numbers. He shook his head in disbelief and smiled—probably for the first time in a couple of hours. The elevator doors slid open again.

"Yeah," said Miller. "And his candy is just about all gone, too."

Now Freddy actually laughed.

"Candy and video games?" snapped Carmelita.

Miller knew that if his wife the shrink were here she would hypothesize that Mrs. Acevedo's fear and concern for her son had just undergone some sort of transference and was coming out as maternal anger.

"*Dias mio!* Freddy, I told you: Carlos needs to go outside and play. He does not need to sit on the couch all day eating junk food and shooting at space people. He'll get fat, Freddy. Obese with the diabetes. I saw it on the television news. He needs to go outside and play football. Baseball ..."

"Yes, dear," said Freddy.

"*Mira*—I mean it!"

"*Sí, querido.*" Fernando Acevedo said it in a way that

made it sound like he was back on familiar ground, a place with rules he understood.

*   *   *

"When the Amber Alert came on the television at approximately twenty-one hundred hours, a patron at the bar tentatively ID'ed the man seated near the windows as a person of interest in the abduction of Carlos Acevedo."

Around 11:30 P.M., Miller sat in the Hyatt conference room with Lieutenant Cimino listening to Officer Sean McManus, a rookie cop, describing what had happened that evening in the Vu Lounge. Also in the room was a representative of the Jersey City Police Internal Affairs Bureau and another man in a suit Miller hadn't been introduced to. This last guy unwrapped a mint from a bowl the management must put in these meeting rooms for businesspeople.

"Then what happened?" Cimino asked McManus.

The man in the suit nodded. Popped the mint in his mouth.

"I identified myself as an off-duty Jersey City police officer, showed him my shield, and requested that he remain where he was."

Cimino cocked an eyebrow. "You said all that?"

"I shouted, 'Freeze!'" said McManus.

"Same difference," said the man with the mint in his mouth.

"Go on," said Cimino.

"I instructed the suspect to slowly raise his arms and

clasp his hands behind his head. That's when I went for a pair of FlexiCuffs I had on my belt."

"You carry cuffs with you at all times, Officer McManus?" asked Cimino. "Even when you're not on the clock?"

McManus nodded. "Yes, sir. I also carry my sidearm."

"Yeah," said Cimino. "We know. We saw the body. You ever fire an automatic before?"

McManus stiffened.

"Take it easy Tony," said the guy in the suit. Miller figured it out: the guy was with the union. The Jersey City Police Officers Benevolent Association. "Sean is the good guy in this situation, remember?"

Cimino nodded.

In fact, the local news stations had already dubbed Sean McManus the Hero Cop. At ten and again at eleven, they'd all led with the story of the off-duty Hero Cop who'd taken down the Halloween Horror outside the Hyatt Regency Hotel in Jersey City, New Jersey. The Hero Cop who'd dropped by the bar to meet his lady friend for a quick drink and ended up chasing Mr. Elwood "Red" Pettus (the police had recovered his wallet and driver's license) out of the Hyatt's cocktail lounge, through the cavernous kitchen, and onto the loading dock.

"I'm only asking about the automatic because," Cimino checked his notebook, "we found eight slugs slammed into the guy's back."

"He was trying to run away," McManus said calmly. "I didn't open fire until I was certain I was clear of any possible civilian casualties."

"Did this man ever threaten you with a weapon?"

"No, sir. Not with any weapon that was readily visible."

"But you figured you needed to pump him full of lead? What—you think all that extra weight might slow him down?"

"Jesus, Tony," said the union guy. "Why are you hocking Sean like this? Why are you busting his balls?"

"Maybe," said Miller, "he thinks your man used more force than necessary to subdue his subject."

The guy in the suit glared at Miller. "Who are you again?"

"Miller. FBI."

"Right. Beautiful. Terrific. So tell me, Tony: why do we all of a sudden need the Fibbies sniffing around in our dirty drawers?"

"Special Agent Miller is a good friend of the Jersey City Police Department."

The guy muttered something under his breath.

"So, why eight bullets, Sean?" Cimino continued. "I figure you could've substantially reduced his risk of flight with a single bullet in the butt. What happened? Finger get jammed up inside the trigger guard?"

McManus's minder stood up. "Okay. That's it. We're done here." He turned to the IA officer. "You need anything else, give me a call and we'll try this again in a more appropriate setting."

Now Cimino stood. "Where's that, Dom? Union headquarters?"

"Like I said, Tony, we're finished here."

13

"You know how proud I am of you. Right, Son?"

"Yes, Dad."

Alexander Schmitz's father stood in the doorway of his son's ten-by-ten bedroom. It was the same bedroom the younger Schmitz had slept in as a child. The same small bed.

The bookshelves over his tiny student's desk were lined with trophies. Dozens of them—all for marksmanship. All the awards looked pretty much the same: a shiny statue of a six-inch-tall hunter, rifle raised, shot lined up—standing atop an inscribed base. Some had a silver dog on point standing alongside the hunter's bent knee.

Alexander had won the trophies at camp: Boy Scouts, NRA-sponsored Shooting Sports Camps, even the church camp he had attended one summer. The Bible was replete with stories of valiant warriors, brave men standing up against tyrants, armed only with the weapons God gave them, their humble shots sailing true with the Lord's guidance.

Draped around the tiny hunter heads on some trophies were the medals and Weapons Qualification badges Alexander had received during his years with the

U.S. Army. He had been classified as an "Expert," which was the highest level attainable, higher than "Sharpshooter" or, the first grade, "Marksman." He had received this qualification on several different weapons systems: Pistol and Rifle, of course, as well as Field Artillery, Rocket Launcher, and Flame Thrower.

Alexander Schmitz had a gift. Extraordinary eyesight. It's why he wore sunglasses, day and night. To protect his eyes—his special gift from God. It's why he could perceive small objects at great distances, why he could hit the tiniest center of any target you placed in front of any weapon he held in his hands. Why his father and others called him the Eagle.

"Where you shipping out to?" his father asked.

"I'm afraid it's classified information, sir."

His father nodded from the doorway. Didn't step into the bedroom.

"What time are you shoving off?"

"It's a ten A.M. flight."

"I'll drive you out to the airport."

"Thank you, sir."

"We'll need to leave the house at oh-seven-hundred hours. Give you plenty of time to pass through the security checkpoints."

"Yes, sir."

He placed a neatly folded stack of white underwear on top of the white T-shirts in his single suitcase. He was also taking four pairs of balled-up white socks and two sets of wrinkle-resistant khaki shirts and pants. He would wash his clothes every fourth day. In the bathroom sink.

"Why'd you shave your head?" his father finally asked. "You look like a cue ball."

"Purifying myself, sir. Preparing for the holy war."

"Jesus, Alex. We're not Arabs. This isn't Al Qaeda."

"They can teach us much."

Dr. Tilley, their spiritual leader, often said so in his Internet postings. They and Al Qaeda shared common enemies. The Jews. The federal government.

"Don't wear your shades in the airport, Son. Especially not with that shaved head."

"The interior lighting will most likely be fluorescent."

"I know, I know. But let it sting for an hour or two. You put on your sunglasses, you'll look suspicious."

"Yes, sir."

"All I'm saying is you want this leg of the journey to go smoothly. No hitches, no glitches."

"Yes, sir."

"You touch any of the guns tonight? Load any cartridges? Because they can pick up gunpowder on your suitcase or your clothes."

"I'm clean, sir. Didn't spend any time in the basement this evening."

"Good. Smart. Any idea when you'll be coming back?"

Alexander shook his head. "No, sir."

"Did Dr. Tilley tell you the target?"

"No, sir. The specifics of my duty have not been relayed to me at this time."

"Yeah. That's smart. Better he keeps us in the dark."

Alexander's father looked like he wanted to say something more profound but words, as always, failed him.

Walter Schmitz was a proud man who had seen the country he loved, the country he had been willing to fight and die for—had there been a war during his own short stint in the service—slip away. That he was now a janitor was beside the point.

"Hit the rack, Alex. Grab some shut-eye."

"Yes, sir."

"I'll wake you up at oh-six-hundred. You want breakfast? I could scramble some eggs."

"I'm good to go, sir. I've packed rations in my carry-on. Protein bars."

"No liquids or gels though, right?"

"Right."

"Good, good."

"Dad?"

"Yeah, Alex?"

"I'm proud of you, too."

His father nodded. Pursed his lip. Nodded some more. It was the most emotion he could muster; the best he could do when sending his only son off to war.

14

Miller and Cimino sat near the big windows in the Hyatt lounge.

They were each sipping the same beer they had ordered half an hour earlier. They hadn't come to the bar to drink. They came to decompress and talk out what happened.

It was a little after midnight.

"You speak to McManus's girlfriend?" Miller asked. "The one he was meeting here?"

"She never showed up. Stayed at a party up in Hoboken."

"She meet somebody better?"

"They usually do."

Miller nodded. Turned the Heineken bottle around in his hand. "What about the guy who ID'ed Pettus?"

"Gone."

"I know, but did you ask him any questions?"

Cimino picked up his beer. "He was gone before we got here. Nobody at the hotel knows who he was. They'd never seen him in the bar before. Probably wasn't even a registered guest. Just some guy who came in for a pop on Halloween night. Maybe he heard they were serving free Devil Wings."

"So he didn't stick around to see if there was a reward or something?"

"Nope. Did his good deed and disappeared."

"You going to track him down?"

Cimino shrugged. "Doubt it. Sure, I'd like to, but it's not what the bosses consider a 'prudent use of manpower.'"

Miller and Cimino were the only first responders left at the hotel. The medical examiner had tagged and bagged Pettus and hauled him off to the morgue. One team of officers drove the Acevedo family home. The others were back out on the streets, back on patrol. Miller and Cimino stayed behind to stare out the windows and puzzle over why this thing just didn't seem right.

Red Pettus wasn't a child molester. If he had grabbed Carlos Acevedo to fulfill some kind of kinky sexual fantasy, he'd probably have done something about it by the time the cops rescued the boy. Instead, the guy had killed time playing video games and sampling Halloween candy.

So why the hell would such a kidnapper pick Carlos Acevedo? Why would he even be trolling for his snatch in Jersey City? If he was looking for a big payday, why wasn't he out grabbing kids in the ritzier suburbs where the money lived?

Miller stared at the skyline of Manhattan. The top of the Empire State Building was no longer illuminated. King Kong had switched off the lights, called it a night. That meant it was late. Real late.

"Guess we should head home," said Miller. "Long day."

"Yeah."

"Maybe, if I'm lucky, Angela left me a couple of those Mr. Goodbars for breakfast."

"Those the ones with the peanuts?"

"Yeah. Spanish peanuts, I think. Kind of round."

"My girls give me the stuff they don't want," said Cimino. "You know: hard candy. The sour balls the little old ladies hand out from their crystal candy dishes."

"Yeah." Miller rubbed his cheeks. Massaged his temples. "Something's wrong here, Tony. Something's not right about how this thing went down."

"Yeah. It's hinky."

"It's what?"

"Hinky. Old cop word. My dad used to use it all the time when he was on the job. Means something's fishy. Doesn't smell right. It's hinky."

"Unh-hunh," said Miller. "And how old is your father?"

"Seventy-two," said Cimino. "Same as you."

Miller laughed. "Don't give me more years than I'm already carrying."

"Ah, you're young at heart, Saint Chris. That's what counts, am I right? Sinatra says so in that song."

"Yeah." Both men reached for their beers again. "You did good, tonight," said Miller.

"I guess. Guess we just got lucky on this one. Lucky that we had an off-duty rookie officer hanging out at a bar because his lady friend stood him up. The case was closed two hours after it was opened."

Miller tilted his beer bottle in a toast. "So here's to good luck."

"Yeah. The luck of the Irish. Here's to Sean McManus, Hero Cop."

The two friends drained the last drops out of their long-nursed beers.

The waitress came over. "Last call, guys. Can I get you another round?"

Miller checked his watch. "No thank you, ma'am. One is my limit."

"Me, too," said Cimino. He reached into his pocket for his cash.

"Let me get this," said Miller.

"Relax, Special Agent Miller. This beer is given to you on behalf of a grateful police force. Thanks for sticking around in case this thing went south."

"Next time, it's my treat."

"Okay, bro," said Cimino. "I'm down with that."

Miller smiled. It was a game they sometimes played: Cimino, who was white, would pretend to talk black. Miller, who, of course, was black but never spoke like that, would try to ignore him.

"Are you two with the police?" the waitress asked. She was young and attractive. Cocktail waitresses frequently were. Tips worked out better that way.

She was also black.

Miller nodded. "I'm with the FBI. He's with the Jersey City PD."

"I see. I thought somebody would've asked me some questions or something."

"Excuse me?" said Cimino.

"About what happened. Guess they were all too busy. With the excitement outside."

"Is there something you want to tell us?" Miller asked.

The young woman nodded. "Yeah. I waited on them."

"Who's that?"

"The two guys. They were together, sitting right here. These same two chairs. The one guy kept ordering Coors and eating all the nuts."

Miller still didn't understand what the girl was getting at. "Who are we talking about, ma'am?"

"You know. The one who got shot. The kidnapper, I guess. And the other one. They were together."

"What other one?" asked Cimino.

"The guy who turned him in. I thought they were friends. Guess I was wrong."

Miller looked at Cimino.

This thing just got hinkier.

15

"Can you please step this way, sir?"

The airport screener pointed his latex-gloved hand to what looked like a doormat decorated with two footprints instead of the customary "Welcome."

"Please extend your arms."

Alexander Schmitz obeyed.

His father had been right. He shouldn't have worn his sunglasses inside the airport. But the sun was blazingly bright at 9:00 A.M. on this first day of November and Buffalo International was a modern cathedral made, it seemed, entirely out of glass. The building had been strategically positioned to draw as much sunlight as possible into the far recesses of the departure hall. It had been designed to torment Alexander's eyes.

"I am now going to check for any concealed items."

The man patted down Alexander's pants. Sides. Back. Front. He narrated every move he made. Thought it made him sound professional, Alexander supposed. Thought his silly TSA uniform made him look like something besides a minimum wage burger-flipper wearing a white military shirt with a patch on the sleeve.

"I am now going to scan you with a metal detector."

The government stooge ran a wand up and down Alexander's chest. He repeated the sweep up and down his back. Alexander kept his arms outstretched. Assumed the stance. Looked like a criminal.

He glanced to his right and saw a uniformed black screener waving *his* wand up and down the ankle of an old man in leg braces who didn't have the strength to crawl off the seat of his battery-powered wheelchair. Alexander's eyes narrowed behind his tinted lenses in disgust. Did the TSA think some geezer was smuggling plastic explosives inside his colostomy bag? Were the old man's Velcro-strapped shoes loaded down with dynamite?

"Are these your bags?"

"Yes, sir."

"I'm going to swab both pieces."

"Yes, sir."

The TSA screener went to his boxy machine, put a fresh strip of cotton fabric into a plastic-handled tool, rubbed it all over Alexander's suitcase and shoulder bag. Made two passes over the handles. Then he put the swatch into a compartment at the front of an electronic box, waited for the machine to tell him what to do next. Alexander knew the box was some sort of explosives detection device. The man was checking for residue. He wanted to make certain Alexander didn't have gunpowder on his hands when he packed his bags.

He wasn't as dumb as these idiots thought. Whenever he worked with his guns or ammunition, he stripped off all his clothes and wore a shower cap and rubber gloves.

"You're all set to go." Duh.

Alexander smiled. Took up his suitcase. Slung the shoulder bag over his neck. Slid the sunglasses up his nose.

No. He wasn't stupid.

These guys? They were morons.

When he landed in New York, Alexander followed the crowds of disembarking passengers past the overpriced restaurants and down the escalator to baggage claim.

He saw a short man in a black suit, white shirt, and skinny black necktie holding up a sign with his name on it.

"I'm Alexander Schmitz."

The guy nodded. Tilted his head toward the baggage carousel.

"Do we need to wait for luggage, sir?"

Alexander tugged up on his carry-on suitcase, tapped the strap of his shoulder bag. "Negative. I'm good to go."

"I'm parked out front. Oh. Here." He reached into his suit coat and pulled out a stack of small cardboard envelopes. "Marriott gift cards. You'll be staying at their Marquis Hotel in midtown."

"For how long?"

"Until you receive further orders."

The driver gestured toward the exit. The two men started walking.

"There's close to ten thousand dollars on those cards," the driver told him. "You could stay at the Marriott for a month. Order room service for every meal."

"Excellent."

"It's a prime location. Right in the center of the city. You'll have easy access to all the bridges, tunnels, and airports."

The driver was obviously hoping for a reaction from Alexander, some hint as to the nature of his mission.

Not knowing what he had been called up to do, he couldn't give the man what he was looking for. But, even if he did know, why would he tell this flunky? Or anyone? That's how wars were lost.

"I look forward to spending time in the city," was all Alexander said in reply.

The driver nodded. Probably realized he had been out of line probing for more. Probably hoped Alexander wouldn't report him. He switched back to tour guide mode.

"Be sure to ask for a room with a view."

"Of what?"

"You've never been to New York City?"

"This is my first visit."

"I see." The man hoisted Alexander's suitcase, led the way out to the sidewalk. "The Marriott Marquis is at the corner of Forty-fifth and Broadway. Get a room with windows facing south and you'll have a great view of the whole thing. The rotten core of the Big Apple."

They waited at the curb for the Walk sign.

"What's the big attraction?" asked Alexander.

The driver looked at him.

"Forty-fifth and Broadway," he repeated. "You're right in the middle of Times Square."

16

"Slow down, Angel. It has to last us all the way to the next holiday."

"Election Day?"

"Nope. Longer. Election Day is not a candy-giving holiday."

Miller sat with his daughter in the kitchen. The contents of her trick-or-treat bag had been emptied out into a big salad bowl. She fished through it, searching for the perfect piece of chocolate to start her day. Miller had already secured a Mr. Goodbar.

"Well," said Angela, standing up on her chair so she could have a better view down at the candy, "what about Veterans Day? That's coming on November eleventh. Mommy says you'll probably get a Monday off on account of it's an official government holiday and you work for the government."

"True. True. But there's no candy involved."

"But it's in red on the calendar."

"I know, honey. But folks don't give each other candy on Veterans Day. No cards, either."

"Really? There's nothing?"

"Well, sometimes you get a red poppy to pin on your shirt, but that's about it."

Angela pondered that. "Doesn't sound like much fun."

It was Miller's turn to ponder.

He had never served in the military. He had gone straight from college to Quantico and then into the field for the FBI. No wars, but he'd fought a few battles on the home front in service to his country. So he wasn't, technically, a veteran, but he knew his daughter was right. Old soldiers deserved more than red-and-black paper poppies sold in the parking lot outside the A&P; more than bank closings and shabby parades nobody bothered attending because they were too busy shopping for a new sofa that the radio commercials promised would be delivered in time for the holidays.

The real holidays.

Thanksgiving and Christmas and Hanukkah. Even Kwanzaa had more going on than Veterans Day.

"Are you two eating Halloween candy for breakfast?" Natalie stepped into the kitchen. "Christopher?"

When she said his whole name like that, when she took the time to linger on all three syllables, Miller knew he was in trouble. But before he could deny all charges, Angela piped up:

"We both get to choose just one piece each, Mommy. Daddy said we have to make my Halloween candy last all the way to Thanksgiving because nobody gives you candy on Election Day or Veterans Day."

Natalie narrowed her eyes. Tried hard to glare at her husband. She even rested a fist on her hip. But Miller knew it was hard to stay mad when your daughter was so damn cute.

It was time to change the subject.

"Did we hear from your folks, yet, hon? Are they coming up for Thanksgiving?"

Natalie smiled. Miller could see she appreciated his tactical ploy.

"I'm sorry," she said. "I thought we were discussing candy and its appropriateness at the breakfast table."

"We were, doc. Hey, you know what—it might be a good idea to have some of those Thanksgiving-style Hershey Kisses around the house for when your mom and dad come to visit. You know—the ones in the brown and gold and silver."

"I'm quite familiar with all of Mr. Hershey's seasonal varieties, Christopher."

"I think they, you know, add a festive touch to the home," Miller said.

Hearing her husband turn into Martha Stewart almost made Natalie laugh coffee out her nose.

"I want to see the Macy's Day Parade!" Angela blurted.

Like so many others, Angela always called the big Thanksgiving Day parade down the middle of Manhattan the "Macy's Day" Parade. The department store had been putting on the show so long, they owned the whole holiday. At least the morning part that came before the feast and the football.

"We will, Angel," Miller said. "We'll watch it on TV like we always do."

"I want to see it in person!" said Angela. "You said I could, remember? Last year. You said we would go into the city and see the Macy's Day Parade when I was older and this year I'm older!"

"You know," said Natalie, "if you want a good spot on the sidewalk, I hear you need to be in the city by six A.M. So, you two should probably catch the train around five. Means you'll need to wake up at four."

Miller could tell his wife was enjoying this. Payback for candy, breakfast of champions. He turned to his daughter. She widened her smile.

Miller knew he wouldn't be sleeping in this Thanksgiving.

"I better get to work," he said.

"You want to take some candy for lunch, Daddy?"

Natalie's expression was hard to read. Maybe he'd forgo another Mr. Goodbar, just to show her he could.

"No thanks, hon," he said and gave his daughter a kiss on the top of her head. He turned to Natalie. "Hey, I've got an idea. Maybe you want to come into the city with us on Thanksgiving morning. We could all catch that early train you were talking about."

"Oh, honey!" his wife gushed. "Great idea. I'd *love* to. But I think I'll need to stay home and put out those bowls of Hershey Kisses. Create that festive touch you were talking about."

Miller nodded. He knew when he was beaten. This game had probably been lost before it even started.

"Something's hinky about it," Miller said to his boss, Charlie Lofgren.

"Hinky?"

"Cop word. Means something's fishy. Doesn't feel right."

"Go on." Lofgren motioned for Miller to take a seat. Lofgren was the Special Agent In Charge of the FBI's Newark Division. His office wasn't anything flashy. None of the offices and cubicles at 11 Centre Street were.

"You ever see that Tom Clancy movie?" Miller asked his boss. *The Sum Of All Fears?*

"No," said Lofgren. "But I read the book."

"Probably better."

"Correct. In the movie, Harrison Ford played Jack Ryan. When I read, *I* get to be the guy who saves the world."

"Okay," said Miller, "remember the nuclear bomb hidden inside the Coke machine? The terrorists were able to smuggle it into Baltimore on a boat—inside a cargo container. Nobody suspected a thing."

"Until the Coke machine blew up the Super Bowl," Lofgren added.

"Yeah. And then it was too late."

"Where you going with this, Chris?"

"That thing I called you about last night. The thug who grabbed my neighbor's boy off the street." Miller leaned in. "Charlie, I spent some time last night with a friend on the job in Jersey City."

"Go on."

"The doer, the kidnapper—he never made any demands. Never asked for money. Just sat in a hotel room playing video games and eating the kid's Halloween candy. So, I have to ask: why'd he grab Carlos Acevedo?"

"I thought you said the father had gambling debts."

"That was my first guess. Last night."

"So what's your second guess? This morning?"

"My neighbor is U.S. Customs. He works over at Port Newark. I think the whole kidnapping deal was a diversionary tactic designed to take Agent Acevedo off the docks because somebody wanted to make absolutely, one hundred percent certain their cargo wouldn't be inspected last night."

"Somebody bringing in another Coke machine?"

"Or drugs. Or a boatload of illegal immigrants."

Lofgren leaned back in his chair. Gestured toward a stack of papers. "The NSA dumped these on me this morning. More wiretaps. They want us to run them down, see what we can learn."

"They suspect something?"

"Yeah. For starters they suspect New Jersey's got the second-largest Muslim population in America. They suspect—no, they know—that in 1993 a group of Muslim extremists from a mosque in your hometown, Jersey City, packed a rented van with fertilizer and tried to bring down the World Trade Center. They also know that right after Nine-Eleven, some of those anthrax letters were mailed from a drop box a few minutes drive from Jersey City."

Miller knew where this was going.

"So," his boss sighed, "the National Security Agency keeps jamming me up with phone numbers. Intercepts. Signals intelligence. All unfiltered. They want us to see if anybody's been speed-dialing Al Qaeda's caves."

Miller had run this drill before. The NSA swamped the FBI with raw data, sending them out to interview innocent folks who just happened to phone their family back home from time to time. Dick Cheney's "vital tool" for combating terrorism was a real drain on man-power. A long run for a short slide.

"We need to check each and every one of these wire-taps," said Lofgren. "That comes straight from Justice. Your other thing? Out there on the docks. Ask your friends at the JCPD to run it down. I need you on this."

"Yes, sir."

Christopher Miller knew when he was beaten.

He just didn't expect it to happen twice in one day.

17

Carl Krieger was eighteen years old and itching for action.

"You saw them go in?" he asked his friend Rolf.

"Yeah," Rolf answered. "Just now. She's white. He's a nigger."

Carl spat into the gutter. "Race Betrayer."

They were standing outside Zad's, a bar on Second Street in downtown Milwaukee. It was the kind of place where you could play pool for free on Monday nights and drink two-dollar bottles of domestic beer before 7 P.M. any day of the week.

Rolf and Carl had never actually been inside the bar. The guy at the front was an asshole who didn't buy their fake ID's and Carl had such a pudgy baby face there was no way to convince the bouncer he was really twenty-two like his phony driver's license said he was. Even the fuzzy beard he had running along his jaw line couldn't disguise his youthfulness.

So they bought their own beer and leaned against Carl's car parked across the street from Zad's where they could hear the muffled thump of an electric bass rumbling through the thick brick walls. The two teenagers smoked cigarettes and slugged big gulps of Meister Bräu from quart bottles tightly wrapped inside brown paper sacks. They both wore black cargo pants tucked into black military boots.

"You want to go inside and kick his ass?" Rolf asked. "The nigger, I mean. I could keep the asshole up front busy while you go after the coon."

"I don't care about the coon," said Carl. "I want to kick *her* ass. She's the one attempting to dilute the race. Turn us into mud people."

Rolf nodded.

Carl had taught Rolf about mud people and the coming demise of the White Race brought on by ignorant white sluts who slept around with niggers. He'd learned it all on his Dr. John Tilley CDs. One, entitled *The Morality of Survival*, was hard work. Thick. Like listening to a social studies lecture in high school. But Carl stuck with it. He liked how Dr. Tilley explained things. Like the White Man's mission: to make certain their glorious Western Civilization, the finest culture the world had ever known, survived. Dr. Tilley assured his listeners that they held the moral high ground in the coming battle: self-defense. The primary law of nature.

"Come on, man," Rolf pleaded. "I'm tired of talking about this shit. I want to *do* something, break some fucking glass."

"Is that her?" said Carl, nodding toward Zad's entryway.

"Yeah."

The white girl was walking out with her black date. She hooked an arm under his elbow.

"Come on."

Carl grabbed the aluminum baseball bat from the backseat of his car.

"Oh, shit, man!" Rolf was giddy. "This is gonna be sweet!"

They marched slowly across the street.

"I'll mess up her face," Carl said, hiding the bat behind his leg. Every time he took a step, it pinged against the heavy heel of his boot.

They were halfway across the street.

The white girl twirled on her heel, went up on tippy toes, kissed her companion's lips. Looked like she wanted to suck his whole face into her mouth. Carl could tell she was totally wasted and incredibly horny. These two would fuck all night long.

He brought the bat up and slapped it against his fist.

A white guy now came out of Zad's, standing behind the couple in the shadowy doorway. Carl could tell he was big. Huge. Had to weigh 300, maybe 350. He stepped out of the darkness.

It was Tiny.

Shit.

Tiny saw Carl and Rolf. Saw what they were up to.

He shot them a look. Shook his head.

Carl rehid the bat behind his baggy pants leg.

The couple turned left, headed up the street. Carl could hear her giggles, his rumbling laugh.

Fucking Tiny.

The inside of the car was fogged with cigarette smoke.

Carl and Tiny sat up front. Rolf was in back.

No one said anything. They just smoked and drained their beers out of the crinkled bags.

Tiny belched. Sucked on his cigarette. "So," he said, "how'd you two punks get so goddamn old school?" Then he laughed. The car seat jiggled with him. "You can't pull that Nazi jackboot shit anymore. Can't whack a nigger with a baseball bat."

"I was going to whack the girl," said Carl.

"Even worse. You two want to play, you gotta play by the rules."

"The rules suck!" shouted Rolf.

The big man swiveled around.

"You want out, Rolf?"

"No."

"Because I'll take you out myself you ever pull that kind of stupid-ass stunt again."

Rolf sank back. Tried to disappear into the seat cushions.

"When the hell are we going to see some action?" asked Carl. *"Real* action—like they're talking about down in Cleveland."

He had Tiny's attention.

"What'd you hear, bro?"

"Me and Rolf went down there couple weeks ago."

"Awesome fucking chili," Rolf added.

"Plus," said Carl, "I picked up some noise on the Internet. Cleveland guys in this chat room. They say the shit is about to hit the fan. Soon."

Tiny wiped cigarette ash off the breast of his leather jacket. "They know anything definite?"

"Rumors," said Carl.

"Like what?"

"The cell over in Buffalo. One of their unit was just called up. Put on active duty."

"Buffalo's not too far from Cleveland," said Rolf. "So we figured they fucking knew what they were talking about."

The fat man grunted. Drained the last drops of beer out of his bottle. Carl could see the tattoo covering his thick forearm: the lady with the winged helmet, riding her horse. He knew she was the one who carried dead soldiers up to heaven.

"So—what's the big plan?" Tiny asked. He flung his empty out the window.

"I've got nothing definite," said Carl. "They call this guy from Buffalo 'the Eagle.'"

"Damn." Rolf was impressed. "The Eagle. Why they call him that? Hunh?"

"Who knows?" said Tiny. "Maybe he's fucking bald."

Rolf laughed.

"This blows," said Carl. "If big shit's finally coming down the pike, how come we don't know the plan?"

"If Dr. Tilley told us," explained Tiny, "he'd be telling the Feds, too. Hell, they tap all his phones. Read his e-mail. So, relax, little brother. Stick to the plan. When our cell is needed, he'll let us know. Until then, we sit tight." Tiny narrowed his eyes. "You cool with that, Carl?"

"Yeah."

"Good." Tiny yanked up on his door handle. Slid out of the car. "I gotta go grab my bike. See you two next week. Stay out of trouble. Defend the pack. But don't venture outside the circle."

Carl nodded.

Tiny walked away, secure in his belief that Carl Krieger was a dutiful and obedient soldier. It never occurred to him that Carl had decided it was time to become what the television commercials called "An Army Of One."

Tiny would hear about it soon enough.

Hell, all America would hear about it.

18

At 8 A.M. on Friday, November 2, Alexander Schmitz exited the revolving door from the street-level lobby of the Marriott Marquis Hotel and pushed his way through the throngs of people bustling toward Broadway.

Acrid smoke accosted him from a pretzel vendor's pushcart. He turned right, maneuvered past the pan-handlers, vagrants, and tourists. He headed south to Forty-second Street.

His room in the Marriott Marquis, one of nearly two thousand in the hotel, was on the thirty-ninth floor of the forty-nine-story building, which rose like a mountain of gray concrete and black glass above the billboards that were the throbbing heart of Times Square.

The wretched crossroads of the interbred world.

Alexander moved through the mobs of mud people. Tried not to touch anybody. He had already showered. He also carried a small vial of Purell hand sanitizer in his pocket.

He could see the NYPD outpost at the base of the building where they dropped the ball every New Year's Eve. Above the police station was a billboard for some kind of torn blue jeans worn by otherwise naked models with breast implants. Above that a stream of headlines zipped along the edge of the building. Above *that* glowed the giant Panasonic TV screen NBC always showed at the end of their evening news broadcast.

Alexander hoped his heroics would soon fill that screen. The flashing headlines, too.

He turned right on Forty-second Street.

He was hungry.

Fortunately, Applebee's had a restaurant just off Times Square. Down Forty-second Street near the Hilton. He wouldn't have to eat the local food. No bagels or pastrami—a type of Jewish meat colored orange and crusted with dirt. He could have wholesome, American food. Pancakes. Eggs. Bacon. He would be, as Applebee's advertising promised, "Eating good in the neighborhood" all month: in addition to the Marriott gift cards, the driver had given him a thick stack from Applebee's.

Alexander felt a buzzing in his jacket.

His new cell phone—another gift from the driver.

He pulled it out. Inserted the earpiece.

The phone was something called a TalkSECURE and consisted of an off-the-shelf Motorola Timeport GSM tri-band cell phone equipped with a clip-in encryption module. This meant nobody could listen in on a conversation between Alexander and his caller, who, anyway, was most likely phoning from a similarly encrypted unit.

"This is Schmitz," he said, moving under the awning to Applebee's Neighborhood Bar & Grill. A crowd of New Yorkers, mostly nonwhite people pushing and shoving like they owned the sidewalk, swarmed around him. He could smell urine and rotting garbage. He could smell New York.

"This is Dr. Tilley," said the voice over the phone.

"Good morning, sir."

"I trust your accommodations are agreeable?"

"Yes, sir."

"Good. But keep your bags packed."

"Sir?"

"You'll be moving out to our training facility on Monday. It's a little further north. I will meet you there."

"Should I check out of the Marriott, sir?"

"Negative. Hold the room. After your training, you'll be returning to the city."

"Yes, sir."

"That is all for now, Alexander. I look forward to meeting you."

The call cut out.

His heart raced. He was actually going to meet Dr. Tilley, the brotherhood's spiritual leader, a visionary and prophet who would certainly know how to best utilize Alexander's God-given talents.

He knew that was why he had been summoned to this godforsaken outpost swarming with human vermin.

To fulfill his destiny.

19

"Terror City."

According to some, that was the FBI's name for Jersey City in the months immediately following September 11, 2001. Less than two weeks after the Twin Towers were destroyed, the *New York Post* ran the headline: "N.J.: A Perfect Place to Hide."

A lot of angry eyes had been looking west across the Hudson River at Jersey City in the fall of 2001. Especially at the Masjid al-Salam, the mosque where Sheik Omar Abdel-Rahman, the blind mullah convicted of plotting the first bombing of the World Trade Center in 1993, had preached.

In the winter of 2001 and all through 2002, Miller and the Bureau's other New Jersey–based agents had investigated more than sixty thousand leads implicating residents in the terrorist attacks. No matter how frivolous the tip—maybe a nervous citizen calling in the license plate number for a cab she saw being driven by a suspicious-looking man wearing a turban, a man who would later turn out to be a Sikh and not an Arab—the FBI was duty-bound to follow it up.

Ninety-nine percent of the tips that came in led nowhere except to the homes of innocent immigrants who quickly learned to fear the FBI. Under the Patriot Act, they knew the drill: if you were a Muslim, you could be made to disappear.

Miller was saddled with a rookie partner for the day.

Dale Krishock was straight out of Quantico and as green as they come. Even worse, what he lacked in experience he made up for with arrogance. The two men spent the day knocking on doors near Journal Square, pounding the pavement in predominantly Muslim neighborhoods, and asking people questions about phone calls.

They parked in front of another drab apartment building.

Krishock undid his seat belt. Sniffed the sleeve of his jacket.

"Jesus. That last house we went in to, what was she cooking?"

"Don't know."

"Smelled like fried goat shit."

Miller pressed hard on the emergency brake. Heard the spring stretch into a click. Typically, he did not apply the emergency brake when parking, but he figured it was a more appropriate use for his leg than kicking the fool sitting next to him.

It was Friday. The weekend was coming. He'd just grind his way through the rest of this bad day. First thing Monday, he'd request a new partner.

"Ghalam Salaam," Krishock read the next name on their list. "What do you think his mother called him when he was a kid? Swami Salami?"

"Dale?"

"Yes, sir?"

"Save it."

Miller rapped his knuckles against the metal door to Apartment 312.

Krishock sniffed the air in the dimly lit hallway. Grimaced. He didn't have to say what he was thinking.

The door opened a crack.

"Yes?" came a frail voice from behind the security chain.

"Mr. Ghalam Salaam?" said Miller.

"Yes?"

"We're with the FBI. We'd like to ask you a few questions."

"I have not done anything, I swear!"

"We'd just like to talk."

"Open the door, Pops," said Krishock. "We need to ask you some questions."

"You are with the FBI?"

"That's right," said Miller, holding up his ID for the man to see. "I'm Special Agent Miller." He didn't bother introducing Krishock.

"Who will pay my bills when you take me away to the secret prison? Who will buy my family food?"

"Mr. Salaam," said Miller, "I assure you—"

Krishock approached the door. Leaned on it hard. "Mr. Salaam? Either you open this door or, I swear to Allah, I'll open it myself."

Miller gripped Krishock's wrist, moved his hand away.

"Stand down," he whispered.

"What?"

"Go wait in the car."

Krishock bristled. "Excuse me?"

"Wait for me. In the car. Go. Now."

Krishock was short and stocky. Built like a fireplug. He glared up at Miller. In his peripheral vision, Miller caught a glimpse of one terrified eyeball widening above the security chain on the other side of the door.

"Go on, son," Miller said gently.

"It's against Bureau protocol for—"

Miller held out his hand. Waited for the younger agent to turn over the paperwork—the printout detailing Mr. Salaam's suspicious phone calls.

"I need the phone log."

Reluctantly, Krishock handed over the rolled-up tube of paper.

Then he turned and walked away.

It took less than five minutes for Miller to establish, beyond any doubt, that Mr. Salaam's federal offense had been calling his mother, who was gravely ill back home in Pakistan.

"I used a calling card. At night, the rates are low."

"I try to call my mom every Sunday after church," Miller said. "Just to keep in touch."

Salaam looked warily at the black man who was a federal agent. Who was here in his apartment and whose very arrival had terrified him.

Then Miller surprised him: he quoted Mohammed. "A man asked the Prophet: 'Whom should I honor most?' The Prophet replied: 'Your mother.' 'And who comes next?' asked the man. The Prophet replied: 'Your mother.' 'And who comes next?' asked the man. The Prophet replied: 'Your mother!' 'And who comes next?' asked the man. The Prophet replied: 'Your father.'"

When Miller finished, Mr. Salaam actually smiled.

"You are a good son, Agent Miller."

"As are you, Mr. Salaam."

"Would you care for a cup of tea? I could put on the kettle."

"No, thank you. I need to go bother a few more of your neighbors." Miller said it without any enthusiasm. "Again, I apologize for any inconvenience my partner and I may have caused you today."

"You partner—he is young?"

Now it was Miller's turn to smile. "You noticed?"

"It is hard not to."

"He'll grow up."

"Let us both pray for it. Have a good day, Agent Miller."

"Thank you. You, too."

The door closed. Miller turned and started up the corridor.

When he reached the stairwell, the cell phone clipped to his belt started chirping. He answered. It was Natalie. She was at Angela's school.

Something was wrong.

Despite Mr. Salaam's sincere farewell, Miller knew there was absolutely no way for him to have a good day.

Not today.

20

A string of orange and white pennants fluttered above the cars parked out front of the Hancock Toyota showroom in Knoxville, Tennessee.

The whole city was decked out in orange and white that Friday afternoon in anticipation of Saturday's football game against the Arkansas Razorbacks, when one hundred and seven thousand members of the Orange Nation would descend upon Neyland Stadium, the second-largest football facility in the country, and turn it into the fifth-largest city in the state of Tennessee.

Thomas C. Hancock stood sucking meat off a rib bone in the party tent. He was a huge fan of the Tennessee Vols. Some called him a jock sniffer. He didn't mind. He was too rich to give a damn what other people thought.

"Son, you gonna whip those Razorbacks tomorrow?" he asked his special party guest.

"Yes, sir," answered the polite young man in the navy blue blazer beside him.

"I can't hear you, boy!" Hancock boomed, loud enough for everybody crowded under the tent to hear.

"Yes, sir!"

"All righty. Damn. That's more like it, son!"

Hancock's prized guest of honor, Darryl Watkins, smiled. He was the leading rusher on the Tennessee team and an early favorite for the Heisman Trophy. He was also black. Everyone else under the tent was white.

Hancock draped his big arm over Watkins's even bigger shoulder. He jangled a set of car keys in front of the young college star's face.

"You sure you're gonna beat them hawgs, son?"

"Yes, sir."

"All righty then!"

Hancock let the keys slip from his greasy fingers. Watkins caught them in a flash. The crowd hooted and hollered.

"What'd I tell y'all?" Hancock's accent was thicker than sorghum syrup. "This-here boy's fast! Now, remember, son, that-there fifty-thousand-dollar Lexus is what we call a 'loaner.' Goddamn N-C-double-A sonsofbitches won't let me *give* it you but they sure as shit can't stop me from letting you borrow it for a couple years, now can they?"

The crowd laughed and clapped and whooped the school's war cries. Watkins climbed into the car. Started it up. More whoops. Hancock strutted around the tent like a prized peacock showing off his orange and white tail feathers. His guests knew the wily businessman donated enough money to UT's athletics program that he was guaranteed any special guest he wanted at his kickoff parties. They knew because Hancock liked to brag about it.

A couple of the party guests also knew about Hancock's secret passion because he loved to brag it as well, but only after the listener swore never to repeat what Hancock said to a living soul.

A truck horn sounded up on the highway.

Hancock grinned when he saw the eighteen-wheeler pull into his parking lot. It was Donny Oglethorpe's car carrier, loaded down with eight brand-new Toyotas—fresh off the boat from Japan.

Oglethorpe climbed down out of his cab, tugged at the seat of his pants.

His Jockey shorts had worked their way up his crack again. Rumbling south on I-81 for a full day would do that to you. He found his work gloves in the pocket of his leather vest and slipped them on.

He shook his head in disgust when he saw the black kid climbing into the fancy new car. A top-of-the-line Lexus.

Of course he knew that Mr. Thomas C. Hancock had so much damn money he could do whatever the hell he wanted, even give expensive cars to nigger ballplayers. Hancock was rich. Private-airplane rich. He had the kind of cash you don't make from selling Toyotas at 10 percent over dealer invoice.

Donny figured the sneaky old bastard was up to something seriously illegal. Maybe smuggling drugs. Maybe moving some of that opium shit out of Afghanistan. The old man had what they called political connections. Could probably get the U.S. Army or the CIA to harvest the poppy fields for him. The cargo he picked up off the Toyota dock in New Jersey was probably loaded down with the stuff. Bags of heroin jammed up inside all the wheel wells.

"Well, how the hell are you, Donny-boy?"

Mr. Hancock was waiting for him when he rounded his rig.

"Hey there, Mr. Hancock."

"You have a good ride down?"

"Yes, sir. Sure enough did."

Hancock held out a stadium cup with cool condensation dripping down its sides. He rattled around the ice cubes. "I fixed you up a Jack and Coke. Thought you might be thirsty."

"Thank you, sir."

Hancock handed him the drink. Donny slugged back a big gulp. He licked at the syrupy drops snagged in his mustache.

"Any trouble up in Newark?"

"No, sir."

Hancock squinted.

"Something troubling you, Donny?"

"No, sir."

"Don't shit a shitter, son. Speak your mind."

Donny drank a little more whiskey and Coke. Cleared his throat.

"Well, sir, how come you just gave that nigger boy a fancy new car?"

"Darryl Watkins? Shit, son, that boy's my prize field nigger. Still want him playin' for me on Saturdays, even after we win the coming conflict."

"I don't know about none of that, sir. I just seen a black boy driving out of here in a shiny gold Lexus that probably cost more than my goddamn house."

"Well, shit, Donny, you live in a goddamn double-wide on a rented patch of gravel down in Shitsville, Georgia."

"Goddamnit, sir, that boy's a darky."

"Come on, Donny. Cheer your ass up! Finish your drink and lower your damn ramp. I need to personally inspect that Sequoia back there." He pointed toward an SUV with black-tinted privacy glass. "I special-ordered it for a friend."

"He want it Bluesteel Metallic like that?"

"I let you in on a little secret, son: my friend don't give two shits what color it is. Just wanted to make sure it came off the boat fully loaded—with lots of special features Toyota don't print up in their damn brochures!"

"Yes, sir."

"He's picking it up tomorrow afternoon. Comin' to the game. Dr. John Tilley."

"Dr. Tilley?"

Hancock nodded.

Donny was impressed. He had some of Dr. John Tilley's CDs up in his truck. Listened to him all the time on long hauls. Knew the man was like Moses, leading white folks to the Promised Land—only Tilley wasn't no Jew.

"What kind of special features did he order?"

"Can't tell you. But I need to check it out. Come on, lower the gate. Hurry up, son."

"Yes, sir." Donny unhooked some chains, worked a lever, and slowly lowered the tailgate.

"Where's the keys to that Sequoia?" Hancock asked.

"You gonna take it out for a test drive?"

"No. I need to check out the back. See what's inside. You stand over there."

*   *   *

In the cargo hold of the SUV, Hancock's gifts to Dr. Tilley and the Cause looked harmless enough—like two five-foot lengths of army-green drainpipe. A sophisticated-looking black box was mounted to one steel tube and both canisters had canvas carrying straps to make them portable.

Hancock, like any good businessman contemplating an enormous expenditure, had done research prior to purchasing the two Stinger missiles from an Israeli arms merchant. So he knew the Stinger was what they called a man-portable, shoulder-fired, guided-missile system. It could be operated by a single soldier to take down any low-flying aircraft threatening his combat zone. The warhead was what the Pentagon boys called a "three-kilogram, penetrating, hit-to-kill" projectile. That meant, when the warhead smacked into something, it'd blow up real good.

"Damn," Hancock muttered. "Hot damn."

One of Dr. Tilley's soldiers could take down a god-damn jet airplane thanks to Hancock's generosity.

Hell, they could take down two.

21

On the Friday after Halloween, some of the kids in Angela Miller's first-grade class were already drawing pictures of Santa Claus.

"Christmas will be here soon enough," the teacher said, sympathetic to their excitement. "But first comes Thanksgiving. So let's stretch out our hands and trace around the edges and draw a big Tom Turkey."

Tyler, the blond boy sitting next to Angela, didn't follow the teacher's instructions. He wanted to draw Santa. He wanted to hurry up and write his letter to the North Pole.

"I'm getting an Xbox 360!" he gloated while Angela carefully ran a crayon around her thumb and four fingers to create her turkey head and tail feathers.

"I'm going to get that Deer Hunter game!" Tyler went on, furiously scribbling on his sheet of paper. "My dad said Santa was gonna bring it to me this year because I'm old enough." He nudged Angela with an elbow. "Check it out!"

The boy held up his crayon and construction paper masterpiece—a scribbled portrait of a wild-eyed Santa Claus with snarling teeth, and two submachine guns jutting out from his hips.

"Santa's going reindeer hunting!"

When Tyler said that, Angela wet her pants.

"We're approaching the one-year anniversary of her traumatizing event," Natalie Miller told her husband. "Usually, the date of an anniversary acts as the trigger. September eleventh. The day a loved one passed away. In Angela's case, it's Christmas and Santa Claus and all the imagery associated with the season."

Miller nodded. His wife had a Ph.D. in Forensic Psychology. She knew what she was talking about. In the headlong rush to the holidays, their little angel would be forced to revisit her nightmare every time she saw a sidewalk Santa or heard "Santa Claus Is Coming to Town" on the radio. Christmas's coming might also explain why Angela had been sleepwalking into their bedroom a lot lately.

"What do we do, doc?" Miller whispered. He could see his daughter's puffy coat hanging on a wooden peg in the foyer.

"I want to talk to a colleague in Pittsburgh. She specializes in Trauma-Focused Cognitive Behavioral Therapy for children."

Miller knew Natalie was switching into shrink-speak to mask her pain. Unfortunately, her daughter couldn't use the same trick.

"Okay, doc," said Miller. "That's good. We'll talk to Pittsburgh. We'll talk to anybody you think can help her. But what do we do *now*?"

"Right now?"

"Yeah."

"We need to be with her, Chris. Let her know that she's safe here—no matter what."

Miller nodded. "I can do that."

"Can you, Chris?"

"Okay. What's that supposed to mean?"

"Your job."

"Don't worry. Charlie can find somebody else to talk to people about their damn telephone bills."

Miller had left work as soon as Natalie called. He'd dropped Krishock off in Newark and broken a few speed limits to make it home even faster.

"Your daughter needs you, Chris."

"That's why I'm here."

"She has to become your number-one priority."

"She is."

"I mean it. We need to give her a sense of safety and security. In her eyes, you represent both those things. She needs to see you around the house. A lot."

"You want me to quit my job?"

"No."

"I'll do it."

Natalie knew he meant it.

"Where is she?"

"Up in her room."

"Okay." Miller headed for the stairs.

His wife's voice stopped him.

"Chris?"

"Yeah?"

"We can expect some regression in her behavior. Some acting out. It's symptomatic of PTSD."

Post-Traumatic Stress Disorder.

* * *

"Patrick Star is Sandy Claws, okay?"

"Okay."

Angela was sitting on her bed, playing with her Beanie Buddies. Patrick was a pink starfish in green shorts decorated with purple flowers. Miller knew Patrick was also a TV star—Sponge Bob Squarepants's underwater sidekick.

Angela wobbled the starfish across her bed.

"Ho, ho, ho. I'm Sandy Claws."

Angela was seven years old. She hadn't called Santa "Sandy Claws" since she was three.

"And guess what?"

"What, hon?"

"Pooky Bear is me!"

She found her teddy bear. Held it tight. Miller recognized him, too, from the Garfield comics.

"No. Wait!" Angela tossed Pooky Bear to the side. Crawled up to the top of the bed. Plucked a white bear off the bookshelf above the headboard. The bear had angel wings sewn onto its back. "I'm going to be Herald, not Pooky, okay? Herald is an angel, see, Daddy?"

She flapped the bear's shimmering wings.

"Sure," said Miller. "Herald the Angel. 'Hark, the Herald Angel sings. . . .'"

He tried to give the traditional carol a Motown groove. Tried to do it like the Temps. Even added a few shoulder dips. His bad choreography usually cracked his daughter up. But Angela wasn't paying attention. She was staring at the bear intently, so intently her eyes crossed.

"I'm Daddy's widdle angel."

More baby talk. What had Natalie called it? Regression.

"Sweetheart," he said softly, "you want to tell me what happened at school today?"

"We drew pictures."

"What kind of pictures?"

"Turkeys."

"Because it's almost Thanksgiving. That's good."

"I went wee-wee in my pants."

"I guess you had a little accident. That's okay."

Angela giggled. "I went wee-wee!"

She raised the stuffed bear above her head, moved it through the air, made believe it could fly.

"What about the picture the other boy showed you? That wasn't a turkey, was it?"

Angela shook her head.

"You know not every Santa Claus you see is automatically bad, honey."

"This one had a gun. Just like the other one."

Miller realized he was in over his head. Was he supposed to talk about the incident? Address the traumatizing event head-on? He'd back off for now. Check in with Natalie. Angela might need her father, but right now her father needed somebody with a degree in clinical psychology.

"I'm gonna run downstairs. Help your mother fix dinner."

"Okay." Angela zoomed the angel down over the starfish.

"I'll let you know when it's time to wash your hands. If you need me, just holler."

Miller stood up. His daughter didn't seem to see him.

He stepped into the hall and his cell phone started chirping. He snapped it open to make it stop.

"Hello?" he said in a whisper.

"Saint Chris. Tony. You okay?"

It was Cimino.

"Yeah."

"You sure?"

"Yeah."

"Then why are you whispering?"

"I'm at home. Angela's lying down. She got sick at school today."

"Oh. Sorry to hear it. Probably just that bug that's going around."

"What's up?"

"Just wanted to give you a little update on the thing at the Hyatt. Remember the waitress's story?"

"Yeah."

"It checks out. We got hold of the security tapes. The two guys are sitting there near the windows sipping beers for like twenty minutes before the other guy waltzes over to watch the TV. He sees the Amber Alert, then goes ballistic."

"So who was he?"

"Don't know. So far, we've got nothing. We're showing his picture around."

"Good."

"We also checked out Pettus. Rolled his fingerprints through the system. Seems he did some heavy-duty time in several of our finer correctional institutions. So, all of a sudden, I'm wondering if maybe his pal might be a brother from behind bars."

"A brother?"

"Yeah. That tattoo on Pettus's left arm? The fat chick in the helmet riding the horse?"

"Looked like a Valkyrie," said Miller. "Comes from Norse mythology."

"No shit?"

"Yeah. The Valkyrie carried slain heroes off to Valhalla."

"Where's that?"

"Heaven."

"Really? Well, she's what all the ganged-up white boys are wearing inside these days."

"Pettus was a skinhead?"

"We think so. Probably a member of some neo-Nazi group."

"And you think his friend at the bar belongs to the Brotherhood, too?"

"Nothing definite. Just a theory. On the security tape, when Pettus first meets him, they do this secret-handshake-type deal. You know, like baseball players tapping knuckles and touching pinkies."

"I see."

"I figure you and the Fibbies might want in on this. I'm starting to think that the grab on the Acevedo boy could've been racially motivated. You still hooked up with that Hate Crimes task force out of D.C.?"

A blur of white and sparkling silver distracted Miller. He looked into his daughter's bedroom.

"Bam! You're dead!" She was slamming the angel against the starfish. "Dead! Dead! Dead!"

"Hey, Chris? You still there?"

"Yeah," Miller told him. "I'm here. But I'm not working that other thing anymore."

He closed up his phone.

Natalie was right: Angela needed her father.

She needed him bad.

22

At noon on Saturday, Carl Krieger stepped into a small Milwaukee shop called Adambomb Tattoos.

It looked like a dentist's office. Clean. Well lit. But instead of before-and-after photos of gap-toothed grins bonded into perfect smiles, the walls were covered with tattoo samples. Thai tribal etchings. Jungle tigers. Jesus with a crown of thorns. Bleeding hearts.

"Can I help you?"

The young guy who stepped out from behind the curtained partition had curly poodle hair and wore a pair of bright-blue latex gloves. He also wore a blue smock. The dork matched the office. He looked like a fucking dentist.

"I need a tat."

"Cool." The tattoo artist pointed to the wall. "See anything you like?"

"I don't want any of this shit." He pulled a folded-up piece of paper out of his black cargo pants. Showed it to the dentist.

"Rad," the guy said admiring the artwork. "Totally Goth."

"Can you do me?"

"Give me like five minutes. I'm just finishing up with another client." The guy gestured toward the crimped curtains.

Krieger leaned left, snuck a peek.

He caught a glimpse of a hot-looking chick lying on her stomach with ratty jeans pulled halfway down her ass. There were wild purple roses and vines swirling out of her thong-strapped crack.

"Now that," Krieger said to himself, "is totally rad."

The tattoo artist was done with Carl Krieger's arm at 1:30 P.M.

"When you get home, take off the bandage," the guy said. "Use a Kleenex or paper towel to wipe off any moisture you see oozing out. But don't wash it, man. Not for like a day. Water content is like a totally major factor as far as healing is concerned. You got Bacitracin at home?"

"Yeah."

"Cool. Smear some on. Wait like fifteen minutes. If bubbles show up on the tattoo, wipe it off with another Kleenex and put on more ointment. Keep doing this like five times until there's no more bubbles."

Krieger nodded. "Cool."

"Rad art, dude."

"Thanks."

"Where'd you say you found it?"

"I told you. On the Web."

"Yeah—but what site? Might want to download it."

Krieger didn't answer. Just stared. He wouldn't go grab his bat, and bash in poodle-hair's brains for being so fucking nosy. Instead, he'd give him the slow eye-burn.

He pulled a roll of cash out of his black pants. Peeled off the bills.

"This cover it?"

"Totally."

It was time to move on. He needed to head over to Walker's Point.

In Milwaukee, that's where all the gay bars were located.

23

Alexander Schmitz stood beneath the fluttering American flags outside the Marriott Marquis Hotel.

Bellmen blew whistles. Guests stood in lines, waited for taxis. Yellow cabs lurched into the concrete terrace that took up the whole block between Forty-fifth and Forty-sixth streets in midtown Manhattan.

It was a little before two on a Saturday afternoon. Alexander had no idea where all these people were going. During his two days in New York City he had gotten used to Times Square. Everybody pushing and shoving to cross the street or gawk up at the whirl-wind of blinking lights and buildings that doubled as plasma-screen TVs with windows cut into the picture. Alexander had grown accustomed to the hordes of human rats chasing after cheap cheese.

It was shadowy in the portico near the flags. The few anemic evergreen shrubs planted in cement tubs were covered with soot. The squeak of rubber and brake pads echoed off the low ceiling. It was like waiting inside a very busy, very crowded, very dirty parking garage at the mall.

He heard two sharp horn honks.

A sleek black SUV pulled in alongside the yellow cabs and Lincoln town cars. Flashed its headlights.

Alexander nodded. Picked up his small gym bag.

It was time to begin the reconnaissance mission.

Time to drive out to JFK airport.

24

Saturday had started out a whole lot better.

Angela seemed to be Angela again.

She had come into her parents' room at 8 A.M.—not sleepwalking or to talk about "Sandy Claws," but to remind her father that it was Saturday morning and he should be downstairs in the kitchen making pancakes instead of sleeping.

"You're sure it's Saturday?" Miller asked through a yawn.

"Yes, Daddy," Angela whispered. "It's your turn to cook breakfast."

Miller pushed back the covers.

"My turn?"

"Yep."

"You're sure about that?"

"Daddy?"

"Okay, okay." Miller swung his feet out of bed. "If it's my turn to cook, then it must be Saturday."

"I already told you it was Saturday!"

"When?"

Miller smiled when he saw her sigh and shake her head in the way that said, very clearly, my daddy might be a big important FBI agent but sometimes he can act so silly I can't stand it. Angela looked just like her mother when she gave him that look.

That was a good thing.

His Angela was coming back.

Miller had been forty-five when his daughter was born. His wife was a whole lot younger. Theirs was one of those May-December marriages, and Miller had the snow up on his roof to show the world which calendar page belonged to him.

"Can we do marshmallows *and* chocolate chips?" Angela asked. She was kneeling on the kitchen counter, already pulling the necessary ingredients out of cabinets.

"Sure we can," said Miller. He saw her juggling a two-pound bag of Toll House morsels and deciding whether to pull down the peanut butter, too. "Be careful, Angel."

"I will." She found a bag of miniature marshmallows that had been twist-tied shut so many times the twisty was frayed and showing its wire.

Miller's bathrobe was pilled and nubby at the elbows and now dusty in the front, from the first cloud of Bisquick out of the box. He cracked open an egg and whisked it into his batter. "You want those chips baked into the pancakes or sprinkled on top?"

"Baked in. The chips don't melt if you just sprinkle them on top."

"And who taught you that?"

"You did!"

"I was just checking to see if you were paying attention."

"I always pay attention, Daddy. I remember everything."

Miller smiled. Tried to hide his thoughts.

Yes, little Angel, you do.

The crazy kidnapper disguised in a Santa suit. The bad man with the machine gun pointed at your head. The horrible things he said he would do to you.

You remember everything.

"Hey," Miller said as the first ladle of batter spread across the pan and started to simmer. "Guess who's playing football this afternoon?"

She climbed down from the counter.

"Notre Dame?"

"Yep."

Angela threw up her arms. "They play *every* Saturday."

"And that's what makes the fall such an excellent season."

"What about the spring?"

"That's basketball. Basketball is good. But Notre Dame football—that's excellent."

"Can I wear your jersey when we watch?"

"Which jersey is that?"

"Number forty-five. Best fullback alive."

Miller grinned. He had taught her that rhyme.

"Of course you can wear it, Angel. Wear it proud."

"It fits better this year."

Miller wouldn't disagree with his daughter even though the jersey was a size XXL and hung down past her ankles. Angela almost tripped on it every time she scurried off to the kitchen during the commercials.

"Good morning." Natalie came into the kitchen. "Coffee?"

Miller flipped the two pancakes bubbling in the pan, and then poured her a cup. He knew she'd miss the mug if she tried to pour it herself this early in the morning. Natalie Miller was a marvelous mother, a foxy lady, and a first-rate psychologist. She was not, however, a morning person.

"Mommy?"

Natalie took a sip from the mug. "What, honey?"

"The Santa Claus in the Macy's Day Parade. He's the real one, right?"

Natalie shot a glance to Miller who stood at the stove, ladling more batter into the pan.

"That's what Daddy says," Angela said.

Miller nodded. Yes. He had indeed said it. It was how he explained all those other Santas, the ones on every street corner ringing bells, the ones Angela had seen eating together at a table in the food court at the mall during their lunch break. Those are Santa's helpers, honey. The real Santa is the one at Macy's.

"It was in that movie, too," Angela continued.

Now Natalie nodded. "That's right, Angel."

"The post office said the Santa at Macy's was the real Kris Kringle and so they took him all those letters and he didn't have to go to jail or stay in the old folks home, either."

Miller smiled. He and Angela watched *Miracle on 34th Street* together every year. Sometimes more than once.

"That's right, honey," Natalie said. "In the movie, the real Santa is the one who works at Macy's."

"And he's the same one in the parade, too."

Natalie knelt down to look into Angela's eyes.

"Is that why you want to see the parade in person this year?"

Angela nodded. "I want to see the real Santa. See if he's still good. See if he's different from the other one."

Miller looked at his wife. Saw her face warming. He figured this must be some kind of breakthrough.

"Then that's where we'll go," said Natalie. "We'll all get up real early and go see the parade and see Santa."

"What about the turkey, mommy?"

"We'll eat a little later, okay?"

"Okay!"

Yes, indeed. Things were getting better.

The Notre Dame game kicked off at 2 P.M.

Natalie made grilled cheese sandwiches and tomato soup and the whole family ate lunch off the coffee table in front of the TV.

During halftime, Miller and Angela went out into the backyard and tossed around a Nerf football. Miller narrated every pass. Added color commentary. Did crowd sound effects whenever Angela caught the ball.

Angela mostly giggled.

During the second half, Natalie made microwave popcorn and served up cold apple cider. The three of them were snuggled into the sofa, enjoying the start of the fourth quarter, when a cell phone chirped.

It was Miller's.

He checked the caller ID.

Charlie Lofgren.

They had a situation.

"A hostage situation, Chris. Milwaukee. We need you on the next plane out."

25

Because of his big-giver alumni status, Thomas C. Hancock had been able to park the Toyota Sequoia underneath the Hancock Motors hospitality tent pitched behind Neyland Stadium.

"You need you another sandwich or something, Earl?" Hancock asked one of his guests: the guy who purchased light trucks for the university's maintenance crews. The Sterno-warmed trays of pulled pork, the mountains of barbecue spare ribs, the never-empty beer kegs, the crates of Jack Daniel's, the gift bags, hell, even the orange and white tent—all of it was tax deductible. Just the cost of doing business in east Tennessee.

"I'm fine, Tom. Just fine."

"Well, that's what I like to hear. Did y'all take that new Tundra out for a spin?"

The man named Earl wiped his mouth with his wrist. His bright-orange sweatshirt was speckled with tomato sauce.

"Sure enough did."

"Now that's a damn truck, am I right?

Earl nodded. Chewed a mouthful of stringy pork.

"We'll talk more on Monday!" Hancock clapped Earl on the back and moved on to another guest: Billy something-or-other. He draped his arm over the man's shoulder.

"How y'all doin'?"

Billy licked his fingers. "Damn fine ribs, Tommy."

"Hell, yeah. I figured we ought to have us some pork this afternoon, seein' how we're about to go inside and slaughter us some hawgs!"

The Arkansas team called themselves the Razorbacks. Their mascot was a wild boar and the fans made hog calls whenever their team took the field. Eating a ton of slow-cooked pork an hour before the game seemed fitting.

"You headin' over to Nashville next week?" the man asked. "For the Vandy game?"

"Hell, yeah."

"Got room on your plane?"

"Sorry, son. Full up. But I'm thinkin' about upgradin' to one of those corporate jets next year. Maybe a Hawker or a Gulfstream."

He surveyed his party guests. Wondered whom to greet next.

That's when he saw him.

Dr. John Tilley. Standing at the entrance to the hospitality tent, signing in with the cute girl who gave everybody their nametags. His face was lined with craggy creases from living out in God's country where the air was fresh and the water clean.

"I'll catch you later, Billy."

Hancock strode over to the sign-in table. The girl handed Tilley his nametag.

"Dr. John Tilley?"

"Yes?"

"Welcome to Tennessee, sir. I'm Thomas C. Hancock." He gripped his hero's hands with both of his own. "Sir, this is an honor and a pleasure. A goddamn pleasure."

"The pleasure's all mine. Thanks for inviting me down."

Tilley had a firm grip. A good handshake. The man was strong, with swept-back white hair and piercing eyes. Cobalt blue. This man's head needed to be carved into the side of a granite mountain for all to admire. Hell, someday, when the coming war was won, it probably would be.

"I can't thank you enough for all you've done," Tilley went on, his voice soft and intimate so no one else under the tent could hear. "Your magnanimous financial support has done more than anything to position us for the coming victory. We built this land, Thomas. Thanks to men like you, we will soon take it back."

"Sir," said Hancock, "I've been reading and listening to you for half my damn life."

"Just doing what the Lord sent me here to do."

"Amen. Let me introduce you around to some of my friends," Hancock said. "Say, you hungry? I'll have one of my boys fix you up a plate."

"Is that the vehicle?" Tilley asked, nodding toward the SUV.

"Yes, sir. She's fully loaded. All the accessories you asked for."

Tilley held out an open hand.

"Oh, right. Nearly forgot." Hancock fished around in his pocket. Found the key ring. "You driving it yourself?"

"Yes."

"You want the paperwork?"

"Yes. You put the title and registration in my name?"

"I meant on the other thing."

"There's paperwork?"

"Some."

"Destroy it."

"It's just a packing slip and bill of—"

"Destroy it."

Hancock and Tilley watched the first half of the Tennessee-Arkansas game from a luxury skybox. They sipped whiskey and smoked cigars. Tennessee scored early and often. The halfback, Darryl Watkins, ran like he had swallowed the engine of his new Lexus and kicked it into overdrive.

At halftime, the Pride of the Southland Marching Band went through its time-honored regimental paces.

When the teams came back on the field for the second-half kickoff, Tilley's briefcase started making a strange sound. A breep. High-pitched and different from any ringtone Hancock had ever heard. Tilley unsnapped the case and pulled out a phone that looked old-fashioned: big and boxy.

"Secure line," Tilley mouthed as he pressed a button. "Satellite phone."

Hancock was impressed.

Tilley pushed some buttons and raised the electronic wonder to his ear.

"This is Tilley. I see. No. Let me handle this. I'll do it from the car. Sit tight."

He switched off the phone.

"I'm sorry, Tom. I need to leave. Immediately."

"Problem?"

"I'm afraid so. Seems we have a situation. Up in Wisconsin."

26

After leaving the Milwaukee tattoo parlor, Carl Krieger had stopped at a nearby 7-Eleven.

"You got Bacitracin?" he asked the sleepy dude behind the counter reading a comic book.

"What?"

"Bacitracin."

The clerk closed up his comic. Started searching through the racks of cigarette packs. Looking for any brand of smokes that began with the letter B.

"It's first-aid shit," Carl said.

"Oh. Try aisle one."

Carl grunted. The clerk went back to his book. Didn't notice the aluminum baseball bat Carl carried hidden behind his leg. Carl shifted its hiding place to the front of his thigh when he turned and headed for the medicine aisle.

He found a tube of the antibiotic ointment in a dusty cardboard tray sandwiched between the diarrhea and constipation crap.

"You find what you need?" The clerk sounded bored. Carl couldn't blame him. Selling cigarettes and beef jerky and microwaved hot dogs all day must suck.

"Yeah. I found it."

The dude closed up his comic. Yawned. Hovered his hand over the cash register.

"Is there a price tag on it?"

Carl pretended to look.

"Nope."

The clerk reached out his hand.

"Let me see. Sometimes they stick it—"

Carl took a solid swing of the bat and cracked open the side of his skull. Whack. Just like playing T-Ball.

The clerk fell to the floor, his blood soaking all the torn straw wrappers and losing lottery tickets. Carl hopped over the counter and tried to jimmy open the cash register with his hunting knife. It had worked at the first convenience store. The one he knocked off prior to his tattoo session. That's how come he'd had the crisp Benjamins to peel off when it came time to pay.

This drawer wouldn't give so he smacked it twice with the bat until it finally popped free. He scooped out the cash and hopped back over the counter.

He snatched a couple pocket packs of Kleenex. Stuffed a few fistfuls of Baby Ruth and Snickers bars into the front flap of his hoody. He'd need food later. Baby Ruths and Snickers had peanuts. Peanuts were good for you.

A bell bonged as he waltzed out the sliding doors. Outside, he saw a stack of Mountain Dew cartons near the newspaper boxes. Grabbed one.

Carl figured he might need the Dew to help him do all that needed to be done that day.

*　*　*

The Flirtini Bar was located at 819 South Second Street in Walker's Point.

According to America Online, it was one of Milwaukee's hottest gay bars.

Carl parked his Pontiac in front of it.

He sucked on a warm can of Mountain Dew then rolled up his sleeve. The bandage covering his fresh tattoo looked wet so he peeled it off.

Underneath, his skin looked pretty gross.

Tiny bubbles were popping up all over the horse. Gunk oozed out of the tip of the fat lady's spear. He crumpled up the smelly gauze and tossed it out the window. Opening the Bacitracin, he did as instructed. He dabbed at the bubbles and stuck a clean sheet of Kleenex on top to act like a new bandage. The tattoo was gooey enough to make the tissue cling in place.

Carl had read about Flirtini on a Web site called The Guide. It had pictures. Men hugging men. An Internet ad for Flirtini said, "There is plenty of eye candy, but get there early . . . especially on weekends."

So that's what Carl Krieger had done. He'd gotten here early because he was on a mission. He was going to do what the Brotherhood always talked about. He would cleanse the country of sinners and sodomites. He would start at the Flirtini. Because God Hates Fags.

That was one of Carl's absolute favorite Web sites: god-hatesfags.com. He had totally burned it into his bookmark bar because it told the fucking truth about hurricanes and the war in Iraq. God hated America because America spit in His face and let homos into its army. That's what caused hurricanes. That's why so many soldiers were being slaughtered over in the desert.

He reached into the backseat and found the Sears Craftsman ax he had purchased for two bucks at a yard sale. The handle was made of stiff fiberglass, the head heavy and rimmed with rust. Carl figured some yuppie bought it so he could wear a flannel shirt, march into his backyard, and pretend he was Ronald Reagan. Then the lazy bastard let it sit for a couple years and get rusty. Men should take care of their tools. That's why Carl had sharpened the ax on the grinder when he got home after hanging out at Zad's with Rolf and Tiny.

He sharpened it until the slightest touch could slice into his thumb and leave a weeping gash.

He stepped out of the car. Hid the ax behind his right leg. Felt its heavy metal bounce against the heel of his boot.

The Flirtini was a crappy building that looked like a repair shack in a railroad yard. Its boxy windows were covered with blackout blinds.

So nobody could see all the sick shit going on inside.

The only indication that the building was a bar came from the neon sign sticking out between the upstairs windows. Flirtini. The final "i" was a wiggly-stemmed martini glass.

Shit.

The OPEN sign was dark.

Fuck.

Carl went to the door. A decal said the place didn't open until 5 P.M. on Saturdays. Of course, it stayed open until three in the morning but that didn't help him. Not now.

It was 2 P.M.

He needed to do this to show Tiny and all the other Wisconsin brothers what they ought to be doing instead of riding around town talking tough.

A shadow swept across one of the window shades.

Carl crouched low. Clutched the ax tighter. Moved to the window. Peered through the crack where the blinds didn't quite reach the side.

He saw a Mexican guy pushing a mop. Short dude with greasy black hair. T-shirt. Baggy pants. He was stacking chairs on top of tables so he could swab down the floor.

Probably a gay. Who else would work in a gay bar?

Carl moved over to the door. Tried the knob. It wasn't locked.

Carl Krieger stepped inside with his ax.

27

"How many hostages?"

Christopher Miller had taken his cell phone into the bathroom so he could talk to his boss without Angela overhearing the conversation.

"Two that we know of, Chris. A witness in Milwaukee saw the suspect drag two men out of the bar. A place called Flirtini. It's in the gay district."

"I see."

It sounded like a bias incident. What the FBI also classified as a Hate Crime—a criminal offense "motivated, in whole or in part, by the offender's bias against a race, religion, disability, sexual orientation, or ethnicity/national origin."

"Who were the two men?" Miller asked. "Patrons?"

"No. One was the custodian. A Mr. Jose Irredo. Hispanic. Mexican we think. The other was the manager. Mr. Geoffrey Gilroy."

"You're certain this wasn't a robbery?"

"Positive. Gilroy had just been to the bank. Cash had been counted out and lined up in the cash registers. None of the fresh bills were taken. The strapping bands weren't even broken. However, the Milwaukee police like our doer for two robberies earlier in the day. The incidents took place at convenience stores and in both cases the clerk manning the register was bludgeoned to death with a baseball bat."

Miller grimaced.

"He had an ax when he left the gay bar," Lofgren continued. "The witness saw him use it to threaten the two men, to force them into his car. A late-model red Pontiac. The witness was later able to ID the perp from the convenience store security cameras."

"When did he cross state lines?"

"About an hour ago. The witness wrote down his plate number, called 9-1-1. State troopers spotted the vehicle on the interstate. Chased the car all the way to Illinois."

"Is he headed for Chicago? That's only about ninety miles south of Milwaukee."

"We don't know. The troopers lost him. Apparently this kid knows more back roads than they do."

"Kid?"

"The convenience store tapes show him to be a teenager. Maybe eighteen. Baby-faced. Chubby. He was wearing a hooded sweatshirt, black pants, and military boots. We know he has the ax and a bat. We fear he may have other weapons as well."

Miller sat down on the closed toilet seat lid. Thought hard.

"Charlie, you don't really need me on this—"

"We think we found a bandage with the boy's DNA on it. It was in the gravel near where he parked outside the bar. We also found an empty Mountain Dew can. We should be able to lift prints off the can, take a sample off the gauze."

"Charlie?"

"Yes, Chris?"

"Why are you calling me?"

"Washington wants to set up a Critical Incident Response Group, ASAP. Some of the guys you teamed up with down there on that Hate Crimes Working Group think this one has your name written all over it. The Special Agent in Charge, Andrew Jackson, asked for you."

Now Miller rubbed his temples. Massaged his brow.

The Working Group was put together back in 1998. Before Angela was born. Miller had liked working with the team. Liked Andrew Jackson. When they met, they joked that they never knew the FBI had so many brothers in its ranks. They all wanted in on the Hate Crimes Group. Some of the African-Americans, including Miller, had first met back in 1996 when they worked together on the National Church Arson Task Force, tracking down KKK firebugs who liked to torch black houses of worship.

Also before Angela was born.

"Chris," Lofgren continued, "it's a hate crime coupled with an apparent kidnapping. Two areas where you can help a whole hell of a lot. Andy Jackson could really use you out in Illinois."

There was a light rap on the bathroom door. Tiny knuckles.

"Daddy?"

Miller covered the mouthpiece.

"Just a second, Angel."

"I need to use the bathroom."

"Use the one upstairs."

"Daddy?"

"Upstairs, Angela."

"Okay." He could see her pouting, even though the door was closed. "Daddy?"

"What, honey?"

"The game isn't over yet."

"I know. I'll be right out."

"Promise?"

"I thought you had to use the bathroom."

He waited until he heard small feet tromping up the staircase.

He pressed the phone to his face.

"Sorry about that."

"Look, Chris, we need to move fast. There's a plane out of Newark in an hour that'll get you to Chicago by seven. We think our doer has gone into hiding because we stopped getting hits on the tags. Nothing for about an hour. He knows we're looking for him. It's all over the radio and TV. Maybe he'll make contact. Try to work out a deal. Negotiate a surrender and release of his hostages. When he does, you and your team—"

"Charlie, we don't have jurisdiction." Lofgren didn't respond so Miller kept going. "Technically, even though the Act specifies hate crimes motivated by a sexual orientation bias, it doesn't give the FBI any power to investigate in those instances. We have to leave those cases to local authorities."

He had spent too much time with the Working Group not to know the law's parameters. But saying it out loud made Miller sound like he was trying to weasel out of the assignment on a technicality.

"I know the rules, Chris. This isn't just a gay thing. The janitor is Hispanic. The manager is black. The perp wrote racial slurs and epithets on the menu board at the bar. He transported two individuals against their will across state lines—"

"Charlie, I'm sorry. You need to send someone else."

"Come again?"

"Tell Andrew and the other guys down in D.C. I can't do it. Not today. Not this weekend."

As soon as the words left his mouth, Miller regretted saying it that way. Now he was worse than a weasel: now he didn't want to come into work on his day off.

"Chris, I realize I'm calling at a rather inconvenient time, but Jackson specifically requested—"

"Not today, Charlie. Send someone else."

28

The Denali took Exit 1 off the Van Wyck Expressway and followed the signs to Kennedy Airport.

Alexander Schmitz didn't recognize the driver. It wasn't the same guy who had picked him up when he flew into New York from Buffalo. This guy had a shaved head and a tattoo creeping up the back of his neck. A swastika.

Alexander sank down in his seat. Pushed up on his sunglasses.

Some members of this movement were idiots. Plastering their necks with such obvious symbols? Nothing too suspicious about that. If he were running things, certain members of the Brotherhood would be the first ones eliminated in the coming race war.

Besides, the driver talked too much.

"So, like I was saying, the big boys expressed an interest in the cargo area out here after *I* told them about it first." His New York accent was as thick as his tattooed neck. "They told me to show you around."

Alexander merely nodded.

"In fact, I come out here the other day, just to make sure it was as easy as I said." The driver maneuvered through a series of confusing off-ramps and wrap-arounds. "You'll see. We can drive right up to the cargo buildings. So close, you could take a piss on the runway. No cops. No security guards. No nothin'. I like Cargo Area C the best. If the wind's blowing right, the planes take off over your head."

Alexander looked out the window. Surveyed the scene. They passed a FedEx building. What looked like a Delta warehouse. It was 4:30 P.M. The sun was already starting to set. Each day was nearly a minute shorter than the day before. Alexander had consulted the sunrise/sunset calendar for November. He needed to be prepared for the job—whatever that job might be.

"It's getting dark out," the driver said. "Maybe you want to take off the shades."

Alexander didn't touch his sunglasses.

They rumbled into a rutted asphalt area surrounded by several single-story warehouses. The sprawling buildings were dumpy, nondescript. Idle freight trucks sat double-parked in front of loading docks. Since it was Saturday, most of the sliding cargo doors were closed, the loading docks deserted.

Alexander heard a huge roar. He looked up and saw the rumbling belly of a 747 groaning into its initial takeoff. The plane's shimmying undercarriage seemed so close he could count the rivets.

"Lufthansa," said the driver. "Flight 686. JFK to Tel Aviv. More Jews heading home to the Promised Land." He turned his thumb and forefinger into a pistol and aimed it at the tail fin. "Or, maybe not!"

The driver chuckled. Alexander didn't.

"Park over there." Alexander pointed to a squat brick building. Something called the Vet Port. Black plywood cutouts of dogs and horses scampered in the garbage pit that must've been a flowerbed once. A banner was bolted above the building's windows: "J.ust F.or K.reatures Animal Hospital."

JFK. Cute. Stupid.

"I want to reconnoiter this area."

"I told you it was good out here. Like shooting fucking ducks in a barrel."

Alexander opened his door. "Fish," he said before climbing out of the Denali.

"Do what?"

"The expression is 'shooting fish in a barrel.'"

"Whatever. You want I should watch your back? I'm carrying."

"No. Stay with the vehicle."

The driver nodded. Looked slightly pissed.

Alexander strode across the parking lot fronting the animal hospital. There were a few cars. An empty horse trailer. He could hear dogs barking. He figured this was some sort of quarantine kennel for traveling animals.

He heard another roar. Reflexively looked up.

Another jumbo jet lumbered up into the sky.

Rush hour.

The driver was right. Here was an excellent firing position. No need to worry about smuggling a weapon past the TSA lackeys inside the terminal. No need to bribe baggage handlers to gain access to the tarmac. You could take Exit 1 off the Van Wyck, follow the signs to Cargo Area C, pull in, park, pop off a single shot, bring down your bird.

It'd be like a turkey shoot where you pay three dollars to shoot a 12-gauge shotgun at a paper target. It was almost too easy to be fun.

There didn't seem to be many security cameras, at least none that Alexander could see. They would need to investigate further.

If they drove to the location in a cargo vehicle, they could blend in. Disappear. Be back on the Van Wyck before the fifty thousand gallons of jet fuel exploded inside the 747's wings.

The TalkSECURE cell phone clipped to Alexander's belt began to vibrate. He answered it.

"This is Schmitz."

"Where are you?"

He recognized the voice: Dr. John Tilley.

"JFK Airport, sir."

"Right. Good. Small change of plans."

"Yes, sir."

"We need you in Chicago. There's a flight at seven. If you hustle, you can make it."

"Yes, sir."

"Have you touched any weapons today? Any gunpowder?"

"Negative."

"Good. Security should pose no problem. Buy a small suitcase. Clothes. I'm certain you can find both items in the airport shops. You'll look suspicious if you approach the ticket counter empty-handed."

"Yes, sir."

"We need to delay our preparations for the main event. Hopefully, this distraction can be dealt with swiftly."

Another jet rumbled past overhead. Alexander had to press the phone closer to his ear to hear anything.

"Was that a jet?" Tilley asked.

"Yes, sir. Swissair. L-10-11."

"Taking off or landing?"

"Taking off."

"Of course. Takeoff is always noisier. You need all that engine thrust because the plane is heavier. Full of fuel."

"Yes, sir."

Alexander waited for more. Tilley remained silent. The Swissair jet climbed into the darkening sky.

"A driver will be there for you at O'Hare," Tilley said.

"Very good, sir."

"Afterward, you and I will meet."

"I look forward to it, sir."

"Good luck in Illinois."

Tilley terminated the call. Alexander put the phone back into its belt holster.

Behind him, a dog snarled and growled.

"Sorry," said a young girl tugging at a pit bull on a taut leash. They had just come out of the Just For Kreatures building. She yanked back on a choke chain.

"Leave it, Maggie. Leave it!"

The dog sank back into its haunches. Every muscle in its massive chest twitched. The small girl pulled harder.

"I said leave it!"

The pit bull bared its teeth and hacked out a chorus of angry snarls. When the beast curled back its lips, it looked like it might be smiling.

Alexander smiled back.

Then he held up an invisible rifle. Aimed it at the dog. Squeezed an imaginary trigger.

"Bang," he said softly. "You're dead."

29

The Forest Preserve District of Cook County, Illinois, operated overnight camping facilities for what they called "properly supervised" youth organizations.

Five years ago, when Carl Krieger had been a Boy Scout, his troop had come down here. They had built a rope bridge across a piddling creek and rubbed sticks together in a fire pit and slept in heated cabins.

He and Rolf made the trip again last year—to drink beer and smash out a few cabin windows and spray-paint swastikas on the cabins where he knew some Hebes from the Chicago YMHA had spent the night.

It was dark. His headlights slashed across naked trees and hit the red sign that told him he had arrived. Camp Reinberg. Dogs must be leashed. Camping by permit only.

Carl didn't have a fucking permit.

He just had two nervous fags in the backseat, their mouths sealed tight with duct tape, their hands tied behind their backs with spare zip strips, leftovers from when he bundled up all his computer cables so his mother would quit bitching at him about the tangle of wires in his bedroom that made it so fucking hard to vacuum.

The cops wouldn't think to look for Carl holed up in a summer camp the first weekend of November.

"Get out of the fucking car." Carl pulled the rear door open. Banged the head of his ax against the sheet-metal roof for emphasis. "Move! Now!"

The two men slid across the seat. Both stumbled when they climbed out. There was no light—no street lamps, no blazing bar neons, no moon—so the queers couldn't see the wet muck underfoot. They both slipped. Fell.

Carl kicked them.

"Get up!"

The small fag, the spic, wore droopy jeans so baggy they dragged down behind the heels of his greasy tennis shoes. The other one was black and seriously gay. Both looked scared to death. The whites of their eyes glowed, like raccoons caught rummaging in the trash.

"Move it!"

The Mexican one pretended like he didn't understand English. So Carl gave his ass another kick.

"Move it! Up the hill!"

They staggered up a path that Carl knew led to the dining hall. The building had a toilet, a couple of electric stoves, running water, and a bunch of picnic tables.

Carl now realized he probably should've planned this thing a little better. Done more than sharpen his ax and get inked up with a Valkyrie tattoo. He probably should've found a gun. Maybe packed some food besides the Snickers.

Of course his plan had been to kill the homos back at the gay bar. That way, everybody would know why they had died: because God Hates Fags. He had scrawled those words on the marker board where they listed the drink specials. Just then a beer delivery dude had showed up at the back door.

So Carl took off with his two captives. But he knew the back roads better than anyone. Lost the cops the beer guy must've called when he got off the interstate.

Carl pushed his hostages up the path. The black one tripped on a tree root.

"Keep moving!"

They reached the dining hall door.

It was locked.

Fuck.

Carl really should have put more time into this.

"Stand back!" he screamed. He raised the ax up over his head, lined up its blade with the doorknob.

He sensed movement to his left.

The little wetback was trying to run away.

"Get back here, you motherfucking faggot!"

Carl took off after him. When he did, the nigger tried to run away, too.

"Stupid sonofabitch!"

He knocked the black queen's legs out from under him with a backswing of the ax, slammed the blunt end of the heavy steel head against the son of a bitch's kneecaps. Heard tendons tear. Screams muffled by duct tape.

Carl pivoted, dashed up the hill toward the road.

The stupid spic homo, wearing ghetto jeans six inches too long for his legs, tripped and tumbled headfirst into a huge rock.

Carl marched to where he lay. Dragged the ax through the leaves behind him. Let it bump and glide along the ground. Not-So-Speedy Gonzalez was all lined up and ready for the slaughter. The rock would make an excellent chopping block.

"You run, you die."

The man moaned. Squirmed. Rolled his body over and stared up at Carl with terrified brown eyes.

"Quit looking at me like that, you sick fuck!" He grabbed the ax with both hands. Swung it up over his head.

A flashlight blinded his eyes.

"What the hell's going on here?" a voice cried out.

Carl squinted. Tried to see who was behind the beam.

The light swung down to the petrified fellow sprawled on his back on the rock.

"Jesus!" The voice sounded horrified.

"Back off, old man!" Carl screamed. "Back off or I swear to God I'll cut off his fucking head."

"Whoa! Take it easy, son."

"You take it easy! Back off!"

"Okay . . . okay . . . I don't have a weapon."

"Yeah? Well I sure as shit do." Carl brandished the ax. "I've got guns," he lied. "Inside. Dynamite, too. So you try anything stupid, I swear to God I'll kill these two homos and blow up this whole fucking place!" Carl squinted again. Tried to size up his adversary. "Who the fuck are you?"

"Park superintendent."

Carl grabbed his prisoner's arm. Pulled him up off the ground. Dragged him backward. Showed the park ranger his ax again.

The flashlight swung up into his eyes.

"Turn that fucking thing off!"

"You're that kid from the convenience stores."

"What?"

"I saw what you did. Saw it on TV."

"Good. Then you know I'll do it again."

He moved backward, using his captive as a shield.

"Take it easy, son," the voice behind the light said. "I'm sure we can work this thing out. There's no need to hurt anybody else."

Carl made it to the porch. He kicked backward at the door with the heel of his boot. Felt the lock give. Shoved one prisoner inside.

The black queen was sprawled on the porch, holding his knee. Carl kicked him in the ribs.

"Get up."

The black guy tried. His knee crumpled.

"Stupid little sissy . . ."

He was about to kick the guy in the balls when the damn flashlight blinded him again.

"Take it easy, son! Don't hurt that man."

Carl froze. Damn, he needed a plan.

"I'm sure we can work this thing out." The voice was practically begging.

Good.

"You call the police!" Carl screamed. "You tell them I want a helicopter and a million dollars. They bring me my money and a helicopter and they fly me to Canada, nobody gets hurt."

"Okay . . . take it easy. . . ."

"Get me my fucking helicopter!"

Carl grabbed the black man's foot. Dragged him across the porch and into the dining hall. The fag screamed the whole way.

Carl kicked the door shut.

A million dollars. A helicopter. Canada.

Finally, he had a plan.

30

On Sunday morning, Christopher, Natalie, and Angela Miller sat in the second-to-last pew of Holy Rosary Church in Jersey City.

The choir finished singing its chorus of alleluias. An altar boy opened a Bible encased in ornate gold plate and held it up over his face to act like a podium for Father Labriolla's reading of the gospel. The elderly priest raised both arms and the entire congregation stood.

"A reading from the Gospel of Luke."

It was the story of Zacchaeus, the chief tax collector. A wealthy man because, in the old days, the tax collector was allowed to skim off a percentage of everything he took in for the government. Sort of like low-level mobsters collecting for the bosses.

Miller's attention drifted in and out as the priest went on about Zacchaeus climbing a sycamore tree so he could catch a glimpse of Jesus passing through town.

Miller was more concerned about whatever Charlie Lofgren's "situation" might be. It wasn't like his boss to call him at home on a Saturday unless it was urgent.

And what about Andrew Jackson? Miller wished he could be out in the field, helping his friend, but Angela needed his help more. Needed him to stay home.

The priest read the part of the story where the people start grumbling because Jesus is willing to eat dinner in the home of a tax collector, a sinner. It was the gospel the priests at St. Peter's Prep used to paraphrase when they dealt with an unruly student: "If Jesus can dine with sinners, I suppose I can tolerate you."

Father Labriolla closed the big Bible.

"This is the word of the Lord."

"Thanks be to God," the congregation chanted and sat down to hear the priest's sermon.

"In the name of the Father and the Son and the Holy Spirit. Amen."

Miller made the sign of the cross. Beside him, Angela did the same, mumbling, "Home plate, pitcher's mound, third base, first," to help her remember head, heart, left shoulder, right.

"I'm sure you all heard the news from Chicago this morning. Maybe you saw the horrible pictures on TV."

Miller glanced over to Natalie. She shrugged. They hadn't turned on the TV this morning. Hadn't listened to the radio on the drive to church. Neither one had any idea what Father Labriolla was talking about.

The priest gripped the lectern. Composed himself. He certainly had Miller's attention.

"Such a senseless tragedy, this murder of a young immigrant. A hardworking man who came to this country to give his wife and children the hope of a better life." Miller could tell that Father Labriolla, himself the grandson of Italian immigrants, was tamping down his rage. "And what an unspeakable crime. A brutal, barbaric beheading."

Miller cringed. Wished Angela wasn't hearing this. Wondered if she knew what "beheading" meant.

"Let us also pray for the hostage still being held and hope that someone can get through to his misguided captor. It is our duty as Christians—no, as humans—to stop the spread of this sort of barbarism here in our own country. It's like Edmund Burke said so many years ago: 'All that is necessary for the triumph of evil is that good men do nothing.'"

Father Labriolla walked away from the lectern, went to his chair, bowed his head, and prayed in silence.

So did the entire congregation.

Everyone except Christopher Miller. He suddenly realized how he could help the "good men" out in Illinois. And he could do it without abandoning Angela.

He turned in the pew.

Natalie was already looking at him. Her jaw set. Her face firm. She reached down and took Angela's hand.

"Go," she whispered. "Hurry."

31

Alexander Schmitz took his time.

The local Illinois liaisons had provided him with a jumpsuit of what the manufacturer called "Fall Mimicry" camouflage. It was the silvery gray and chalky black of moth wings with just a touch of autumn leaf color tossed into the pattern to allow him to blend in completely with the Cook County Forest Preserve.

He moved twenty yards west. Froze.

He had come into Deer Grove from Hicks Road, about a half mile east of all the excitement.

Now he could see them.

Down the hill. Police, FBI, and ATF agents were everywhere, the backs of their navy blue windbreakers emblazoned with bright-yellow initials. They had established a wide perimeter. Roads were blocked. Roof lights swirled on top of SUVs and patrol cars. Nobody was allowed in or out without some form of federal or police ID.

Nobody except Alexander Schmitz. Then again, the federal army didn't know he was here. A half mile away. Keeping his distance.

He didn't need to be close to do his job.

He kept parallel to the bicycle path that made a 2.6-mile loop through the eastern sector of the forest.

No bikes were on the path today. In fact, the whole preserve was locked down. No one could slip in unless, of course, they had been trained to do so by another branch of the federal government. The U.S. Army.

"Mr. Krieger?" a tinny voice squawked in the distance.

It was one of the federal agents, calling through a bullhorn.

"We're finalizing the details," the amplified voice continued. "I just talked to the Air National Guard. Your helicopter is on the way."

Alexander assumed the Feds were lying to the boy. They'd tell him anything at this point to avoid a fire-fight. The kid had already killed one hostage. Did it Al Jazeera style: lopped the man's head off with an ax. Did it on the porch so the TV crews, which, earlier, had been allowed past the perimeter, could see. The networks and CNN wouldn't show the "graphic images" on their morning news broadcasts but video of them was no doubt looping like crazy on the Internet.

Now the TV people had been pushed back and were no longer allowed anywhere near the standoff.

There was a shrill beep and another burst of static. The bullhorn.

"I repeat: your helicopter is on the way."

"What the fuck is taking so long?" shouted someone from inside the dining hall. Alexander assumed it was Carl Krieger. The young man sounded tired. Angry.

"As we told you, the morning fog at the Air National Guard base—"

"You've got an hour! You hear me? If that fucking helicopter isn't landing where I can see it in sixty fucking minutes, I'm chopping off the nigger's head and blowing up this whole goddamn building!"

According to news accounts, the young man doing the screaming was extremely well armed, with enough dynamite and plastic explosives, he claimed, to bring down the dining hall. He seemed very willing to commit suicide rather than be captured by armed agents of what he called the ZOG—the Zionist Occupational Government, the people who really ran the United States of America.

"Tell you what, Carl," said the man on the megaphone. "We're going to toss in a cell phone so we don't have to shout at each other like this, okay?"

"Fuck that! You want to teargas me! Toss in a flash-boom!"

"No. It's just a cell phone. I promise."

"Fine. I'll put the nigger in the door. Toss it to him. If it's a fucking gas canister, his ass is the one you're gonna fry!"

Alexander headed further up the hill toward a thick oak standing at the crest of a ridge. Most of the trees in this section of the forest preserve were spindly, hardly worth preserving. The oak up the hill had a massive trunk, wide enough to offer ample cover.

He had no radio to relay in the coordinates of his final position. He had no cell phone to alert the Illinois militia as to his movement. He was alone in the battle zone—just the way he liked it.

All he had packed in on the mission were his canteen, some beef jerky, and his H.S. Precision Pro-series 2000

HTR, also provided by the local militia. The 2000 had a fully adjustable stock, detachable magazine, stainless-steel fluted barrel, and a German-made Schmidt-Bender scope—optics so good you could shoot a lion in the dark with nothing but the light from your flashlight.

It was an excellent HTR: Heavy Tactical Rifle.

It also happened to be the same sniper weapon system currently being carried by the FBI's sharpshooters, all of them secretly hoping Carl Krieger would soon step in front of a window so they could take him down.

32

Carl grabbed the cell phone the FBI bastards tossed to Gilroy the second the black man crawled back inside the dining hall.

"Get back under the sink."

Gilroy did as he was told. He squeezed under the counter, hugged his knees.

The phone rang.

Carl sank down on the floor. Propped his back up against a wall. He knew better than to stand near any windows. Knew the ZOG army had SWAT teams and sharpshooters hidden in the woods, just waiting for a clean shot to take him down. The FBI's rules of engagement were always the same, ever since Ruby Ridge: if you see him, shoot him.

Carl would make damn certain they couldn't see him.

"Yeah?" he said into the phone.

"Carl?"

"What?"

"My name is Andrew Jackson."

"Bullshit."

"I'm an agent with the FBI."

"You a nigger? You sure as shit sound like one."

There was a pause.

"I am an African-American."

"Damn if that don't beat all. A nigger named after a white president, a goddamn white hero! You think we're ever gonna put a nigger's face on the twenty-dollar bill?"

"Andrew was my father's name," came the calm reply.

"You a fag? You got the hots for Gilroy? That why you want him outside so bad?"

"Mr. Krieger, there is no need for you to hurt Geoffrey Gilroy, or anyone else, for that matter."

"Bullshit. This is war, Andy. Time for those of us who built this country to fight back against the Zionists and their nigger henchman and Hollywood homos who took it away!"

"Your helicopter is coming, Carl."

"What about my million dollars?"

"It will be on the helicopter as you requested."

"Unmarked Canadian currency, right?"

"Yes."

"Good. The Jews don't rule Canada. Not yet. My brothers up there will protect me."

"I'm sure they will. How is Mr. Gilroy doing?"

"The fag is fine."

"Are you two hungry? I could send in some food."

Carl was starving but he wasn't stupid. They'd put poison in any food they sent him. They'd mash up sleeping pills and hide them in his hamburger so he'd be woozy when they stormed the dining hall.

"Fuck you, Andrew Jackson. Don't call again unless it's to tell me my fucking helicopter has landed." He checked his watch. "It's noon, nigger. You have thirty more minutes or your girlfriend dies."

33

Andrew Jackson closed up his cell phone and stuffed it into a front flap on his flack jacket.

"I am absolutely the wrong individual to be talking to this goddamn cracker," he said to the other agents of the Hostage Response Team assembled at the command post set up inside the Winnebago. "Ed, are the sniper teams in place?"

"Roger that," said the man on the radio with a soft southern accent. "They are locked and loaded, ready to take Krieger down hard and fast."

"Tell them to stand by."

Jackson wanted to talk the boy out of the dining hall. Wanted to stop any more senseless bloodshed. The crazy kid had already killed three people. Two convenience store clerks and the busboy from the bar in Milwaukee. Jackson, who was thirty-four and on the job with the Bureau for a dozen years, wished his old friend and mentor Christopher Miller were there to suggest what he should try next. Miller had seen more of this crazy shit than anybody on the team.

Not showing up for a tough assignment wasn't like Saint Chris. Wimping out on the Bureau and his brothers. Unwilling to help apprehend a boy who hung with the Brotherhood, a group that the Hate Crimes team had been tracking for over a decade.

There was a light rap on the camper's metal door.

"Yeah?" Jackson said without looking over to see who or what it might be.

"Agent Jackson?"

"Yeah."

"I'm Dale Krishock. Special Agent out of the Newark field office."

Jackson swiveled around in his chair.

"Newark?"

"Yes, sir. I report to Charlie Lofgren."

"I know who folks report to in Newark."

The agent in the door nodded. He looked like a kid just out of college. Wore a brand-new navy blue windbreaker. Probably still smelled like the plastic bag it came in.

"Long way from home aren't you, Agent Krishock?"

"I flew into Chicago this morning."

"Really? Why?"

The kid blinked. Up where his jacket zipper ended, Jackson could see the knot of a necktie. Only rookies wore ties on field assignments.

"What brings you all the way out here on a Sunday morning? Itching for some action, son? Eager to try out that shiny new Glock they gave you down in Quantico?"

"My Agent In Charge said you needed help."

Jackson bristled. He never needed "help." Sometimes he needed assets, like Christopher Miller, a skilled negotiator, but he never needed "help" from some young pup who figured shooting real men might be as much fun as blasting holes in those paper targets down on the FBI firing range.

"I'm sorry you flew all the way out here, Agent Krishock. Sorry Lofgren's gonna have to eat the cost of your airplane ticket."

"I flew out on my own dime."

"And used your Fed creds to get past my perimeter?"

"Yes, sir."

"Look, son, we're very busy. I need to ask you to clear out of my command center and—"

A telephone near the radio gear jangled.

The radio operator snatched it up. "This is Delroy, go ahead. Just a second." He cupped his hand over the mouthpiece. "Andy, it's Chris Miller."

"Is he on his way?"

The radioman went back to the phone. "Where are you, Chris? Okay. Hang on." He shook his head. "He's still in Jersey City."

Jackson took the phone. Noticed the kid named Krishock was still hovering near the door.

"Yeah, Chris?" Jackson nodded. "I understand. But—" Jackson listened.

"It's a pretty heavy chip to play."

He nodded. Miller was making sense.

"Make the call."

Jackson hung up the phone. Turned to the kid standing in the step well near the screen door.

"Agent Krishock?"

"Sir?"

"Go check with Barb Szydlowski outside. She's running tactical support. She'll tell you where she needs you."

"Yes, sir." He closed the door behind him.

"So?" the radioman asked. "What'd Miller suggest?"

Jackson stuffed his hands into his jacket. Frowned.

"That we play an ace we've been holding on to since nineteen ninety-nine."

34

The cell phone chirped again.

Carl Krieger checked his watch.

"Did you hear a helicopter?" he said to Geoffrey Gilroy. "You better pray they're calling to tell me my goddamn whirlybird just landed or I might need to take a couple whacks at your neck, boy."

Gilroy didn't answer. Kept his head bowed.

"You fucking praying? Might be a good idea— considering your current situation. Only one problem. God don't listen to prayers from fucking apes."

The phone rang a second time. Carl snapped it open. "What?"

"Carl?"

It was Tiny.

"Shit, bro! How'd you get this number?"

"I told those stupid FBI goons that I was your fucking father. Told them I could talk some sense into your thick fucking skull."

"No shit. And they fell for it?"

"Hook, line, and sinker, bro."

"Fuck. That's awesome."

"How you doing?" Tiny asked. "You hanging in there?"

"I'm cool. A little sleepy. Kind of hungry. Hey, maybe you could hop on your Harley and bring me a pizza or something."

"Yeah. Maybe." There was a pause. "I thought I told you to lay off the Nazi jackboot shit, bro."

"I know, man. But I got tired of sitting around. Waiting for Dr. John Tilley to call us up."

"He called me."

"Who?"

"Tilley."

Shit.

"When?"

"Ten minutes ago."

"No shit."

"Yeah. He's been watching CNN and he ain't too happy."

Carl slid a little further down the wall. His stomach growled. This wasn't good. He had pissed off the leader of the whole goddamn movement.

"He ain't, huh?"

"You're attracting way too much attention. You told me yourself—big shit is about to go down. This stupid little stunt could totally fuck it all up!"

"Tiny?"

"What?"

"Should you be talking about this? I mean on the cell phone and all? What if the FBI is listening? They're the ones who gave me this phone."

"Relax. I'm on a scrambler. Got a sixteen-digit code churning out algorithms. They tap this shit, all they'll get is one hell of a headache."

Carl laughed. It was good to talk to his big buddy. Tiny had his shit together. Knew how to deal with The Man.

"So what should I do? The FBI has me pinned down and half of them outside are niggers with itchy trigger fingers."

"They ain't gonna shoot you, bro. They can't afford another Waco or Ruby Ridge."

"So what do I do? Surrender?"

"That's what Dr. T. suggested," said Tiny. "This thing with the eagle takes priority over any other actions."

"That's just a rumor."

"Tilley confirmed it."

"No shit. He tell you about the rocket?"

"What rocket?"

"The guys in Cleveland said Tilley had his hands on some kind of missile or some shit like that."

Tiny didn't say anything.

"Sorry, man. I should've told you sooner."

"Whatever," said Tiny. "But this thing you're doing now—you see how it could totally interfere with the fucking bigger picture?"

"I'm sorry . . . I didn't mean to . . . I was just—"

"I know, man. I don't blame you. I hear where you're comin' from."

"So, what should I do?"

"Tilley says you end it now. So, walk out. Let them haul your ass off to jail. As soon as the war starts, we throw out the ZOG and take over. And guess what's the first thing we do?"

"What?"

"We release all the POWs, bro. You'll be out in six months."

"Six months? I don't know, man. There's a lot of niggers inside."

"The Brotherhood will cover your ass. Hell! You'll be their goddamn hero."

Carl chuckled. "Yeah."

"You ready to do this thing?" Tiny asked.

"Yeah, bro. Thanks."

"Okay. I'll call the FBI bastards. Tell them you're coming out."

"Cool. Tiny?"

"Yeah?"

"We built this country."

"That's right, bro. And, we *will* take it back."

35

At 12:25 P.M., Carl Krieger came out of the dining hall door with both hands held high.

"That's it, Carl," said the voice over the megaphone. "Nice and easy. No one wants to hurt you."

"Tell your men to put down their weapons!" Carl called out.

"They already have."

"I mean it, man!"

"So do I. Hey, Carl?" The voice on the megaphone suddenly sounded friendlier. "You hungry?"

"Yeah." He kept walking forward. "Kind of." Hands raised, he started down the flight of steps at the front of the porch.

"We have some food," said the megaphone. "Here in the van. You like pizza?"

"Yeah."

"We got it at Pizza Hut. It's still hot."

Carl moved down the staircase.

"Okay," he said, looking down to make sure he didn't trip. "Pizza Hut is cool."

His foot found the pathway. His hands went higher over his head.

The report of a rifle cracked through the air.

Carl Krieger's head exploded in a pink cloud. He stood motionless for an instant.

Then his legs gave out.

He forgot how to stand.

He toppled into a limp heap.

Half his skull was gone.

One shot. It's all a good hunter ever needed.

Behind the oak tree, Alexander Schmitz lowered his rifle and slipped away.

36

Miller sat in the front room watching the ten o'clock news.

Watching it all for the hundredth time.

The FBI agents carrying Krieger out of the woods. The black vinyl body bag being hoisted up into the back of a rescue vehicle. The bloody stains on the porch bench—the chopping block where Carl Krieger executed Jose Irredo. Fox 5's handheld video camera swooping around the insides of the Camp Reinberg Dining Hall, checking every corner, every cabinet, looking for signs of a weapons cache; finding nothing.

The news reports had stopped showing their interview clip with Geoffrey Gilroy, the rescued hostage, around 6 P.M. His relief at being set free was no longer the hour's top story.

If it bleeds, it leads. Carl Krieger sure as hell bled when that sniper round blew off the top of his skull.

"Many are calling today's incident a tremendous tactical blunder," a stern reporter voiced over the footage. *"The FBI's shooting of eighteen-year-old Carl Krieger while he was attempting to surrender may be a misstep worse than the Bureau's bungling at the Branch Davidian*

compound in Waco or their bloody standoff with a white separatist family in Ruby Ridge.

"Now, the FBI assures us they are investigating what happened here, attempting to determine which of their riflemen violated orders and shot Krieger. Andrew Jackson, the agent in charge here at Camp Reinberg, has flown down to Washington, where, I'm told, he'll be asked to answer some very tough questions.

"Meanwhile, a thorough search of the dining hall area has turned up no weapons. At the end of the day, the FBI used lethal force to take down a teenager armed only with a Sears Craftsman Ax and a Louisville Slugger. Michelle?"

The scene shifted back to the newsroom. The male and female anchors looked solemn. Shook their heads in what Miller assumed was dismay.

"Thank you, Tony," said the woman. *"Sad story."*

"Indeed," said the man. He was older. Had some gray at the temples. *"Up next: Roseanne Scarlotti talks turkey."*

The man and woman smiled at all their friends beyond the cameras.

"Roasting or deep-frying? What's the right word for your bird this Thanksgiving?"

Miller snapped the TV off.

He knew none of Andy Jackson's men had shot the kid. There was no immediate threat, therefore no need to use lethal force. The boy was in the process of surrendering, which is all the FBI ever wanted.

But if not the FBI, who? Who wanted Carl Krieger dead?

"Chris?"

Natalie came into the room. She hugged one of Angela's storybooks tight against her chest.

"Yeah. What's up?"

"Angela wants her daddy to read her a story."

Miller massaged his eyes.

"Tell her I'll be right up."

Natalie looked him in the eye. Surprised him. "I'm starting to think that helping Andy might be the best way for you to help Angela."

"I'm confused. I thought I needed to stick close to home. Give her a sense of safety and security."

"She heard Father Labriolla this morning. She probably heard the TV."

"I tried to keep the volume low—"

"That's not my point. Angela knows more bad men are out there again doing evil things. And if you don't go out and stop them—"

"Whoa! Hold up. How am I supposed to do that?"

"Work the case, Chris. Don't sit here moping in the dark."

"Dammit, doc—"

"Terrorist groups have leaders and they have followers. Do you think Krieger was a leader?"

Miller shook his head.

"Of course not," said Natalie. "He's one of the sheep. A classic follower. Group membership gives losers like young Mr. Krieger a sense of belonging to something, a feeling of potency they've been denied everywhere else."

"Sort of like a religious cult?"

"Exactly."

"Okay. What about the leaders?"

"Unstable, uninhibited, self-interested, and unemotional."

"You're saying they're psychopaths?"

"I'm saying they feel no guilt or empathy."

"Even if they have to kill one of their own followers."

"Exactly. In fact, the act sends out a very vigorous message. 'Stay in line, do as I say. If not, I'll have you killed.'"

"You remember all this stuff from school?"

"I've been upstairs. Surfing the Web. Rereading some old textbooks. Figured it might prove more productive than sitting down here watching CNN all night."

"I was watching Fox."

"Even worse."

"You have no idea."

Natalie moved closer. Miller opened up his arms. They sandwiched the flat storybook tight between them.

"First things first." She pulled back, handed him the book.

Miller studied the cover: a fat man in thick glasses and a Santa suit offering an overstuffed deli sandwich to a couple of reindeer.

"*How Murray Saved Christmas?* Who's Murray?"

"Murray Kleiner," said Natalie. "Owns a deli. Takes over one Christmas when Santa's out of commission. Santa loves Murray's chocolate chip cheesecake."

Miller took the book. "You sure you're cool with me following this thing through with Andy and the team?"

Natalie nodded. "So is Angela."

"Hmmm?"

"Why do you think your daughter requested this particular book tonight?"

Miller flipped through the pages of the illustrated storybook.

"A deli owner saves Christmas, hunh?"

"Yeah," said Natalie. "Guess our daughter is trying to tell us that it's *your* job to save the rest of the year."

37

Zeigert's Pine Tree Lodge in New York's Catskill Mountains was nothing like the Marriott Marquis in Times Square.

"Hebes by the hundreds used to come here," Alexander's driver said as they bounced up the dirt road. "They called it the Borscht Belt. In the summer, it was worse than Jew York City."

Alexander peered through the windshield at a dilapidated four-story building at the top of a hill. The porch ceiling sagged. So did the shingled roof.

"What's borscht?" he asked his driver.

"How the fuck should I know? I think it's something they eat. So, I guess it's not a fucking pork chop, hunh?" The man laughed and rasped the top of his stubbly head, which, apparently, he had forgotten to shave this morning. With each rub, the swastika inked into the skin at the base of his skull stretched and contorted.

He was the same driver who had taken Alexander out to the cargo terminal at JFK Airport on Saturday. The same thick-necked goon who had picked him up when he flew back to New York City from Illinois on Sunday night. Now they had driven two hours north of the city. Alexander was growing weary of the man's company.

"What a dump, hunh?" the driver said as he pulled to a stop in front of a rickety porch.

Alexander didn't respond. He opened his door. Stepped out of the vehicle. Surveyed the scene. In the distance he spied a lake with the rotting remnants of a dock and boathouse. Probably where the summer campers had kept their canoes. His companion hauled suitcases, provisions, and sleeping bags out of the back of the SUV.

"You don't want to sleep in the big house," he said. "Place is fucking falling apart."

"I didn't come here to be comfortable."

"I'm just saying we might be stuck up here a couple days is all. We fixed up this one building out back. Waterproofed it. Put in toilets and electricity. It's base camp whenever we come up here for maneuvers and shit."

"Fine." Alexander started down the hill.

"Hold up! Got a shitload of stuff to haul down. I could use a little help."

Alexander didn't turn around. It wasn't his job to carry the bags.

Alexander claimed his room.

There were six in the refurbished bungalow. He took the first one off the communal entrance hall. Inside it, there was a cot, sink, footlocker, and bedside table with a lamp and wind-up alarm clock. The toilet and showers were down the hall. He'd seen worse barracks.

"Hey!" It was the driver. He was sweating. He dropped a box filled with cans and jars on the wooden floor. He mopped the top of his head with a rolled-up knit cap. "You allergic to work or something?"

Alexander didn't answer.

"Listen up, bro. You need to start pulling your weight. You may be some hot-shit hotshot, but, to tell you the truth, I don't give a flying fuck."

The man rested his hands on his hips to make his massive chest look even bigger.

"What's your name?" Alexander asked.

"What?"

"Your name. It's probably printed on your driver's license if you're having difficulty remembering."

His companion moved closer.

"My name is Trochmann. Kirk Trochmann. People call me Truck Man, and there's a fucking good reason. You understand what I'm saying?"

"Yes."

"So you gonna help me unload the fucking car?"

"No."

Alexander closed the door. He heard the big man say "fuck" and "shit" and "fucking shit" a few times.

But then he heard "Truck Man" walk out the door to fetch the rest of the luggage.

It was his job.

Hopefully, Alexander would learn the details of his own task, soon.

38

The Toyota arrived at 2:00 P.M.

Dr. John Tilley drove up the gravel driveway and parked beside the Denali. He was tired of driving. It was beneath him.

It had taken twelve hours spread over two days to travel here from Tennessee. Tilley never exceeded 55 mph. The last thing he needed was to be pulled over by an overzealous state trooper, who might, for whatever reason, want to inspect his vehicle.

A big man came thumping out of the dilapidated hotel, smoking a thick cigar. The old floorboards creaked under his weight.

"Dr. Tilley?"

He was grinning at Tilley like a giddy girl.

"Yes?"

"Kirk Trochmann. Fuck. I mean—wow! I can't believe it. Dr. John Tilley himself. I listened to all your CDs. Read your books, too. And I don't usually read books, just yours, sir!"

"Where's the Eagle?" asked Tilley, impatiently.

"Who?"

"Our guest."

Trochmann grimaced. "Down the hill."

"Kindly tell him I've arrived."

"Yes, sir." His expression remained sour.

Tilley walked around the Toyota.

"Need a hand with your bags, Dr. Tilley?"

"No. I'll wait for Mr. Schmitz to assist me."

When he said that, the big man laughed.

Alexander Schmitz knelt in the driveway and secured the Stinger tube onto its launcher, and attached the battery coolant unit to the handguard.

"You bought it from an Israeli?" he asked Tilley.

"Indeed. When the FBI does their forensic workup they'll figure that out. Should foment strong anti-Zionist sympathies among the masses."

"Excellent PsyOps, sir."

"Have you trained on such a weapon system before?" Tilley asked.

"Yes, sir. I am Stinger certified. Officially, it's an FIM-92. This is, of course, a disposable, single-round canister."

"With information etched inside," said Tilley. "Serial number. Lot number."

"Facilitating tracing it back to the Israeli arms merchant."

"Exactly."

"How much ammunition do we possess, sir?"

"Two rounds."

"Shit," Trochmann grumbled. "What if the kid misses?"

Without turning, Tilley said, "Unfortunately, two warheads were all we were able to procure. However, one shot is all a good shooter ever needs. Especially when utilizing a weapon system this lethal."

"Roger that," said Alexander. He rocked back on his knees, sat on his ankles. "Exactly what is the job, sir? Antiaircraft?"

Tilley smiled. "Later."

Alexander peered through his sunglasses. Saw Truck Man eagerly soaking up everything the two men said.

"Yes, sir. Understood."

Tilley gestured toward the missile launcher. "Do you find it satisfactory?"

"We're good to go."

"Excellent." Tilley opened a side door on the Toyota. "I'd like to take a photograph," he said. "Of you and our new acquisition."

"Is that wise, sir?"

Tilley showed Alexander his camera. "Don't worry. It's a Polaroid. There will be no digital record to be carelessly spread over the Internet. This photograph will only be shown to a select few members of the council— the gentlemen who financed our rather expensive weapon purchase."

"Of course, sir."

"Good. Prop it up on your shoulder."

"You want me in the picture?" Trochmann asked almost shyly.

"No, thank you." Tilley depressed the button. The camera flashed and churned out a sheet of photo paper. "Now then," he said, "since we have two rounds, I think a test fire is called for. We should make certain our generous benefactor didn't get hold of a lemon. How about that boathouse down there? That's what—three hundred yards? Think you could hit it, Mr. Schmitz?"

"Easily. But perhaps we should add a heat source to our target. Make certain the warhead's heat-seeking heads are fully functional."

"What do you suggest?" asked Tilley.

"Do you have another cigar?" Alexander asked Trochmann.

"Sure."

"Please fire it up and place it in the window down there."

Trochmann laughed. "You saying you could hit something as tiny as the hot tip of a cigar?"

"I believe that's why they call him 'the Eagle,'" said Tilley.

"You're on!" Trochmann jammed a fresh cigar into his mouth, clicked his Zippo. Miniature smoke signals followed him down the hill to the boathouse.

Tilley shook his head as he watched the big man trot off.

After Schmitz fired the Stinger, there would be no way to determine whether he had, indeed, hit the glowing tip of the cigar. The warhead would first be propelled out of the tube with the tremendous thrust of a launch rocket. After a few seconds, that first stage would fall away and the main engine would ignite. The warhead would quickly accelerate to a speed of Mach 2.2. It carried a three-kilogram hit-to-kill shell. It would simply obliterate the boathouse. Vaporize it.

Tilley moved to a protected position behind the hood of the parked SUV.

*   *   *

Alexander placed the weapon on his right shoulder.

Activated the electronics. Took aim. Waited.

He saw Trochmann run inside the boathouse and disappear behind its rotting walls. Soon, he reappeared at the remnants of a window. Placed his cigar on the sill.

The Stinger beeped to let Alexander know his target had been fully acquired.

He breathed a sigh of relief.

Thank God.

He would be driving back to Manhattan alone.

39

"I'm curious," Agent Krishock said to Christopher Miller. "Are you the one who actually made the call to take the kid down while he was surrendering?"

"Come again?" said Miller.

"I was there when you phoned Jackson. Fifteen minutes later, Krieger comes walking out the door with his hands up over his head. Ten seconds after that, he was dead."

"What's your point, Dale?"

"This disaster has your fingerprints all over it."

"Is that so?"

"Big-time."

Miller shook his head. Stepped to the right to move around him. Krishock countered. Blocked the fullback.

"You really don't want to be getting in my way today," Miller said with studied politeness.

"Do you ever think about retiring, Agent Miller? Getting out of *everybody else's* way?"

People were starting to stare over the tops of cubicles.

Miller thought about grabbing the tubby man's necktie. Hoisting him up out of his tasseled shoes. Tossing him out an open window.

"Chris?"

It was his boss. Charlie Lofgren.

"Yes, sir?"

"You got a second?"

"Sure."

Krishock stepped aside. Smirking.

"Good morning, Phyllis," Miller said to the secretary stationed outside Lofgren's office.

She pretended not to hear him. Stared down at some papers on her desk.

After nearly thirty years on the job, this was shaping up to be the worst Monday ever.

"Come on in."

Lofgren held open the door. Miller stepped inside.

"Take a seat."

Miller did. Lofgren didn't.

He went to the window, peered through the blinds.

Miller broke the silence: "You mind telling me what Dale Krishock was doing in Illinois this weekend, Charlie?"

"Helping out."

"Did you send him?"

Lofgren kept staring out the window.

"Dale Krishock volunteered," he said without looking at Miller. "Paid for his own plane ticket. Didn't take his weapon because I told him not to. However, I figured he could use the field experience and Jackson could use an extra hand on deck."

"I see."

Now Lofgren turned around.

"It's the kind of thing you used to do, Chris. Back in the day."

"Yeah."

"How's your family?"

"Fine."

"Natalie's good?"

"Yeah."

"Angela?"

"Better."

"You think they'd both be okay if you went out of town today? Took a trip down to D.C.?"

"Yes."

"You don't need to phone home? Ask permission?"

Miller and Lofgren had been friends for a long time. Ten, fifteen years. Today looked like the day that friendship would officially be over.

"No," said Miller flatly. "I'm good to go."

Lofgren rolled his chair aside so he could pick up a yellow legal pad from the desk.

"Special Agent Andrew Jackson has requested your presence at a two P.M. meeting down in D.C. Follow-up, he said, to this thing that went down Saturday. Of course, I didn't even know you were involved with the mess out in Illinois until Agent Krishock told me about it."

"I was just trying to help. Made a few phone calls."

"I see. Let your fingers do the walking. Easier than flying out there like I asked you to do."

Yeah. This could be the day. Game over. Friendship done.

"I'll head over to the station. Hop on the next train."

"Yeah. Great. Good."

"Anything else?"

"No, Chris. I think we're done."

"Yeah," said Miller. He didn't think it, he knew it. They were definitely done.

Miller was the first one into the conference room.

"Hey, Chris." Andy Jackson came in carrying a stack of manila folders and a mug of coffee. "Thanks for coming down on such short notice."

"No problem."

Jackson put his things on the table. He, of course, looked older than Miller remembered. When they'd worked together on the Hate Crime Work Group, Jackson had been the eager new agent, Miller the seasoned pro. They made quite a team.

"Andy?"

"Yeah?"

"Sorry about Saturday. I should've flown out."

"But you couldn't. Family thing?"

"Yeah. Angela."

"How's she doing?"

"Better. It's the holidays, you know? The anniversary of the thing that went down last year."

Jackson nodded. He understood. "I figured that's what was jamming you up. You did the right thing, Chris. Family comes first."

"You need me to talk to the bosses about how I screwed up?"

Jackson shook his head. "You didn't screw up, Chris. You figured out a way to get the boy to surrender. For that, I am eternally grateful."

He motioned for Miller to take a seat at the table. The two friends sat down. Jackson put on his reading glasses. He hadn't needed them the last time he and Miller worked together.

"So why'd one of our guys take him down?" Miller asked.

"Wasn't an FBI bullet."

"Local cops?"

"Nope. We did a weapons check. Not a single shot was fired by any of the law enforcement personnel on-site. Plus, we did the ballistics. The shot that cut down Krieger came from outside the perimeter. About a half mile up the hill."

"Jesus. A half mile?"

"Yeah. Whoever did this, the guy is good, Chris. Scary good."

Miller nodded. "Natalie called it. She profiled it as one of the guys at the top calling in a hit to rein in a gung-ho young recruit, independent thinking not being encouraged in the Brotherhood's ranks."

"Great minds," said Jackson. "I agree."

"But why'd they assassinate Krieger? I mean, restraining the troops and shoring up discipline is one thing, but this took serious organization and planning. Plus, they moved pretty damn fast. Why was eighteen-year-old Carl Krieger worth all the extra effort? Why not just let us get him? Come on, he was a kid. A sad, small fish."

"Well, let's say it was a hit called in from the high command," Jackson mused. "But let's also say they didn't do it to teach everybody a lesson about obeying orders and staying in line. Maybe it wasn't even about shutting Kreiger up. What if the Brotherhood is protecting something bigger?" Jackson looked at Miller.

"What've you heard?"

"We're picking up a lot of chatter. The usual Web sites and sources."

"How can I help?"

"What about Angela?" Jackson now asked him.

"She's cool with me doing whatever you need, Andy. She wants me to be like Murray."

"Who?"

"Deli owner. The guy who saved Christmas."

Jackson gave a small smile. "Okay. So, Murray, can you shake free back home?"

"Yep." Miller gave Jackson a small smile in return.

"Lofgren won't mind?" Jackson peered over his reading glasses.

"Hardly. He's been informed that the fiasco on Saturday was all my fault." Miller wasn't smiling anymore.

"Forget that noise, Chris."

"I already have. But I don't think Charlie has any immediate plans for me—except, of course, suggesting that I apply for that Voluntary Early Retirement we got the memo about last month. I mean I am over fifty, with twenty years of creditable service."

"You're not actually thinking about putting in your papers, are you?"

"No. Not until some of the bad guys start putting in theirs."

"I'd follow this thing through myself—"

"But the brass has you booked solid: testifying to subcommittees of subcommittees."

"I figure I'm screwed through New Year's."

"Which year?"

"That, my friend, I do not know."

Miller leaned forward. Reached for the files stacked on the conference table.

"What've you got?"

"Whole lot of bits and pieces," said Jackson. Then he picked up the phone. "Alma? Send in Jim Fitzgerald. Thanks." He put the receiver back in its cradle. "Have you ever met Fitzgerald, Chris?"

"No. I mean, we've talked. But only on the phone."

"Man, wait till you see this guy. Got hair down to here, big old bushy beard. Looks like a biker."

"Guess working undercover has it perks."

"Yeah. Apparently, you get to eat whatever you want. Fitz is huge. Three hundred, three hundred fifty pounds." Jackson laughed.

"What's funny?"

"His nickname."

"So what is it?"

"Tiny."

40

Alexander Schmitz slid the remaining Stinger canister into the hard-sided rolling golf bag Dr. Tilley had purchased at the sporting goods store in a nearby mall.

"As the salesman pointed out: I've spent a fortune on my clubs. It only pays to protect my investment. It's their top-of-the-line model."

"Yes, sir."

Tilley stared down the hill to the lake.

"An effective weapon, no question."

"Does the job, sir."

The boathouse was a smoldering ruin, a scattering of charred lumber bobbing up and down in the water, torn from its moorings by the blast. Scavenger birds swooped in wide circles above the lake. The bravest soared across the water and dove low to snare a tempting tidbit floating on the surface.

"Looks like the raptors are enjoying the feast you prepared for them," said Tilley.

Alexander grinned. "What should we do with the empty canister?"

"Stow it in the barracks. I'll have the local unit tidy up after we're gone."

"Yes, sir."

"You were wise to eliminate our friend Trochmann," said Tilley. "The fewer people, in and out of the movement, who know the full extent of what we're planning, the better."

Alexander nodded. "Such was my assumption."

Tilley leaned forward. "However, next time, I would prefer that you check with me, first. In the future, kindly wait for my orders before you take out a human target. Agreed?"

"Yes, sir."

Tilley beamed proudly. "You know, I wish I had more soldiers like you, Schmitz. Your dedication to the cause is inspirational."

"Thank you, sir."

"Now, then, please take care of that canister. I have a plane to catch."

"Yes, sir. Are we taking the Denali?" Schmitz asked.

"No. We'll leave that for the locals as well. You and I will travel south in the Toyota. Less conspicuous."

"Yes, sir."

Tilley gazed out at the lake again. Seemed in a contemplative mood. "Tell me, Alexander, which holiday would you say is the most meaningful to those of us in the Brotherhood?"

Alexander thought about it.

"The Fourth of July, sir?"

"Interesting choice. Interesting. Overthrowing tyrants, always something worth celebrating. But, personally, I would choose Thanksgiving, the day set apart for we White Americans to give thanks to God for bringing us into this, his Promised Land. North America. An entire continent set apart for White Christians brave enough to sail across a storm-tossed sea in much the same manner that Moses and his people once crossed the desert. Of course, it didn't take the *Mayflower* forty years to complete its journey. Christians were at the helm. Not argumentative, greedy Jews."

"Yes, sir."

Tilley looked up at the thin white lines criss-crossing the sky—the contrails left by jetliners flying five miles high.

"Can the Stinger hit a target that high?" he asked.

"Doubtful, sir. But I'm willing to give it a go."

"First things first."

"Yes, sir."

"You will return to the city. Store the 'golf clubs' in your hotel room. I will fly back to Wyoming, where the Grand Council is meeting to decide final target selection." Tilley pulled a thick envelope out of an inside pocket. "More gift cards. For the hotel and the restaurant."

"Thank you, sir."

"Use your secure phone to call your father. Tell him you won't be home for Thanksgiving dinner. I'm certain he'll understand."

"Yes, sir. Is the target JFK Airport, sir?"

"JFK is in the mix. As is LaGuardia. We're also looking at Grand Central Terminal. The Lincoln and Holland tunnels. At this juncture, only one part of the plan is set in stone. The date."

Of course. That's why Tilley gave Alexander the little speech about holidays.

"Thanksgiving Day, sir?"

"No, Alexander. Thanksgiving will be the day we celebrate our triumph. You will actually strike the day *before*. On the Wednesday prior to the holiday. As you know, it is always one of the busiest travel days of the year."

41

Andy Jackson was right: the man the Wisconsin Brotherhood knew as Tiny was huge.

"Saint Christopher!" FBI Field Agent Jim Fitzgerald strode into the conference room.

"Good to finally meet you, Jim," said Miller, reaching over to shake his hand.

"Same here. When I was a little kid, my dad and I used to watch you run the ball for Notre Dame. You moved up the middle like a freight train, man."

Jackson motioned to the chair next to his. "Have a seat, Jim."

"You can call me Tiny." He grinned.

The three men sat down.

"Did you enter the building undetected?" asked Jackson.

"Yeah. I think so. Took the usual precautions."

"Tell Chris what you think is going down."

Tiny nodded. "They definitely took the kid out," he said. "Called in a pro to do the job. I think Krieger was drawing unwanted attention to the movement at a time when they'd prefer to keep a low profile. You're familiar with Dr. John Tilley, right, Chris?"

"Sure. Andy and I have tangled with him before."

"When we first set up the Hate Crimes Working Group," Jackson added.

"Yeah," said Tiny. "The old fart's been talking trash for a long time."

Jackson agreed. "Too long."

Miller knew Tilley had been one of the more vocal leaders of the White Supremacist movement for over two decades. He had first heard Tilley preaching on underground audiocassettes that circulated among his many disciples. He was also known for the advice he generously passed along to all those who might one day encounter the police or FBI: If the authorities ask you anything, Tilley advised, always give the same response: "I have nothing to say." His Five Little Words were a cornerstone of the Tilley gospel. His followers understood that one day they might indeed have cause to use them.

"Why would a leader of the White Aryan Resistance, or whatever they're calling themselves these days, want to eliminate an eighteen-year-old foot soldier?" asked Miller.

"I'm not a hundred percent certain," said Tiny.

"Go ahead and guess," suggested Jackson.

"Okay. I knew this kid up in Milwaukee. Carl Krieger was a hothead. Probably borderline psychotic. Always itching to smack somebody down. I can't tell you how many times I had to haul his ass out of bad situations. Look at him the wrong way, he'd be ready to whack you up the side of the head with a baseball bat."

"Like he did with the two clerks," said Jackson.

Tiny shook his head, disgustedly. "Usually Tilley doesn't mind when the lowlifes go out and play storm trooper. He lets them smash out a few windows, paint swastikas, even crack open a couple heads. Hell, that's the reason most of these peckerwoods sign up in the first place."

"So what's different now?" asked Miller.

Tiny shrugged. "Signs point to something big coming down the pike."

"When?"

"Soon."

"How soon?"

"I dunno. Before the holidays. Definitely this year."

"What've you heard?"

"Talk at the meetings. On the Internet. 'Judgment Day is nigh.' 'The ZOG's days are numbered.' 'Don't worry about sending out Kwanzaa cards, the end is near for niggers.'" Tiny's eyes darted from Jackson to Miller and back again.

The two black men remained stoic.

"Sorry, guys."

"They said it, not you," said Miller. "Go on. Do you have any details?"

Tiny shook his head. "No. Like I said, it's pure hunch, with a total absence of any corroborating data."

"Unfortunately," said Jackson, "we can't apprehend and arrest on a hunch."

"No," said Tiny. "Now if they were Arabs, we might be able to get away with it. We could book 'em for looking funny and wearing turbans."

"So, what do you need, Agent Fitzgerald?" asked Miller. "How do we dig up something more concrete?"

"I don't know. I think I need to head out to Cleveland."

"Why Cleveland?" asked Miller.

"Well, Krieger went down there a couple times. Dropped in on a few meetings. Heard some wild tales about a coming Messiah. Guy called the Eagle." He pulled a folded sheet of lined notebook paper out of his leather jacket. "Here's a list of Web sites you should definitely check out. Especially the chat rooms where some are saying the Eagle is a pilot all set to crash a crop-duster into the side of a Federal building. Maybe a courthouse." Tiny reached for the water jug in the center of the table. Wiped some sweat off his forehead. "Others are saying he's a sniper gearing up to assassinate somebody. Somebody big. Even Krieger had a theory. Shared it with me on Saturday before I talked him out. He said the Eagle has a rocket."

"Jesus," said Jackson. "What kind of rocket?"

"Don't know. Like I said, I need to be in Cleveland. Find this meeting. Talk to these guys who seem to know so much."

Miller nodded his agreement. "Anything else?"

Tiny pulled another folded sheet of paper out of a different pocket of his jacket.

"Hot off the presses. I rented a computer at Kinko's this morning, printed it out. Some dude claiming to be the Eagle's father posted it."

Tiny swiped at his brow so the sweat wouldn't tumble down into his eyes.

"He tells the faithful to sit tight. His son, the Eagle, will 'give them much to be thankful for this Thanksgiving.'

That's why I think whatever it is they're planning, it'll go down soon."

"Damn," said Jackson. "Thanksgiving is, what—three weeks from now?"

Miller corrected him. "Eighteen days." They needed to move fast. "We'll check the father's ISP. See if we can nail him that way. Can you make it to Cleveland tonight?"

"Yeah. It's only a six- or seven-hour bike ride."

"Is it safe?" asked Jackson. "I mean you're the guy we called to talk Krieger out of the building."

"They don't know that. As far as my white brethren are concerned, the thing in Illinois was just another royal FBI fuckup. A new Ruby Ridge for them to rant about." Tiny peeled off his leather jacket. Rolled up his shirtsleeves. "Man, this room is like a sauna."

"What's that?" said Miller, pointing at Tiny's forearm.

"Part of the disguise. A lot of the guys have the same tat to show their commitment to the cause."

It was the lady in the helmet on her horse.

"Krieger had the same thing on his arm," said Jackson.

"Really?" said Tiny. "I never saw it."

"It was brand-new. Had it inked on right before he started his rampage."

"The Brotherhood has this thing for Norse mythology," Tiny explained. "The Valkyrie is one of the twelve handmaidens of Odin. She rides her horse over the field of battle and escorts the souls of slain heroes up to Valhalla. The Muslim martyrs may get sixty virgins but these boys get a free pony ride."

Miller wasn't smiling.

He, of course, had seen the Valkyrie before. In Jersey City. On the loading dock behind the Hyatt Hotel.

The guy who kidnapped Freddy Acevedo's son on Halloween.

He had the same tattoo.

42

"Can I help you with your golf clubs, sir?"

"No. The case has wheels. I can handle it."

Alexander Schmitz returned to the Marriott Marquis after dark on Monday. Around 8:30 P.M.

The crowds swarming out of the hotel's revolving doors were somewhat thinner at this hour. The Broadway shows all had eight o'clock curtains. Alexander had planned his road trip so he could avoid the pretheater crush that swept through the covered forecourt every evening. He wanted no delays hauling his luggage up to his room, securing the Stinger.

He rolled the bag across the concrete plaza and headed toward the revolving doors into the lobby.

"Sir?"

He turned around.

Another guy on the Marriott payroll.

"What?"

"Your claim check. For the car."

The young man handed him an orange cardboard stub.

"Any time you need your vehicle, call this number. We'll have it up in fifteen minutes."

"Fine."

The garage attendant scribbled on the back on his portion of the orange ticket. "Would you like this charged to your room?"

"What charge?"

"The garage, sir. It's fifty dollars per night with an additional ten-dollar fee every time you take out the car."

Alexander couldn't believe it. No wonder they called it Jew York City.

He needed to stay cool. Calm down.

"Fine," he said. "Please charge it to my room."

"Very good, sir."

The garage guy stood there smiling.

Jesus.

Schmitz fished an Applebee's gift card out of his back pocket.

"It's good at any location," he said and handed the car monkey his tip.

Everything in the hotel room was just as he left it—except, of course, the bed was made, the floor vacuumed, and the stationery items and room service menus were tucked in their proper slots inside the leather binder atop the small writing desk.

Alexander went to the window. Looked down at Times Square.

He was confined to this cesspool until the Wednesday before Thanksgiving.

He pulled the missile canister out of the carrying case. Laid the olive-drab tube across the bed.

There was a knock at the door.

"Housekeeping," said a thickly accented voice.

Another rap of knuckles.

"Housekeeping."

Now the click of the lock responding to an inserted card key.

"Just a minute!"

He dashed to the door.

He glanced over his shoulder. He was confident the launch tube could not be seen from the entryway.

Alexander pulled the door open two inches. Saw the dark lady in the maid uniform clutching clean white towels against her chest.

"Housekeeping," she said.

"I have towels."

"Would you like the bed turned down?"

"No."

The woman smiled. Handed him two gold-foil coins. Chocolates. To put on his pillow. He didn't take them.

Closing the door, he grabbed the Do Not Disturb sign and hung it on the doorknob for all to see.

He needed to call the front desk. Request that, henceforth, Housekeeping leave his room alone.

He replaced the launch tube inside the rolling golf bag. Wheeled it against the back wall of the closet. Hung the extra bathrobe in front of it to further conceal it.

When he called to request a suspension of Housekeeping, the operator asked him if there was some problem.

"No. Just have the maid leave the sheets and towels in front of my door. I prefer to make my own bed."

They bought it.

Now the phone rang again.

"Yes?"

"Mr. Schmitz?"

"Yes?"

"This is the front desk, sir. I'm sorry to bother you, but I noticed that we forgot to charge you for valet parking during the first four days of your stay with us."

"I didn't have the car then."

"Excuse me?"

"You can't charge me for valet parking when I didn't even have a car!"

"But you checked in on Thursday—"

"I didn't have a fucking car on Thursday, okay?" Alexander found himself screaming into the phone.

Damn fucking Jews! Trying to suck him dry. Bleed him for every penny he had.

He wanted to march down to the front desk with his shoulder rocket and blow the hook-nosed desk clerk away, blow away the whole damn desk!

Instead he took in a deep breath, steadied his voice.

"It's a rental. I picked it up this afternoon."

"Oh. I see. My mistake."

"Yes."

"Again, my apologies, Mr. Schmitz. If there is anything any of us can do to make your stay at the Marriott Marquis more enjoyable, please let us know."

Alexander hung up the phone.

The Wednesday before Thanksgiving.

Only seventeen more days of this torture.

Seventeen fucking days!

43

At 10 A.M. on Tuesday, Miller was at the Jersey City Police office on Erie Street visiting Tony Cimino.

He was carrying two cups of coffee in a brown bag.

"I thought you weren't working this thing anymore," said Cimino. "In fact, a couple days ago, when I called you at home, I specifically remember you giving me the bum's rush."

"Yeah," said Miller. "I was having a bad day."

"Really?" Cimino took the paper container his friend handed him.

"Yeah."

Cimino nodded. "I can dig it. Only kind of days I seem to have anymore. So, what brings you down here so bright and early?"

"We need to find Pettus's friend. The one he had the beers with at the Hyatt."

"You mean the guy who fingered him?"

"Yeah. I think you were right. I think the two of them were members of some secret supremacist group. Maybe old prison pals. Remember the tattoo on Pettus's left forearm?"

"Sure. The fat lady in the Viking helmet."

"The kid out in Illinois had the same thing on his arm."

"So what?" said Cimino. "All of a sudden you think there's some sort of connection between the guy gunned down on the loading dock behind the Hyatt and the punk kid shot out there in East Bumblefuck or wherever?"

"Yeah. Something's fishy. It's . . . what's that word you used?"

"Hinky."

"Yeah. This whole thing is seriously hinky. Too many tattoos."

Cimino took another sip of coffee. "Okay. One neo-Nazi snatches the Acevedo boy here on Halloween. A couple days later, another skinhead abducts some guys out of a gay bar. In both incidences, the kidnappers wind up dead."

"Exactly."

"You're right. This thing is one hundred percent hinky."

"We need to find that other guy, Tony. The one who was knocking knuckles with Pettus a half hour before turning him in."

"Trust me, we're trying. But other than his mug shot from the hotel security cameras, we've got nothing. Nobody knows him. Nobody's seen him. He paid for his drinks with plastic."

"Could you trace his credit cards?"

"Wrong kind of plastic. He had these Hyatt gift cards. Same as cash. No ID required."

Miller slumped down in his seat. "Nothing."

"Exactly."

"What about our local hero cop? McManus was in the bar before the thing got hot. Maybe he remembers something."

Cimino nodded. "While you were off having your bad days, I went over to the North District to ask him a few questions."

"And?"

"Turns out he's put in his papers. One week he's a TV star, the next week he's quitting. Technically, he's only on the job till next Friday. Gave Division his two weeks on account of he's moving to Scranton."

"Why?"

Cimino shrugged. "Maybe he's got family out that way. When I ask him what he remembers about that night at the Hyatt, he tells me he no longer feels obligated to answer any of my questions—seeing how he's packing it in and all. But I don't give up easy. I keep pushing. Did the guy have an accent? A distinguishing body mark, maybe a tattoo?"

"And?"

"He turns into a hardass. Gives me the same answer over and over, like a broken record. 'I have nothing to say. I have nothing to say.' Same frigging answer to every question. 'I have nothing to say.'"

Miller winced, like someone just kick-started his brain.

"Where's McManus now?" he asked, leaning forward in his chair so he could tap the lump at the base of his spine and make sure his Glock was still there. It was an old habit. Check your weapon because you might need it.

Soon.

McManus had used Dr. Tilley's "five little words."

Cimino rode with Miller to the North Division on Central Avenue.

"Hey, Frankie," Cimino called out to the desk sergeant, "you seen McManus?"

"Yeah."

"So where is he?"

"Took an early lunch."

"What? It's ten thirty."

"Maybe it was brunch. I hear these cop hero types do that sort of thing. Go out for mimosas and your eggs Benedict and whatnot."

"Any idea where he might've gone?" asked Miller.

"Dunkin' Donuts. It's cheap. It's close."

Miller and Cimino strode up the block.

"He's in on this thing?" Cimino still couldn't believe it.

"Yeah. I think so."

"So maybe he didn't just *happen* to be at the Hyatt on Halloween. Maybe he was waiting for the other guy to finger Pettus."

"Exactly," said Miller. "Maybe it was Pettus's job to grab the kid, their job to nail Pettus so he couldn't talk."

Cimino, who was twenty years younger than Miller, was huffing and puffing, trying to keep up.

An orange-and-pink Dunkin' Donuts sign jutted out from a building two doors up the block.

They heard a scream. Female. Terrified.

Now they were running.

The door to the Dunkin' Donuts shop burst open. A man bolted onto the sidewalk, shoved pedestrians out of the way. The woman inside screamed again.

"Sir?" Miller yelled at the man's back, but the man kept moving up the sidewalk. Fast. "Sir?"

Other people tumbled out the door. They pushed and shoved. Panicked. Some had powdered sugar on their lips, cake crumbs on their chest.

"Oh, Jesus," groaned Cimino.

Miller swung around. Looked through the plate glass window. Saw what Cimino just saw: a man slumped sideways in an orange plastic chair.

"That's him," said Cimino. "That's McManus."

They barged into the store.

"I'm with the police," shouted Cimino as he flashed his badge at the terrified counter worker. He went over to the slumped body. Tried to find a pulse. Shook his head. There wasn't one.

Miller looked down at the table. Two doughnuts sitting on tissue paper across from each other. The one in front of whoever had been McManus's brunch buddy was chocolate-frosted and had a toothy bite chomped out of it. The bavarian cream in front of McManus hadn't been touched.

Two cups of coffee sat on the table. The one near the chocolate-frosted still had its lid on. The one in front of McManus was tan from added milk and half gone. There were two tubs of nondairy creamer near his coffee cup. Their foil seals had been peeled back.

"We need to secure this evidence," said Miller.

"Poison?" asked Cimino.

"Maybe. Probably. Send the coffee in McManus's cup out to your lab. Analyze the doughnuts and those creamer tubs, too."

"That was the guy," said Cimino.

"Who?"

"The one running out the door. That was the guy who fingered Pettus."

"You sure, Tony?"

"Absolutely. I've been showing his face around town since Halloween. That was him. I'll call it in. Don't worry. He won't get far."

Miller unbuttoned the dead man's shirt at the cuff. Rolled it back. Exposed Sean McManus's forearm. Found what he knew he'd find.

Officer Sean McManus, late of the Jersey City Police Department, had the same Valkyrie tattoo they all had.

Tiny.

Carl Krieger.

Even Red Pettus, the foot soldier this same cop had drilled with eight bullets to the back on Halloween night.

44

The first Tuesday in November was the third *yahrzeit* for Marvin Oskard—the third anniversary of his death.

"Take a right turn when we pass the lake. You'll see a sign."

"Yes, Mom."

Sarah Oskard-Klein had agreed to drive her mother up to White Lake in the Catskills, to help her commemorate her husband's life in the place where they first met.

"Pay attention or you'll miss it."

"I thought you said there's a billboard."

"I said there should be a sign. Not a billboard. Is it still there? I don't know. I haven't been back in thirty years."

"I see the sign."

"That's where the turnoff is. At the sign. It says 'turn right.'"

"I see it."

"Your father never did. Take the right."

"I'm taking it."

"You should slow down."

"I'm slowing down."

The car turned off the road and headed to "Zolt's Pine Tree Lodge." The narrow lane leading to the hotel was choked with weeds. They rumbled over a boulder.

"Slow down! You want both your parents should die on the same date?"

Sarah stared out at the ghostly gray trees lining the road.

"I guess in the summer, it was pretty up here," she said.

"Oh, you have no idea. It was gorgeous. Absolutely gorgeous."

Her mother stared out the window, seeing happy summers where Sarah saw spindly trees.

"They called the Catskills the Jewish Alps. Every morning, we'd eat bagels and pickled herring. Maybe *challah* French toast. In the day we'd swim or go on pony rides. Flirt with the busboys. Of course this was back before you were born."

Sarah smiled but saw no need to indicate that, yes, she knew her parents met *before* she was born.

"Your father was so funny. Such a wisenheimer. It's no wonder Mr. Zolt made him the tummler. That's what they called the social director. Like on a cruise."

"I know, Mom."

"He kept people entertained all day long. He'd tell jokes. Wear silly hats. Lead the Simon Says games around the pool. One day, I'm sixteen, he sees me in my bathing suit. One thing leads to another. . . ."

Her mother waved her hand to signify that she wasn't going to divulge any details. They crested a hill and saw the silhouetted gables atop the old hotel.

There was a car parked in front of the porch. An SUV.

"Oh, my," said Sarah's mother when she saw the dilapidated building.

Sarah slowed down. Gravel crunched beneath her tires.

Sarah's eyes darted all over. Took in the sagging porch. The chunky remains of cement picnic tables. Rust-encrusted barbecue grills and swing sets.

Sarah's mother sighed. "What a mess. Now I'm sorry I made you schlep me all the way up here."

Sarah pointed to scorched dock pilings sticking up at the edge of the lake.

"Looks like they had a fire."

Her mother clucked her tongue. "There used to be a boathouse there."

"Somebody burned it down."

"Kids," said her mother. "Hooligans with nothing better to do than play with matches."

Sarah looked at the SUV. Its windows tinted black.

"We should leave," she said.

Her mother unbuckled her seat belt.

"In a minute."

"Mom?"

"What? We've come this far."

"I don't like the looks of this."

"Me, neither." She opened her door. "The place is a dump!"

"Mom?"

"I want to show you the swimming pool."

Her mother walked up the driveway toward the far side of the hotel. Sarah had no choice. She opened her car door.

"Wait for me."

The two women trudged along the remnants of a path, passed through a grove of trees, went over to where Sarah's mother remembered the bungalows and swimming pool used to be.

"Oh my god."

The first thing they saw were the giant swastikas spray-painted on the cracked walls of the empty pool.

"Who would do such a thing?" her mother gasped.

Sarah thought about the scorched pilings down by the lake. She headed for one of the bungalows.

"Sarah?"

"I want to see what else they did—"

"No, Sarah. We should leave."

Now Sarah was the one who wouldn't turn back.

45

Alexander Schmitz ate an early lunch at Applebee's on Forty-second Street.

He had been awake since 5 A.M. and had already spent four hours in the Marriott Marquis Fitness Center— lifting weights, running on the treadmill, stretching.

"Will there be anything else?" asked his waitress.

She was his favorite. White. Tall and skinny with extremely slender fingers. Her name was Anna. Said so on her name tag. He tried to sit at one of her tables every day.

"No, thank you."

"How was the Cowboy Burger today?"

"Good."

She picked up his empty Coke cup, crumpled napkins, and red plastic burger basket. She balanced everything against her flat chest. Her red collared polo shirt was unsnapped, revealing a strong, sinewy neck.

"You must like it," she said.

"Excuse me?"

"The Cowboy Burger. You order it every day." She smiled. It softened the sharp lines of her face. "Is that why you have all those cards?"

"Pardon?"

"The gift cards. I've never seen anybody use so many."

"It's all I wanted for Christmas last year."

"Miss?" A group of obvious tourists waved at the waitress. "Miss?"

"So," she said to Alexander, "we missed you yesterday."

"Miss?"

The waitress spun around. Three men. Three women. Dark-skinned. Probably Pakistanis.

"Sorry," she said. "That's not my table."

The tourists looked around. Other than Alexander, they were the only customers currently seated in this section of the restaurant. They looked around some more. There were no other waitresses.

"Whose table is it then, please?" one of the men asked.

"I don't know," replied Anna. "I'll ask the manager when I see her."

She turned back to face Alexander.

"The manager's out front grabbing a smoke," she whispered.

Alexander smiled.

The girl looked to be twenty-four or twenty-five. About his age. She was pretty, in a wholesome, unadorned, pink-cheeked way. Her eyelashes were long and dark, framing her pale blue eyes.

"Can I ask you a question?" she said.

"Sure."

"I don't mean to be rude or anything. . . ."

"I'm certain you won't be."

"Okay. Here goes: why do you always wear those sunglasses? I mean, we're indoors."

"I need them to protect my eyes."

"Oh. Are you legally blind or something?"

"No. Far from it. In fact, my vision is considered exceptional. The army doctors advised that I take steps to keep it that way."

"You were in the army?"

"Yes, ma'am."

"Iraq?"

"Yes, ma'am."

"Wow."

The six tourists got up from their table. Made a big show of leaving.

A smile blossomed on the waitress's radiant face. "Good riddance," she said under her breath.

Alexander tried to resist. Knew his mind should be focused on the coming mission, whatever the target might be. But there was something about this girl that drew his interest in ways he couldn't explain.

"Would you like some dessert?" she asked.

"No. I need to go back to my hotel. Do you live close by?"

Anna snorted. "Me? I couldn't afford it. This is midtown. The center of the city. Rents are outrageous because the landlords are all . . ." She didn't say it. She didn't have to.

"I see."

"I live with my parents out in Queens."

Alexander nodded.

"You sure you don't want dessert? The Blue Ribbon Brownie is pretty good."

"No, thank you." He handed her a twenty-five-dollar gift card, even though the Cowboy Burger only cost $15.99. "I'm expecting a very important phone call."

"Okay. I'll put this in, bring you your change."

"Keep it. Please."

"All of it?"

"Yes, ma'am."

"Wow. You're very generous."

Alexander smiled. Pulled off his sunglasses. Let her gaze into his eyes for just a second.

"You earned it," he said.

The secure cell phone chirped at 1 P.M.

"This is Schmitz."

"Good afternoon, Alexander."

"Good afternoon, sir."

"It was a pleasure meeting you yesterday."

"Likewise, sir."

"I met with the Council this morning."

"Yes, sir."

"Are you familiar with Trans African Airlines?"

"No, sir."

"Please use the computer in the Marriott Business Center, visit their Web site. Go to the home page and pay particular attention to the tail markings on their planes. Very colorful. An assortment of geometric shapes. Green, red, gold, blue, crimson. Almost looks like a flag. An African flag."

Alexander was jotting down notes on the bed-side pad.

"Yes, sir."

"I take it you're familiar with the silhouette of a jumbo jet. Specifically a 747."

"Yes, sir."

"Good, good. We need you to go back to JFK. A driver will meet you in the lobby first thing tomorrow morning. Six A.M. Sharp."

"Yes, sir."

"A T-A-A jumbo jet en route to Lagos, Nigeria, is scheduled to depart JFK airport at seven-thirty A.M. on the Wednesday before Thanksgiving. You, of course, may wish to be there a little earlier. To greet it."

"Yes, sir."

"You will be assigned a three-member tactical team. The men are all former military and will provide cover, should that prove necessary. They will be armed with conventional weapons. Rifles, sidearms, grenades."

"Good."

"You will travel to the target site in an unmarked cargo truck. We suggest that you park the truck in such a way that you can simply roll up the rear door, take your shot, roll the door back down, and take off. In the ensuing chaos you should be able to escape undetected."

"Yes, sir."

"Talk all this over with the squad leader. We leave the operational details to you men on the ground."

"Squad leader, sir?"

"One of the military men. William Brewster. The Council has assigned him full oversight on the operation to ensure that you can remain focused on the one thing you do so well."

"I see. Sir, if I may—I'm quite certain I could perform both tasks. Lead the team and take the shot."

"We see you continuing to operate in a specialist capacity, Alex."

His left eye twitched slightly.

Tilley remained silent.

"Very good, sir."

"We'd like to give you one additional responsibility."

"Sir?"

"In the unlikely event that you and your support team should be discovered, we cannot jeopardize the entire movement."

"Understood."

"You would martyr yourself to the cause?"

"Only after dispatching the other three team members to Valhalla first, sir."

"Excellent."

"I'll need an appropriate weapon. Something quick, clean, and quiet."

"A package will be delivered to you this evening."

"Thank you, sir."

"Have you spoken to your father recently?"

"Yes, sir. He knows I won't be home to carve the turkey this year."

"You may call him again."

"Thank you, sir."

"Use your secure phone, then make no further contact with him or any other family members until a full week after the job is done."

"Yes, sir."

"I'm sorry you won't be home for Thanksgiving this year."

"Not a problem, sir."

"We built this country, Alex."

"We will take it back, sir."

46

Traces of hydrogen cyanide were found in Sean McManus's bloodstream.

Miller and Cimino were back at the Jersey City Police office on Erie Street. It was 2 P.M. They'd grabbed sandwiches and were attempting to inhale them so they could get back on the street and join the hunt for the Mystery Man who poisoned the Hero Cop.

"Cyanide?" Miller said. He bit into the pickle that came wrapped up with his turkey on rye. "Like in spy movies?"

"Not a bad choice," said Cimino, wiping his hands on his sweater since he'd already used all the napkins that came with his meatball sub. "Works fast. Interferes with the enzymes controlling the oxidative process."

Miller made a face to let Cimino know he was impressed with the man's detailed knowledge.

"Prevents the red blood cells from absorbing oxygen. The victim basically dies from what you might call internal asphyxiation. He can still breathe, but the oxygen ain' goin' anywhere."

"Okay. I have to ask. How come you know all this?"

"My brother—he's an exterminator. Fun guy to talk to at a barbecue, you know what I'm saying?"

"Yeah."

"Maybe our Mystery Man picked up a couple tubs of creamer from a Dunkin' Donuts somewhere, took it home, used a syringe to squirt a drop or two of the cyanide into the white stuff. This morning, he makes like he'll be the guy to go grab the napkins and sugars. While he's playing fetch, he does the switcheroo. Anyway, we'll know soon enough."

Miller nodded.

"You ready to rumble?" Cimino stood, jingled the car keys in his pocket. "I'll drive."

"Fine by me."

"You sure your bosses are okay with you spending the day on this?"

"Yeah. I'm on special assignment with the D.C. team."

"That mean somebody in Newark is still pissed at you?"

"Exactly."

They walked out of Cimino's office and into the police station's lobby just as two uniformed cops were hauling in the handcuffed Mystery Man.

"Well, whaddya know? We grab lunch, they go out and grab our guy!"

The Mystery Man had a tattoo on his neck.

It wasn't the Valkyrie ferrying souls of valiant Aryan warriors up to Valhalla. It was a pair of S. S. lightning bolts partially filled in with three skulls. There was room for more to be added later. If Miller remembered correctly, the three skulls meant three kills on enemies of the white race.

Miller sat in the viewing room while Cimino grilled the suspect.

"What's your name?" Cimino asked for the tenth time.

"I have nothing to say."

"Why'd you kill officer McManus?"

"I have nothing to say."

"Why'd Pettus grab the Acevedo boy? He want his Halloween candy?"

"I have nothing to say."

"Where'd you pick up the cyanide?"

"I have nothing to say."

"Is your name Gilbert Winslow?"

"I have nothing to say."

"That's okay. Your fingerprints already answered that one. You left them on the creamer tub. So, do your friends call you Gil or Bert, Gilbert?"

"I have nothing to say."

"Kind of sissy name, isn't it? *Gilbert Winslow.*"

"I have nothing to say."

"How come you didn't finish your frigging doughnut this morning?

"I have nothing to say."

"Just seems kind of wasteful, you know? You take one bite, leave the rest."

"I have—"

"Yeah, yeah. You have nothing to say because you're a frigging no-neck moron."

Cimino left Winslow sitting alone at the interrogation

table under the watchful eye of an armed guard stationed near the door.

"He's got nothing to say," said Cimino when he entered the observation room.

"So I heard."

Miller's cell phone chirped out its ring tone.

"That the Temptations?" asked Cimino.

"Yeah. 'My Girl.' Angela picked it."

"Nice."

Miller checked the caller ID. Washington area code. FBI prefix. He snapped open the clamshell.

"This is Miller."

"Chris? Andy. What's shaking up there?"

"We just ID'ed two more brothers. One was a Jersey City cop. He's dead. Poisoned by this other white brother. They were both involved with that Halloween kidnapping. The customs agent's kid."

"Why?"

"Don't know. Plan to find out."

"Good. We found a new den, too," said Jackson.

"Damn. These guys are everywhere, suddenly."

"You need to see this, Chris. Could be a big break."

"What've you got?"

"Meet me at the Sullivan County airport. Tomorrow. Ten A.M. I'll show you when you get here."

"That's up in the Catskills, right?"

"Yeah. Near a town called White Lake."

"Figures. What'd you find?"

"I'm not sure."

"You're not sure, or you're not telling?"

"Let's just say, whoever's been here believes in serious firepower."

"You mean like the Eagle?"

"Maybe. If so, Tiny was right. That particular bird got its claws on a rocket."

47

Alexander Schmitz was doing push-ups in his hotel room when the telephone rang.

"Yes?" he said, panting slightly.

"Mr. Schmitz? This is the front desk. Sorry to disturb you. But there's a gentleman here with a package."

"Send him up."

"I could have one of the bellmen bring it to your room."

"No."

"Very good, sir."

Three minutes later there was a rap on the door.

"Hang on."

He unchained the door. Flipped back the hasp lock. Turned the deadbolt.

When he opened the door, whoever had knocked was gone.

Schmitz looked right. Nothing. Left.

A man was walking along the hallway, a balcony ringing the cavernous atrium. He was headed toward the bank of elevators shooting up and down like glass space capsules.

"Hey!" Schmitz called out.

The man kept walking. Didn't react.

Schmitz looked down at his feet. Saw a Nike shoebox sealed with plastic strapping tape. The box was big enough to hold a pistol.

And ammunition.

Teflon-coated, silent bullets.

Schmitz slid a magazine up into the stock, racked a bullet into the chamber, then stowed his new gear inside one of the golf bag's zippered pockets where it would be easy to retrieve should the mission go south. He closed the closet door and went to the cabinet housing the television set. He slid open the goody drawer, ignored the Toblerone chocolate bars, and helped himself to a small jar of cashews. It would be his dinner this evening. A good mix of protein, fat, and carbohydrates. The tiny jar probably cost fifteen bucks. The gift cards would cover it.

He popped a nut into his mouth. Sucked on the oily salt. At least fifty cents a cashew, he figured.

He moved toward the windows and pushed aside the gauzy drapes so he could look down at Times Square. The nightly carnival had begun. The human cockroaches were swarming.

After the Trans African Airlines plane was a flaming shell of shattered titanium and roiling jet fuel, he would never return to this hideous Marriott. A truly godforsaken place in the center of a truly godforsaken city. However, he still had two weeks to kill in Manhattan. It seemed like too much time. Surely Trans African Airlines had other flights departing JFK sooner. Why wait until

Thanksgiving Eve? Because it was one of the busiest travel days of the year, he reminded himself. Fine, but wouldn't it be better to sew the seeds of chaos a week before the holiday, terrify the Zionist Occupational Government, make the race traitors tremble, send them to their churches to beg God for forgiveness?

Maybe. But it wasn't his call to make.

Strategy should be left to the politicians. The thinkers. The Council.

Alexander was a soldier.

He would do as he was ordered.

He would wait.

Perhaps Anna, the girl from Applebee's, could help him kill some time.

Tomorrow morning, at breakfast, he would ask her for her phone number. They could go to a movie. There were two multiplex theatres on Forty-second Street, right across the street from each other. Together, they had thirty-eight screens. He and Anna would be able to find something to watch together.

He checked his watch. 6:30 P.M. His father should be home.

Alexander took the secure cell phone out of his gym bag.

It was time to make the final call home before going dark, initiating even stricter security measures.

"Hello?"

"Dad?"

"Alex! Goddamnit, it's good to hear your voice."

"Likewise, sir."

"You sure it's okay for you to call me like this?"

"Dr. Tilley insisted. He's like us, Dad. Family first."

"I know, I know. But what if the ZOG goons bugged your phone?"

"Impossible, sir. My line is secure."

"What about mine? Sometimes, when I'm on the phone, I hear these clicks, you know what I mean? Click, click, click."

"We can assume your line is safe, Dad. Otherwise Dr. Tilley would not have suggested that I place this call."

"I don't know, Alex. The FBI could be bugging me. Probably the CIA, too."

Alexander realized his father might be right. Perhaps the government was aware of his affiliation with the Brotherhood. Maybe they had tailed him after one of the meetings at the bowling alley. Maybe they had infiltrated the cell.

"Go to Pasquale's," Alexander suggested.

"The pizza place?"

"Call the Marriott Marquis in Times Square. Ask for my room."

"You're using your real name?"

"Yes. Dr. Tilley instructed me to do so."

"Alex, that's stupid!"

Alexander felt hot blood rushing to his cheeks. Nobody called him stupid—not even his father.

"Call the hotel. Ask to be connected to my room. When I pick up, immediately tell me the number for Pasquale's pay phone. I'll call you back."

"I can't believe you used your own name! The Feds have your fingerprints, Alex! From when you were in the army!"

"Sir, if you think your home phone line has been compromised, it is imprudent for us to continue this conversation."

Alexander pressed the end call button.

God, he hated it when his father rode his ass like that. What the hell did he know about any of this, anyway? He was just a janitor.

His son was the Eagle.

48

"You can't tell anybody."

"Alex, I've been doing this longer than you. I know the rules. We trust nobody outside the movement. Period."

"I'm sorry I won't be home for the holidays."

"How about Christmas?"

"My future is uncertain."

"Jesus, you're not going to go all Arab on me and blow yourself up after you blow up this plane full of niggers, are you?"

"I have no intention of becoming a suicide bomber. And, sir—please watch your language. You're in a public place."

"Pasquale's has a booth."

"I know. That's why I recommended that you go there."

"Smart call, Alex."

The old man was learning. The Eagle was not "stupid."

"I'm not sure I like you using a missile launcher bought off a Jew, Alex."

"It's all part of the plan. Misdirect suspicion. Have the postmortem forensics implicate the Israelis. Incite fratricide between the Jews and the Blacks."

"You remember Uncle Bob?"

"Sure."

"He's one of us."

"I didn't know that."

"Because, like I told you, I know how to keep a secret."

"You can't tell him anything."

"I won't, Alex. Of course not. Not until after."

"Have you contacted him lately?"

"No. I mean we swap e-mails now and then. I told him you might bring home another trophy. Told him 'the Eagle has landed.' Like they said on the moon, you know?"

Alexander knew his father. Knew he liked to pop open a few cans of Genny every night, sit down at his computer, send out e-mails and funny cartoons to everybody in the movement.

"Dad? Don't send Uncle Bob any more e-mails."

"He's your godfather!"

"So?"

"So—he'd be proud to see how good you turned out!"

"Not a word, Dad."

"Okay, okay. Can I at least tell him not to fly anywhere? Once you do this thing, flights are going to be backed up all over the country. They'll think it's Al Qaeda again. Ground all the airplanes. Strand people at airports."

"Not a word."

"Okay. I think they do Thanksgiving there in Cleveland anyway."

"Good. Cleveland should be safe."

49

"Tiny" swiveled on a stool at the counter of the Blue Bird Diner in Cleveland, Ohio.

It was early. 7 A.M. He reached for the bottle of Tabasco sauce, shook it, and splattered it over his eggs and home fries.

"You like it hot," said the cadaver working behind the counter. He was skinny. Ashen skin. Thick and waxy gray hair. Sixtyish.

"Only way to go," said Tiny.

"Haven't seen you in here before."

"Yeah."

"I'd remember you if I had. What do you weigh? Three hundred? Three hundred fifty?"

"Something like that."

"I'm good at guessing weights."

"Unh-hunh."

"I know most of the early birds. The regulars. Maybe not the names, but I know the faces."

Tiny grunted. Crunched toast.

His new friend swiped at the stainless steel with a shabby rag.

"See the same ones. Day in, day out. Same faces. Never seen you before is all I'm saying."

He was pretty chatty for so early in the morning—just like Fitzgerald figured he'd be, once the guy caught a glimpse of the tattoo on his forearm. The drawing started at the undercover agent's thick wrist and didn't stop until the tip of the Valkyrie's spear disappeared in the fleshy folds of his elbow. It was no accident that he was going out of his way to flash it here. The FBI knew that the back room of the Blue Bird was where the Cleveland cell of the Brotherhood held their meetings.

"You need more coffee?" The counter man gestured toward the Bunn machine.

"Thanks."

The counter guy pulled the pot. Tiny drained the last drops from his mug and slid the empty down the counter. He flashed his arm with every move.

"So—you new in town?"

Tiny nodded. "Yeah. Blew in about an hour ago. That's my hog out front."

"Just passing through?"

Now Tiny shrugged. Dipped a triangle of toast into egg yolk. "Maybe. Depends."

The counter guy poured the coffee. "On what?"

"Whether I'm too late."

"Too late for what?"

Fitzgerald smiled.

"I heard there was some action here back in 'ninety-nine. Wish I'd been here for that. You know what I mean?"

The counter man smiled back. "Yeah. 'ninety-nine. That was really something."

It had been the year when the American Knights of the Ku Klux Klan held a rally in Cleveland.

"Trust me, friend," said the skinny man, "you like action, stick around."

"Where?"

"Right here."

Tiny pretended to be surprised. Checked up and down the counter. Saw nothing but sleepy-eyed losers too worn out from the night before to worry about the coming day.

"Here?"

Now the counter man looked around, seeming to scan every face. Waited for a busboy hauling a rubber tub full of clinking glasses to pass. The busboy was black. When he was gone, the counter man slowly rotated his arm, laid it wrist up in front of Fitzgerald, and gave one more glance around the diner.

He rolled up his watchband to reveal *his* hidden tat. A miniature Valkyrie—wrinkled in places where the metal watchstrap pinched his skin.

Fitzgerald put down his knife and fork. Sat back on the stool. Studied the older man's milky eyes.

"We built this country," the counter man whispered.

Fitzgerald nodded. "We will take it back."

"Ten P.M. Tonight. Use the back door. Park your bike behind the Dumpster or up the street."

Another nod. "Will do. By the way, my friends back home call me 'Tiny.'"

"Really? Tiny?"

"Yeah."

"I'm Bob," said the counter man. "Bob Schmitz."

50

Jennifer Stevens volunteered at the animal shelter every Monday, Wednesday, and Friday morning before heading into Manhattan, where she worked for one of the big law firms on Wall Street.

The commute into the city took over an hour. The rescue group rented kennel space at The Vet Port at JFK Airport.

"I'll take Maggie out," Jennifer told the security guard seated behind the front desk.

The guard grunted. "Good luck, honey."

Jennifer smiled. Everybody knew Maggie—the meanest dog in the building.

"I'd rather take one of those snakes out for a walk!" the security guard said. "That Maggie is psycho."

"She's just scared," said Jennifer.

"I don't blame her. I'm scared whenever I'm near her, too!"

Jennifer entered the kennel. A deafening chorus greeted her. Two German Shepherds. Three Rottweilers. A beagle with a howl. A lab with a throaty roar.

"Good morning, Maggie Mae!"

The tiger-striped pit bull swayed her bottom wildly,

slapped a happy tail against her cage's bars.

"You ready to go for a walk, girl?"

The tail wagged even faster. Jennifer slipped a modified choke collar over her massive, fist-shaped head.

"Let's go!" She unlatched the door. Maggie bounded out. "Easy, girl. Easy."

Maggie slowed down. Panted. Smiled.

"Let's go!"

They entered the lobby.

"Oh, Lord, here comes trouble," said the security guard.

Maggie snarled.

The security guard held up her hands. "I'm just sayin' is all."

"I've got her."

"Use both hands on that leash, girl."

"Come on, Maggie."

They headed out into the parking lot. A jumbo jet lumbered overhead, thundering into its initial ascent. Maggie went up on her hind legs and lunged. She wanted to chase after the big silver bird screaming across the sky.

"Come on, girl. Easy." Jennifer tugged at the leash. Regained control. "Who wants to go for a walk? Let's go for a walk!"

She gave two quick tugs and they set off down a sidewalk that wound its way around the warehouses and parking lots of Cargo Area C. It was early. The morning air was still pretty fresh, only slightly tinged with the bitter scent of jet fuel. Jennifer led Maggie toward a picnic table, her favorite spot to pee.

They walked alongside a boxy white cargo truck.

Maggie growled.

"What's the matter, girl?"

When they reached the rear of the truck, Jennifer saw what Maggie had already smelled: four muscle-bound men in gray coveralls milling about in the road. Three of them formed a cluster around the fourth—a guy wearing sunglasses and peering through his fist at the sky.

All four were bald. Their heads shaved clean.

Maggie hunched low and rumbled.

"Easy, girl," Jennifer whispered.

Maggie barked.

They turned.

Maggie let loose a barrage.

"Sorry!" Jennifer called out.

"Yo!" said one of the men. "We better roll."

The man in the sunglasses nodded.

Suddenly, out of nowhere, another jumbo jet screeched into view. Its wheels were moving up into its wings. Its underbelly shimmied.

Maggie went ballistic. Snarls. Lunges. Bared teeth.

"Restrain your animal!" one of the men shouted over the deafening roar.

"Sorry!" Jennifer shouted back. She yanked on the leash. Dragged Maggie up the sidewalk. The dog resisted. Tried to dig its claws into the cement.

"Is that a pit bull?" one of the men yelled after her.

"Yes. Part pit."

"Only niggers keep pit bulls. Fucking niggers and spics."

"Let's roll," said the man in the sunglasses. It sounded like an order.

The guy to his right raised an arm to salute him. Held it out straight and stiff, like the German soldiers in World War II movies always did.

"Yes, sir, Mr. Adler!"

The other men laughed. It was the kind of laugh Jennifer remembered hearing very late on Saturday nights on the sidewalks outside the bars where all the guys had had too much to drink and were looking to take it out on somebody.

She turned. Lowered her eyes. She didn't watch them pile into their truck. But she heard them. The front doors swinging open and slamming shut. The rear cargo door rolling up then rolling down.

She tugged Maggie up the sidewalk. The dog was straining so hard against its collar it was choking. Gasping.

"I know, Maggie. I know."

They had to be skinheads. She'd heard about them. Seen them on the TV news. Read about the kind of awful things they sometimes did at synagogues. She'd even seen a few on the streets in the East Village.

But what the hell were four of them doing watching airplanes take off from JFK Airport at 7:30 on a Wednesday morning?

51

Miller drove the 120 miles from Newark to White Lake in just over two hours.

Special Agent Andrew Jackson was waiting for him near the porch of a ramshackle hotel. Miller could see that the old Catskill resort was literally falling apart: big chunks of shingles and siding lay scattered around the crumbling stone foundation.

"You made good time," said Jackson. He pointed down the hill to the charred remnants of what Miller figured used to be a dock.

"This was their practice range. Wasn't much of a challenge."

"How so?"

"Stinger missiles have a range of about five miles."

"Stinger?"

"Yeah. We found the launch engine about halfway down the hill."

"Jesus."

Miller knew about Stingers. Back in 1996, the army and FBI had run computer simulations to determine whether just such a shoulder-launched missile had downed TWA Flight 800 after it took off from JFK airport. Witnesses reported seeing something streak toward the aircraft just before it burst into flames.

"How the hell did they get their hands on a Stinger?" Miller asked.

"Undoubtedly the black market. Trouble is, we left a lot of these things behind in Afghanistan when they were fighting the Soviets. Of course, it'd take some serious cash."

"What's the going price?"

"Got an MSRP of twenty-three thousand dollars. That's when the army buys one wholesale from Hughes or Raytheon. The street price is higher. You want a black market Stinger, it'll cost you over two hundred thou."

"And these boys bought at least two," said Miller. "Because they sure as hell didn't spend a quarter of a million dollars just to take down a dock that was blocking their view of a lake."

"We figure this was a weapons check," said Jackson. "Chance to make sure the system was fully operational before taking it into the field against their primary target."

"Okay," said Miller. "We're talking half a million dollars. Maybe more. Should be a money trail."

"We're already on it."

"Good. So, how can I help?" Miller asked.

"Find the shooter. Who's their trigger man? We find him, Chris, we find the weapon. You spend half a million dollars on weaponry, you don't let just anybody handle it."

"The Eagle."

Jackson nodded. "That's what I'm thinking. All that chatter we've been picking up. Could be the guy."

"Probably ex-military," said Miller. "Probably in his mid to late twenties. Definitely findable."

"I just heard from Agent Fitzgerald in Cleveland," said Jackson. "He's made contact and is keeping his ear to the ground."

"Okay. So, we're getting somewhere."

"Yeah. I just don't know if it's fast enough. Come on." Jackson started for a stand of trees.

"Where we going?"

"I want you to do a walk-through of these buildings over here."

They hiked down to a small cluster of cabins.

Miller followed Jackson and thought how this could be a lot of folks' worst fear come true. A Stinger missile in the hands of a terrorist group operating on American soil. Al Qaeda had Stingers. So did Hezbollah. Now it seemed the Brotherhood did, too.

They entered a cabin and stepped into what appeared to be a small bedroom. Miller noticed the neatly made cot topped with a tightly tucked-in wool blanket. A storage locker stood at the foot of the bed. Everything was squared away, ready for inspection.

"You dust in here for prints?" Miller asked.

"Absolutely. If, as we suspect, the shooter is ex-military, we'll find a match on the IAFIS," Jackson said, referring to the Bureau's Integrated Automated Fingerprint Identification System.

"Somebody cleaned up in here," Miller noted. "Made the beds. Mopped the floors. See how there's no dust or dead bugs in any of the corners?"

"Yeah. They must've figured someone heard the blast."

"Is that how you found out about all this?"

Jackson shook his head. "No. A woman named Miriam Oskard discovered it. She lives in Manhattan."

"What was she doing up here?"

"Taking a trip down memory lane with her daughter. They went into that other cabin. Across the courtyard. The walls were plastered with Nazi propaganda."

"Look there." Miller pointed at the floor. "That sheet of flooring. It doesn't line up with the others. Did your guys find the canister? The empty tube from the fired round?"

"No. We figured the cleanup crew hauled it away."

"Maybe. Or maybe they didn't know where to dump it. You can't just haul it out to the curb in a Hefty bag."

"So you think they stowed it here?"

Miller bent down, studied the seam where the two sheets of plywood met. "You got a crowbar?"

Ten minutes later they had ripped up the four-foot square that made up half of the floor underneath the cot.

Sitting in the dirt between the joists was a five-foot-long metal tube. Scorch marks charred the open end.

Inside the canister, Miller knew they'd find a serial number. The folks at Hughes Missile and General Dynamics liked to keep track of their inventory.

Jackson had his team carefully remove the empty casing.

Miller now knew they were definitely back in the game. With the numbers etched inside the canister and the fingerprints possibly blotted up and down its sleek steel sides, they might be able to track down the shooter.

Jackson's cell phone chirped.

Miller waited. When his friend snapped the phone shut, he was smiling.

"What's up?"

"More good news. A woman who works out near JFK just called in a report of suspicious persons. Skinheads. She only caught one name—Mr. Adler."

"So? The phone book's full of Adlers."

"It's German, Chris. Means 'Eagle.'"

52

Alexander Schmitz had time to kill.

He had reconnoitered the firing zone, felt confident he would be able to bring the bird down. Of course, the Stinger was "fire and forget" smart and he was a lethally gifted marksman. There was no way to miss.

He had made his own evacuation arrangements and would drive west from New York on Thanksgiving Day. In the late afternoon. He'd wait a day because police activity would be heaviest immediately after the attack. There were sure to be roadblocks and other traffic hassles.

He also had the Russian-made PSS silent pistol—the weapon delivered to his hotel-room door—packed inside his mission kit. Should things go south, he would take out the three-member tactical team and then, in the worst-case scenario, put the pistol to his own head. No need to take aim, just the courage to pull a trigger one last time.

Alexander fervently hoped his mother would learn of his heroic exploits. Wherever she might be. Whoever she might be currently sleeping with. He knew all about his mother's whoring ways. Her filthy exploits had been his nightly bedtime stories, the grim fairy tales told by his rightfully bitter father.

Maybe that's why he enjoyed spending time with Anna. She was his kind of woman, hardworking and honest. And faithful. If she said, "I do" in front of a priest, she'd mean it.

Two weeks to kill.

Or, in this case, two weeks *until* the kill. But he didn't intend to sit in his room flipping through channels on the television set.

He would spend as much of the time as he could with Anna.

"Do you have gift cards here, too?"

Alexander smiled.

"Yes."

"Is that why you invited me to your hotel?"

"Yes."

"Is that the only reason?"

They were seated at a small table in the lounge at the Marriott Marquis. Anna looked charming. It was the first time Schmitz had seen her in anything other than a navy-blue polo shirt—her Applebee's uniform. Her hair was clean. Fluffy. No longer scented with airborne fryer oil or tied back in an efficient ponytail.

"So, what'd you do today?" she asked. Alexander stared into her narrow face. The skin was so tight and white against her cheekbones it seemed to glisten.

"Met some business associates out at the airport."

"So, tell me—what is it that you do?"

"I'm a consultant. I work with defense contractors. Homeland Security. Stuff like that."

"Shit," she said.

Her sudden outburst shocked him.

"Is something wrong?"

She nodded. "Behind you."

Alexander swiveled around. Four businessmen were sitting down at the neighboring table. They looked like Pakistanis. The men were boisterous. Loud.

He turned back around.

Anna's face was frozen in terror.

She leaned in across the small table. "In Pakistan," she whispered, "Muslim men rape Christian girls. The judges let them. Whole families gang-rape girls. They raped my little sister. She was a missionary there. They tore her apart." Her eyes were like slits.

"I'm sorry." And he was.

"Is there somewhere else we could go?"

"Well, yes. There's a restaurant upstairs."

"What about room service?"

"Excuse me?"

"Can they bring dinner to your room?"

"Yes."

"What about breakfast?"

"Yes," said Alexander, his mouth dry. "Room service is available twenty-four-seven."

"Good."

53

Jim Fitzgerald pulled into the small parking lot behind the Blue Bird Diner.

Taking off his helmet, he ran his fingers through his tangled, shoulder-length hair.

"Tiny?"

He turned around. It was Rolf. The other kid from Milwaukee. Carl Krieger's best bud.

"Hey! What you doin' down here?"

Rolf shrugged. "Checking out the scene."

They headed toward the restaurant's rear door. Rolf gave the door four knuckled knocks. Two long, two short. There was a bumper sticker plastered above its small rectangle of security glass: "These Premises Insured by Smith & Wesson."

Fitzgerald soon realized that the Cleveland cell of the Brotherhood had a pretty big voice on the Internet for a group so small. There seemed to be only three members. The counter man from the diner. An even older guy in a VFW cap. A scrawny kid in coveralls trying to dig crankcase grease out from under his fingernails.

Fitzgerald figured it was Bob Schmitz who did most of the blabbing in the online chat rooms. The other two didn't look like they could string more than three words together. Besides, if the mechanic had a computer it was doubtful he could even use it anymore—too much sludge on the keyboard

"Good to have our brothers from up north with us tonight," said Schmitz. The five of them were sitting in a circle of upended milk crates in the kitchen. Giant pots hung off steel racks over their heads. The whole room smelled like a spent Brillo pad mixed with onions.

"Sorry about what happened to your buddy," Schmitz said to Rolf.

"Fucking Feds. We should rent a Ryder, make one of those damn rolling fertilizer bombs."

Bob Schmitz nodded. "Don't worry, Rolf. Payback is coming. Trust me."

"When? We keep saying we're gonna hit back but we never do jack shit!"

"It's coming."

"How do you know?"

Schmitz stood. Looked around at his assembled crew. Looked with what Fitzgerald recognized as pride. "The Eagle has landed and is ready to strike."

"Bullshit. I'm tired of your fucking Eagle crap. What the fuck do you actually know?"

"Trust me—your friend's death will be avenged."

"When?"

"Soon."

"I don't believe you."

Schmitz held up his hand. "Listen, son, I can't say anything more. What's going down is highly confidential. None of you are gonna breathe a fucking word about it to anyone. You do, we'll find out and we'll come after you, understood?" He looked at all the men seated in the circle. They all nodded, stiffened their backs, and sat up a little straighter.

"Okay," said Rolf. "We get it."

"But what's the plan?" asked Tiny. "I mean there might be some way we can offer backup, or maybe execute some kind of diversionary tactic. I just hate feeling so far on the outside on something this huge. I came here looking for action. How about the rest of you guys?" He looked around.

"I can't tell any of you any more," Schmitz insisted.

"Come on," Tiny urged. "We need more! Especially me and Rolf and everybody else up in Milwaukee. Carl was our brother, man."

"Too fucking bad," snapped Schmitz.

"So how do we know you're not just blowing smoke up our butts with this Eagle bullshit?" asked Tiny.

"Take my word for it."

"Aw, that's just more bullshit," said Tiny.

"Hey, I know what I know for a good reason. A very good reason. A blood reason!"

"Blood reason?" asked Rolf. "What the fuck does that mean?"

"My nephew," Schmitz admitted, with a pleased little smile.

"Your nephew, huh?" Tiny said. "Who the fuck is

your nephew? What kind of payback can your nephew set up for us?"

"Well, for one thing, he's in New York City, okay?"

"And?"

"And . . . I still can't tell you anything else." Schmitz shook his head.

"Jesus. If your nephew's such a tough dude," Tiny needled him, "how come he needs you to run interference for him?"

"That's not what I'm doing here."

Tiny rolled his eyes. "Well, whatever you're doing, it sure seems pretty pussy to me."

The grease monkey in the corner laughed when Tiny said "pussy."

Schmitz darted his eyes around the room. "Look, what if I told you assholes that the Eagle, my fucking nephew, was going to shoot down a whole fucking jet packed with niggers heading home to Africa? You still think that's pussy? You still think *he's* a pussy?" Schmitz smirked.

Tiny shook his head. "Wow," he said softly. "Awesome. Totally awesome."

"The day before Thanksgiving," Schmitz added. "You'll see."

Tiny had no trouble looking impressed. Truth was, it was always amazing what people will tell you if you make them mad enough.

54

It was after 10 P.M. when Miller finally headed south from the Catskills.

The drive down the relentlessly monotonous Garden State Parkway gave him plenty of time to think, make connections.

The Halloween kidnapping of Carlos Acevedo.

The Stinger missile.

What if, as Miller had long suspected, the kidnapping had simply been a dramatic diversion to pull the boy's father, Customs Agent Fernando Acevedo, off the docks? What if Halloween had been the night the Stinger had been smuggled into the country?

It made some sense. Helped explain why the kidnapping had left such a lethal wake.

They needed to find out how the Stinger had come into Port Newark. How it was transported up to White Lake and the Pine Tree Lodge. If they could put that information together with a hit from the fingerprint database and intel from Agent Fitzgerald's undercover work in Cleveland, they might be able to snare the Eagle before he took flight again.

Miller pressed a speed-dial number into his hands-free phone. Gripped the steering wheel a little tighter. He was excited about bumping this thing up the line.

The call went through to Charlie Lofgren's home number.

"Hello?"

"Charlie, Chris Miller."

"It's late."

"I know. We need some warrants."

"Now?"

"First thing tomorrow morning."

"For what?"

"All records pertaining to cargo shipments coming into the docks at Newark on Halloween night."

"Why?"

"That's the night the customs agent's son was kidnapped."

"And?"

"We now have reason to believe that a terrorist group staged the hijacking to pull Agent Acevedo off the docks in order to facilitate the smuggling of a Stinger missile into the country."

There was a pause.

"A Stinger?"

"Yes, sir."

"Who did this? Al Qaeda? Hezbollah?"

"No, sir. White supremacists."

"Domestic terrorists?"

"Yes, sir. That's the working theory."

"So this is coming out of the Hate Crimes Group?"

"Yeah. Andy Jackson and his team have—"

"Chris?"

"Yeah?"

"Why aren't you asking Special Agent Jackson's superiors down in D.C. to initiate your warrant requests?"

"Because the Newark field office has a more immediate working relationship with the Port Authority of New York and New Jersey."

"Oh, they're going to be thrilled to hear from me. Do you know how many ships come in and out of that port every day? And you want paperwork on all of them?"

"Just the ones that unloaded Halloween night."

"I see. Look, Chris, as you might remember, the Newark field office has its own mandates and priorities. I can't be spending my already thin resources on Hate Crime jobs for your friends down in D.C.—"

"Sir, time is of the essence."

"I know. I'm on a deadline with these NSA phone logs. You're on loan to Jackson. Other guys are putting in for vacation time because of the holidays—"

"Charlie—we have the serial number off a spent canister."

"They've already fired the weapon?"

"Once that we know of."

"Do they have another round?"

"We suspect so."

"Tell me what you know. Not what you suspect."

"I know we need to move fast."

"And do you know how many of these cargo vessels sail under foreign flags?"

"Almost all of them."

"Correct. So if you want to search shipping records from foreign carriers, you'll need a warrant from the Foreign Intelligence Surveillance Court. Do you have a tangible link between these white supremacists and some foreign national or government?"

"No. We can assume they purchased the Stinger on the black market. Overseas."

"But you have no link? No concrete proof?"

"It all hangs together—"

"You press for a warrant based on a hunch, Agent Miller, it could seriously jeopardize your career."

"Charlie? Come on, man—"

"Applications for special intelligence court warrants are exactly the kind of thing that can land an FBI agent in serious trouble."

"Hell, I've been in trouble before. Remember?"

"If you have no link, no concrete proof, I cannot recommend the issuance of warrants."

Miller punched the top of the steering wheel.

"Furthermore," Lofgren continued, "the focus of the Newark field office is and will be for the foreseeable future the investigation and apprehension of radical fundamentalist *foreigners*. If you and Jackson wish to pursue this warrant, regardless of the consequences to your careers, I wish you all the luck in the world. Good night."

The phone went dead.

Damn.

He tugged at the chain hanging around his neck. His medal.

If anybody was counting on Miller to protect them tonight, they should know the truth: Saint Chris was currently flying solo.

55

Tiny and Rolf stood in the parking lot behind the Blue Bird Diner.

"You want to go grab something to eat?" Rolf asked.

"No thanks. Gotta hit the road. You heard the man. Shit's about to hit the fan."

"I'm hungry," Rolf complained.

Fitzgerald pulled on his motorcycle helmet. It was molded to look like the ones the Nazis wore in World War II.

"Suit yourself," he said to Rolf. "I'll grab breakfast when I hit home."

"You driving all the way back tonight?"

Fitzgerald nodded. He needed to lose this kid and phone in what he just learned, but Rolf kept tagging along like an annoying little brother who insists on going to the movies with you and your hot date.

Fitzgerald kick-started his motorbike. The Harley engine rumbled to life.

Rolf stuffed both hands into the front pockets of his hooded sweatshirt. Looked like he was pouting.

"I talked to Carl," he suddenly shouted.

"What?" It was hard to hear though the hard plastic shell covering his ears.

"I talked to Carl!" Rolf screamed.

"When?"

"When he was in that cabin! Right before they nailed him."

"You talked to him? How?"

Fitzgerald undid his chinstrap. Took off the helmet. He didn't want Rolf yelling this crap loud enough for the three guys still inside the diner to hear.

"They gave him a cell phone. Tossed it in so they could, you know, communicate with him. Talk him down. Talk him into surrendering."

Fitzgerald gave Rolf a pained look, hoping that's what the kid needed to see. "Bastards."

"He told me to watch TV. Said he was coming out. Said he was going to be fucking famous."

Now Fitzgerald shook his head. "Poor Carl. The fuckers double-crossed him."

"He also told me he'd just talked to you."

"What?"

"He said you were the one who told him to walk out of there. That he should fucking surrender."

Fitzgerald laughed. Shook his head. "That is such bullshit."

"You told him to surrender 'cause it's what Dr. Tilley wanted."

Rolf's hands had been in the sweatshirt pockets. Now they came out. He had a pistol. A nasty-looking semiautomatic. Fitzgerald's own weapon was strapped to his right ankle inside his cowboy boot. He needed to buy some time.

"Look—"

"You fat fucking liar." Rolf raised his weapon. Aimed it at Fitzgerald's chest. The kid was only three feet away. The gun was closer. The boy's hands were trembling but Fitzgerald realized the unpleasant truth: he was the equivalent of the broad side of a barn and Rolf was definitely close enough to do some serious damage.

"Whoa. Easy, there!"

"You and that bastard Tilley set Carl up, man! You sent him out the fucking door so the fucking Feds could blow off the top of his fucking skull!"

Fitzgerald raised both his hands. "Come on, bro. Put down your gun and we can talk—"

"Don't you tell me what to do, you fat fucking liar!"

"Come on. You heard the man. There are bigger things happening than your bad guesses about what really went down out in—"

Rolf squeezed the trigger. Six times. One right after another.

He watched Tiny's chest explode.

The fat fucking bastard had killed his best fucking friend.

What Schmitz had said in the meeting was so totally true: it was fucking payback time.

56

Miller sat at the kitchen table sipping his first cup of coffee.

Angela sat across from him. Slurping spoonfuls of milk out of her Cheerios bowl.

"Eat some cereal, Angel."

"I like the milk better."

"How much sugar did you use?"

"Just two or three spoons."

Miller closed his eyes. Massaged his eyelids. He hadn't gotten home until after midnight, and when he fell into bed, he couldn't sleep. His brain kept rewinding and replaying his conversation with Charlie Lofgren. This morning, the inability of senior FBI officials to see the seriousness of the threat posed by members of the Brotherhood toting Stinger missiles was still working his nerves: he hadn't seen his daughter spoon half a bowl of sugar into her cereal and turn her milk into syrupy sludge.

He rose from the table.

"Let me pour you a fresh bowl, Angel. You don't need all that sugar."

"It tastes good."

"So do Hershey bars. But we don't eat Hershey bars for breakfast, now do we?"

"Yes, we do. The day after Halloween."

"That's different. Yesterday wasn't Halloween."

"I know. But do you know what's exactly two weeks from today?"

Miller emptied the sugar soup into the kitchen sink. Poured a fresh bowl of Cheerios from the box.

"Two weeks from today?" He played dumb. "Thursday—just like today."

"It'll be Thanksgiving! The Macy's Day Parade!"

"Oh, yeah . . ."

"There's going to be a Dora the Explorer Balloon and SpongeBob and Bumpus Balloonicles—"

"And we're going to see it all," said Natalie.

Miller's wife stepped into the kitchen. She looked good, even in a ratty red bathrobe and pillow-tousled hair. Cozy. She shuffled over to the coffee machine. Smacked a badly aimed air kiss in his general direction.

"Good morning. What time did you get home?"

"After midnight."

She nodded. "Find anything interesting up north?"

When she looked up from her mug and into his eyes, Miller glanced toward their seven-year-old daughter.

"Yeah," he said. "Real interesting."

Natalie understood.

"I need to head into the office."

"Do you have to work on Thanksgiving, Daddy?" asked Angela.

"I don't think so."

"Good! Because we're going to a hotel in New York City!"

"We are?"

"Uhm-hmm," said Natalie. "Booked a room near Times Square. Place called the Novotel. I figured checking into a hotel Wednesday night beat waking up at four A.M. Thursday morning to catch a train."

"Uhm-hmm. And how much is this room going to cost?"

"You don't want to know."

"They're going to have marching bands and Big Bird," said Angela. "And Santa! The *real* Santa."

"Chris," Natalie asked, "are you sure you and Andy won't be busy on this thing you're working on?"

Miller shook his head. Almost laughed. "Not if our bosses have anything to say about it."

"What do you mean?"

"Nobody wants to press for warrants. Could prove hazardous to the health of one's career."

"What's a warrant?" Angela asked.

She wasn't eating her Cheerios. She was hanging on Mommy and Daddy's every word.

"Something a judge writes," Natalie explained. "To help the police do their job."

"Do you need a warrant, Daddy?"

"Yeah, Angel. I do. I need one real bad."

Six hours later, Christopher Miller needed *two* warrants and nobody at the Newark field office seemed interested in helping him obtain either one.

"Now you guys want a *criminal* warrant?" Lofgren said when Miller was finally able to grab twenty seconds with him in the hall.

"We found fingerprints. Matched them against military records."

He showed Lofgren the e-mail that just came in from D.C.

"Perfect match. Alexander Schmitz. United States Army."

"Uhm-hmm."

"We need to search his house."

"Where does he live?"

"Buffalo. With his father."

"You talk to Brown? He's the SAC in western New York."

"Yes, sir. He said I should talk to you."

Lofgren glanced at his watch. Shook his head. Miller could tell: he had already eaten up more of Charlie's time than Charlie had wanted him to.

"I have a meeting, Chris. Have Jackson run point out of D.C."

"Charlie? Alexander Schmitz is armed and dangerous and poised to strike."

Lofgren frowned.

"What about the container ships thing? You still looking for that warrant?"

"Yes."

"Well, kindly keep my name out of it. Do you know how much excrement will hit the fan if you simultaneously pursue a warrant from the Foreign Intelligence Surveillance Court *and* a criminal warrant?" Before Miller could answer, Lofgren did it for him. "The surveillance court gets mighty ticked off if they suspect you are exploiting their lower standard and then using the information obtained to prosecute *criminal* cases. I don't know about you, Chris, but I'd like to spend the holidays with my family, not an army of lawyers!"

And that was that.

End of conversation. They were done.

Lofgren went up the hall to his meeting. Miller went back to his cubicle. He wondered if he'd even be invited to the office holiday party this year.

At 5 P.M., the horrible day got even worse.

Andy Jackson was back in D.C., facing the same sort of obstacles Miller kept slamming into up in Newark.

He was having absolutely zero luck convincing his bosses to give a damn about Alexander Schmitz and his white brethren. Former U.S. soldiers who had become radicalized right-wing nut jobs were not currently listed on the Bureau's high-priority list, no matter how many times Jackson reminded folks about Timothy McVeigh and Oklahoma City.

September 11, 2001, had changed everything.

The big fish were foreign terrorists. The FBI agents making their names and building careers brought in radical Muslim Jihadists, not KKK crackers.

"We're on our own, Chris."

"Well, at least we've got Tiny."

And that's when Jackson told him the worst news of all:

"We lost him, Chris. The Cleveland police found his body stuffed behind a Dumpster."

57

Dr. John Tilley escorted his guest into the great room of his Wyoming lodge.

Sinking back into an overstuffed leather chair, he swirled a curved crystal glass of single malt Scotch.

"Handsome, aren't they?" he said, indicating the trophies mounted on his massive stacked-stone fireplace.

"You shoot them yourself?" his visitor asked. "Even that moose up there?"

"Yes. Of course."

His guest shrugged. "I figured you hired somebody to do it for you. You're rich enough."

Tilley smiled. "One can never be 'rich enough.'"

"Yeah." His guest put down his glass. "You got any beer?" His Brooklyn accent was thick. "I never went in for this other stuff. Too brown. Whaddya call it?"

"Bowmore Single Malt. Costs nine thousand dollars a bottle. Then again, it is aged for forty years."

"Forty years? Jesus. Must be why it tastes like lighter fluid. Personally, I prefer Bud. Has that 'brewed on' freshness date stamped right on the side of the can. Never more than a couple months old."

"Mike," Tilley said with a patronizing smile, "your clients find themselves in a very serious predicament."

"From which you can extricate them."

"Indeed."

"That's why I came out here to East Bumfuck—not to watch you sit there sipping that shit or to have that moose staring down at me with its glass eyeballs. How much we talkin' here?"

"You certainly cut to the chase."

The man named Mike shrugged once again. "I find it gets me out of East Bumfuck faster."

Tilley knew 'Mike' wasn't the man's real name. He was a professional go-between, the sort of man who lurked in the shadows and fixed things for other men. Scared men such as the board of directors at Trans African Airways.

"Fine. I would like two hundred million dollars."

"Jesus. What are you on besides Scotch? No way are my clients going to pay you two hundred mil."

"I actually think the price tag is quite reasonable. Correct me if I'm wrong, Mike, but a Boeing 747 sells for somewhere between two hundred and two hundred and fifty million dollars. Seen in that light, my offer is extremely generous."

"Trans African Airways doesn't buy Boeings. They lease them. So maybe we'll just call the cops instead. The cops and the FBI work for free."

"That, of course, is your prerogative, Mike. Call whomever you choose. However, once word leaks out that TAA is a known terrorist target, I'm quite certain their bookings, not to mention their stock price, will plummet."

"Guess you'd be the one doing the leaking?"

"I'd consider it my civic and Christian duty."

"Two hundred million dollars . . ." Mike shook his head again.

"Just think of all the money you'll be saving your clients. An untold fortune in P.R. expenses. No interruption to the revenue stream. If a TAA airliner is blown out of the sky the day before Thanksgiving, customers may seek alternative carriers for months, maybe years to come."

Tilley handed a photograph to his guest. A Polaroid.

"This the nut?"

"Yes. And there—on his shoulder—that's his rocket launcher."

"You guarantee you can stop this guy?"

"Quite easily. Perhaps you noticed how we dealt with young Carl Krieger when he became a liability?"

"Yeah. Impressive. The Stinger guy. He work for you?"

"No. He, like Krieger, is merely a misguided follower."

"Where is he? New York? Los Angeles?"

Tilley smiled.

"That's the beauty of our arrangement, Mike. You don't have to worry about any of that. I handle all the details. All you need do is wire me my money."

"Half up front, half on Thanksgiving Day."

"Exactly."

"This could take some time. I have to talk to my clients. They gotta scrape together the dough."

"Of course, Mike. But talk and 'scrape' quickly. We have less than two weeks."

"You'll give my people the Stinger?"

"Better. I'll give them the shooter."

"Good. Because they're gonna want his head on a platter."

Tilley smiled. Glanced up at the animal heads jutting out above the fireplace.

"That, I am quite certain, is something that can be arranged."

58

Miller tapped his computer keyboard.

He wanted to see just how hard it would be to play his hunch about the Stinger being smuggled into the docks on Halloween night—a trail that might lead to Schmitz and his weapon.

According to the Port Authority's Web site, New York Harbor handled 14.5 million tons of cargo per year. They had fifty-four container cranes to haul the big boxes off the boats. Thirteen hundred acres devoted to stacking off-loaded containers the size of tractor-trailers on top of each other.

Fourteen point five million tons of cargo a year.

About 1.2 million tons a month.

Forty thousand tons a day.

A Stinger missile weighed 34.5 pounds, fully loaded. Call it seventy pounds for two.

So, net-net, they were searching for seventy pounds out of the eighty million that probably came into Newark on Halloween night. They were looking for a narrow-gauge needle in a hundred-acre field full of haystacks.

He picked up the phone. Pressed in numbers.

"This is Customs Agent Acevedo," said the voice on the other end.

"Freddy? Chris Miller."

"Chris! Good to hear from you. Things okay?"

"Yeah. You?"

"Never better."

"Carlos still doing okay?"

"Beautiful. But he thinks Santa Claus should bring him extra presents this year. On account of how he didn't really get to do much trick-or-treating on Halloween."

Freddy laughed. Miller smiled. It was a good thing—being able to joke about what, just a couple of weeks earlier, was almost a tragedy.

"Freddy, I need a favor."

"You name it."

"Can you find out what cargo came in on Halloween night?"

"Which docks?"

"Any and all that might've fallen under your jurisdiction."

Freddy whistled. "That's a lot of paper to track down. Shipping manifests, invoices . . ."

"I'm sorry to ask, but—"

"No, man. I'm just sayin' it's a lot of paper to let you know it might take me a little time is all."

"But you'll do it?"

"Absolutely. I owe you, Saint Chris. You brought Carlos home safe. I owe you big-time."

59

The strike force met in the squad leader's room at a place called the Novotel. The hotel was located at Broadway and Fifty-second Street, eight blocks north of the Marriott Marquis.

Alexander Schmitz stood at the window. It faced south. Times Square. Was there a hotel room in this city without a bird's-eye view of all that was wrong with the world, the swirling filth of the human circus?

"You need to be here, Schmitz," said William Brewster, the squad leader.

Alexander hadn't been listening.

"Come again?"

"I want you here. Oh-seven hundred hours, every morning. We do P.T. in the Fitness Center. We do it together."

"Well, that's stupid."

"Excuse me?"

"The three of you associate together?"

"Affirmative. These two leave their hotels, meet me in the gym, we work out."

"You're exposing yourself to surveillance cameras."

"The brothers should rehearse in advance!" the so-called leader replied, spouting more of the crap he apparently memorized from the Al Qaeda training manual. "The success of this mission depends on us functioning as a cohesive unit."

"No. That's where you are wrong, Mr. Brewster. The success of this mission depends on you transporting *me* to Cargo Area C at JFK. The success of this mission depends on *me* targeting the aircraft, lining it up, bringing it down. In short, the success of this mission depends upon *me* and *me* alone."

"We don't even need you," said another member of the team. "I was in the army, too. That Stinger is a fucking fire-and-forget weapon. Got a goddamn infrared guidance system and all kinds of gyroscopes stuck up its nose. Hell, I could point that thing at an airplane and shoot it down."

"Could you?"

"You bet your sweet ass."

"You wouldn't lose your nerve—even if you saw a mother and child, their faces pressed against a window?"

"No problem."

"Then, please. Be my guest."

The third man in the room had a painful look of confusion contorting his face. "You can see through the window? Even when you're, like, completely underneath the airplane?"

Alexander didn't answer.

He was working with imbeciles.

He decided it would, indeed, prove necessary to eliminate all three of these men after completing his mission.

Even if they were in no danger of being apprehended, each man would receive one bullet straight to the heart. Dr. Tilley would thank him for it.

60

Saturday morning, Miller went out to JFK airport, where he met Jennifer Stevens, the volunteer dog-walker who had called in the report of "four skinheads" in Cargo Area C.

"You think they're terrorists or something?" she asked.

"It's something we're investigating."

"Maggie didn't like them."

"Does she work here with you?"

"No. She's a dog."

An angry bark came from the squat building behind them. They were standing in the Vetport parking lot. The warehouses around them were closed for the weekend.

"It looked like they were in some kind of army," Jennifer said.

"How do you mean?"

She waited for a jet to finish its thundering takeoff.

Miller had never realized how easy it was to get so close to the underbelly of a jumbo jet on its initial ascent. He felt as if he could pick up a chunk of gravel and, without much effort, hit the big metal beast right in its rivets.

They both watched the plane as it sailed east. Miller tried *not* to imagine the jet being hit by a shoulder-launched rocket and bursting into flames and crashing into the ocean and tossing torn seat cushions and luggage and severed limbs and baby doll debris into the rolling whitecaps of the Atlantic Ocean.

He tried.

"They acted like these soldiers my little brother has in one of his Xbox games. These computerized Marines always move around in a tight little clump of four soldiers. Timmy, that's my brother, he says they automatically take up positions to protect the man on point."

Miller nodded. She was describing a Marine firing team. A squad covering each other while simultaneously moving forward.

"This one guy kept staring up at the sky. Scanning it. He had on sunglasses. The other three, the big ones, they were like secret service agents around the president."

"Would you recognize this man in the sunglasses if you saw him again?"

"I think so. Yeah."

Miller pulled a folded sheet of paper out of his pocket. It showed six different photographs from United States Army personnel files. Five were selected at random. One was Alexander Schmitz.

He handed the paper to Jennifer Stevens. Without hesitation, she tapped on the fourth frame.

"That's him. Number four."

Alexander Schmitz.

"I don't recognize anyone else. The three who were protecting him, their pictures aren't here."

Miller took back the sheet of paper. It wasn't as good as a lineup, but it might be enough to finally convince a criminal court to issue a warrant. He had already initiated his "warrantless" search down on the docks, thanks to Freddy Acevedo.

"Thank you, Ms. Stevens. You've been extremely helpful."

"Are these guys up to something?"

"They might be. We're not certain. But we need to look into it."

But first, of course, he needed that warrant.

61

Thomas Hancock unscrewed the cap to the flask of Jack Daniel's whiskey.

"You sure you don't want a nip, sugar?"

He offered it to the big-chested blonde sitting next to him in the copilot's seat.

"Nuh-uh. I'm already drunk as shit from all that beer."

She swiveled around as best she could. The control yoke forced her to spread her tan legs a little wider. Made her tiny skirt move higher up her thighs.

Her name was Connie. She worked at Hancock Toyota. Up front where the men coming in to look at trucks could look at her first. She was twenty-two. Flunked out of U.T. Business School. But, hell, this girl didn't need a damn degree to sell Toyotas. Her body would work just fine.

He took another sip of hooch and felt it burn its way down his throat. Shivered.

"Damn. That's good."

"You sure you're okay to drink and drive?"

"Hell, girl. I ain't drivin'. I'm flyin'! Ain't no highway patrol up here to pull us over and give me a damn DUI."

The plane bounced.

"Relax, sugar. Just a little turbulence."

He tapped a finger against the glowing radar screen in the control panel near his knees. The sweeping circle was filled with angry green blotches.

"Them there are rain clouds."

"Rain?" Connie looked out the window and saw nothing but blue sky. "It's not raining out!"

"Yes it is. Underneath us."

She seemed bewildered. "If it's raining, how come the sky is so blue?"

Hancock looked at her. Smiled. Gave her one of his best winks.

"God painted it that way to match your eyes, honey pie."

She blushed. "I need to use the potty."

"You know what they say. . . ."

"What?"

"You can't buy beer, only rent it."

"Shit. That's funny, Tommy!"

He beamed. "You want to see somethin' even funnier?"

"Hell, yeah."

"Grab my briefcase on your way back."

"What is it?"

"Picture I found on the Internet."

"Is it dirty?"

"Just bring me my briefcase and I'll show you."

She fumbled for her seat belt. Found it. Twisted around to unsnap it. Gave Hancock a fine, full view: first her enormous breasts, then, when she stood up, her well-rounded butt.

Damn, but he was on top of the world.

His Tennessee Vols were enjoying a winning season, might even make it to the National Championship. Sales were skyrocketing at the dealership. He was a well-respected member of several national organizations. Hell, he was Dr. John Tilley's number-one benefactor.

Connie worked her way around the cabin seats. Staggered toward the bathroom.

They were flying up to Lexington for the Tennessee-Kentucky game. Caterers had stocked the plane with sandwiches and liquid refreshment. They'd be on the ground at Blue Grass Airport in plenty of time for kickoff.

He flipped on the autopilot switch, fumbled under his seat, and found the quart bottle of Jack Daniel's. Charcoal aged. Smooth. Old Number 7. He needed to decant another pint into his flask.

"Don't go anywhere without me," Connie said as she wiggled into the small lavatory at the rear of the aircraft.

The plane rocked. More turbulence.

Connie stumbled sideways.

Her head bumped against the ceiling.

"Ouch."

"You hurt yourself?"

"Nah. I'm so drunk, I can't feel a thing."

She yanked on the handle but the bathroom door didn't close all the way. Another air bump and it swung wide open without her noticing.

Hancock watched Connie tug at her orange thong and slip it down her thighs.

"Tommy? Are you peeking at me?"

She giggled, pulled the bathroom door shut.

The twin prop engines set up a soothing hum. Hancock yawned, looked over at his aluminum attaché case. He'd spent a fortune for it over in Hong Kong because it was some sort of high-security deal. Fireproof. Tamper-resistant locks. Made him look and feel like James Bond.

Inside were business papers and other important documents, including the funniest photograph he'd ever seen: Hillary Clinton servicing O. J. Simpson.

He'd show that one to Connie.

Then, maybe he'd show her the shipping manifest.

He'd kept it.

The paperwork from the Israeli arms dealer. Hell, why not? It was his money. Young Connie should know what sort of important man she was keeping company with. A true southern gentleman, able to drop half a million for a pair of Stinger missiles.

The briefcase seemed to switch seats. Then it moved back. Looked like it couldn't make up its mind. Kept switching from the right seat to the left seat and back again.

Then Hancock realized: his eyes were kind of crossing. The briefcase was sitting still. It was the airplane cabin that was spinning all around.

He might've had him a little too much Jack Black.

Should probably eat a little something.

One of them pimento cheese sandwiches back in the galley. Pimento cheese sandwich and some potato chips.

Maybe drink him a Coke-Cola to dilute the alcohol. There was Coke in the cooler with the beer.

He undid his seat belt. Twisted around in his chair.

Stumbled up. Staggered backward. Bumped into the yoke.

He put the plane into a nosedive.

62

For eight days, Alexander Schmitz filled his time as best he could.

He worked out in the gym at the Marriott Marquis.

He ate breakfast and lunch at Applebee's.

Reluctantly, he continued to meet with his strike team at the Novotel—but only in the squad leader's room, not in any of the hotel's public spaces, which were, undoubtedly, under the watchful eye of hidden surveillance cameras.

He ate dinner with Anna after her shift ended at Applebee's, usually in the Encore Lounge of the Marriott, where they served American food. They stayed away from the sushi bar. Sushi was the Japs' revenge for World War II. Mercury poisoning. The raw fish was full of it. It was a slow-moving death but every bit as lethal as an A-bomb over Hiroshima.

Anna spent the night in his hotel room on several occasions. Together, they watched pay-per-view adult movies, but that was as far as their sexual relationship went. They kissed a few times. One night, he cupped her miniature breasts. The rest, they would save for after they were married. Those were God's rules.

* * *

For eight days, Christopher Miller waited.

He waited for Freddy Acevedo to go through the tedious process of piecing together a record of what ships were unloaded on Halloween night, what cargo came ashore, what merchandise moved off the docks.

He waited for his superiors to give him permission to go to a court for a warrant to search Alexander Schmitz's father's house. He requested surveillance on the house. It was denied. There was a manpower shortage in western New York State. All agents were needed to assist the Canadians investigating a new threat originating in a Toronto mosque.

When he finally received reluctant permission to pursue his search warrant, he had to wait for the judge.

Down in D.C., Andy Jackson had uncovered one fresh lead: the man who worked the counter of the Cleveland diner where Undercover Agent Fitzgerald's body had been found just happened to be Alexander Schmitz's uncle.

When interrogated, he, of course, repeated the party line: "I have nothing to say."

They had nothing to hold him on. But they had another link back to Alexander Schmitz. Another argument for the issuance of a warrant.

It proved to be the tipping point.

Three days before Thanksgiving, Judge Osgood Throckmorton granted Special Agent Christopher Miller and the FBI Hate Crimes Working Group a warrant permitting them to search the last known address of one Alexander Schmitz in Buffalo, New York.

*   *   *

On the day before that warrant was issued, Dr. John Tilley received the first payment from Trans African Airlines. One hundred million dollars was wired to his offshore banking account in the Cayman Islands.

That same Sunday, Alexander Schmitz received a telephone call from his father at his room in the Marriott.

"You aren't supposed to contact me! Not until the job is finished."

"They're talking to Bob!"

"Who?"

"They're watching me!"

"Who?"

"The FBI! They've been tailing me for about a week. I've seen them. At work. In the neighborhood. There's a car parked outside right now. Two men in the front seat."

"Dad?"

"Yeah?"

"If it's the FBI, they've probably tapped your phone, too."

"Oh, shit. Jesus."

Alexander didn't say good-bye. He simply hung up.

He would need to move.

Change locations.

He would need to do so immediately.

Fortunately, he had planned for just such a contingency. There were other Marriotts in New York. They all accepted gift cards. The closest was located on West Fortieth Street, four blocks south, one block east.

So he moved out, taking the rolling golf bag with him.

63

On the Monday before Thanksgiving, Christopher Miller met Andy Jackson's team in the parking lot of the Northtown Plaza Shopping Center in Buffalo, New York.

"How many agents do we have?" he asked.

"Not as many as I'd like," said Jackson. "Everybody's up in Canada, checking out that thing at the mosque."

"Can we set up a hard perimeter?"

"Yeah. We're eight, altogether. You, me, three guys from the Buffalo field office, three Buffalo PD. We set up four two-man teams. We can station a vehicle behind the house." He tapped a map. "Here on Carmen Road. Put a van at each of these corners. We do that, they're pretty much boxed in."

"And who goes knocking on Schmitz's front door?"

"That's easy. The A-Team. You and me."

Miller nodded. "Sounds like a plan."

The other vehicles rolled out first. Took up flanking positions.

Miller and Jackson checked their weapons. Climbed into a rented Ford sedan. It was a bright November morning. Blue sky. Damp air. Colder than Jersey, because this was Buffalo and the wind came whipping in from Canada across Lake Erie, the threat of a blizzard always on its breath.

They eased onto Eggert Avenue, turned right down Emerson Drive. The houses on the street all looked pretty much the same. Red brick. Single story. Tidy lawns. Two trees in each front yard. Probably looked the same way when the houses were brand-new back in 1955.

"You think Junior will be home?" Jackson asked as the car crawled down the street.

"Doubtful. We know he was up in the Catskills with the Stinger. Then that girl ID'ed him at Kennedy. My guess is he's in the New York area, waiting for his orders. I'm hoping we'll find something here to point us in the right direction."

"Like his father?"

Miller nodded.

"And if the dad has nothing to say?"

"Maybe his phone records will do the talking for him." Miller drummed the search warrant against his thigh. It covered everything discovered on the premises of 102 Emerson Drive.

They pulled into the driveway.

They could see the backside of a pickup truck through the window of the closed garage door.

"Looks like somebody's home," said Jackson.

"Yeah."

The two agents stepped out, easing the doors shut. They didn't want to announce their arrival too noisily.

They moved up a concrete walkway.

Took the two short steps up to the front stoop. Jackson rang the doorbell.

No answer.

He rang it again.

Still nothing. He pressed a third time. Again, no answer. No sounds of movement inside the house.

Miller knocked. Hard.

"Mr. Schmitz? This is the FBI. We have a warrant! We need to search the premises. Mr. Schmitz?"

Nothing. He banged harder—hard enough to rattle glass in the door's little window.

"I'll swing around back," said Miller.

"Right."

He went down the steps.

"Chris?" called Jackson.

"Yeah?" Miller turned around. Saw Jackson had drawn his weapon. "Might be a good idea."

Miller nodded. "Yeah." He reached around, pulled out the Glock. Held it out in front of him with both hands.

He sidled around the garage. Made his way up a dirt path. Stepped into the backyard. He saw a rusty grill and a soggy bag of charcoal sitting in the middle of the dead sod. Two faded lawn chairs, their plastic strapping torn and frayed, lay rusting on their sides near the grill.

At the back of the house Miller saw another short set of steps. The rear entrance also looked locked up tight. It didn't look like someone had just hightailed it out the back door.

Miller moved toward the stoop.

The glass window of the storm door was cluttered with decals. Mostly American flags and yellow ribbons that said "Support Our Troops." One of the flags was clenched in the talons of a screaming eagle.

There was no doorbell so Miller banged on the aluminum doorframe.

"Mr. Schmitz? This is the FBI. We have a warrant to search these premises. Mr. Schmitz?"

He knocked again. Harder. The metal door was as cold as the chill November air. He felt like he was banging his fist against the inside of a steel-lined ice chest. Miller wanted somebody to open a damn door— soon. He breathed steam into his hands. Rubbed them together.

"Mr. Schmitz?"

He cupped his hands to block the sun's glare, pressed his face against the glass.

He saw a shadowy shape sprawled on the kitchen floor.

A man.

The legs and arms were spread out at awkward angles.

His eyes adjusted. Took in more detail.

Now Miller could see a thick pool circling the man's head.

Blood. A black lake of it.

64

At the start of the new business day, Dr. Tilley prepared to make a satellite call to his team in New York City. He levered up the thick antenna.

The TAA wire transfer had cleared. His account in the Cayman Islands was one hundred million dollars healthier. It was the easiest money he had ever made. Even easier than selling audiotapes full of flimflam to disgruntled truck drivers.

"Abort the mission," he said into the phone. "Affirmative. Abort."

He depressed the power button. Terminated the secure connection.

He sipped tea from elegant bone china.

He wondered how close the FBI was to finding Alexander Schmitz.

He picked the boy because he could be so easily traced. He was military and the military kept records. Fingerprints. Dental records. Service records. They inventoried their human stock as diligently as their ready-to-eat meals.

Besides, Tilley had left the Feds quite a trail. Made it ridiculously easy for them—like tracking a sluggish bear through wet cement.

Surely they had monitored the "chatter" he had initiated online about "the Eagle."

Surely someone had heard the rocket blast up in the Catskills. In fact, it's why Tilley had insisted that Hancock procure *two* Stinger missiles. He needed one to fire early in the game to help the FBI track down Schmitz.

It's also why Tilley had made certain that his cleanup crew hid the fingerprint-laden canister so ineptly.

It's why Tilley'd instructed Schmitz to check in at the Marriott under his real name.

Why he'd kept the boy parked in the same location for over three weeks.

People would recognize him. Bellhops. Chambermaids. Front-desk clerks.

If Tilley couldn't stop the boy, he was certain the FBI—before Wednesday—would do just that.

The people who might try to thwart Tilley's plans, who might try to protect Alexander Schmitz and, thereby, permit him to shoot down the TAA jetliner, had already been dealt with.

Including the boy's father.

Yes, a hundred million dollars in an offshore account was nice.

Two hundred million would be even nicer.

65

Alexander Schmitz slept late on Monday.

Only two more days and he would be famous.

Immortalized.

The sun was slanting in through the vertical slit he had inadvertently left in the heavy rubber-backed curtains when he closed them last night. The stark light of the new day scorched his retinas. He reached for his sunglasses on the nightstand.

He and Anna had checked into the Courtyard Marriott on West Fortieth Street the night before. Actually, Alexander checked in. Anna joined him in the new room around midnight.

They had been up until 3 A.M. The adult movies had overstimulated them both. Alexander would need to shower this morning. Vigorously cleanse his genitals.

They would certainly need to get married, now. As soon as possible.

His secure cell phone rang on the small desk near the window.

"This is Schmitz."

"This is Brewster."

"Yes?"

"Where are you?"

"In my hotel room."

"The Marriott Marquis?"

"I have made alternative arrangements."

"Why?"

"Reasons of no concern to you or our mission."

"That's what I'm calling about. The mission is off."

Alexander was stunned. "Come again?"

"The mission is canceled. Repeat, the mission is canceled."

"Why?"

"Wasn't told. Didn't ask. I received my orders ten minutes ago."

"From who?"

"My superior officers."

"Was it Dr. Tilley?"

"I am not at liberty to discuss this matter in any further detail."

"Did you receive authentication? Are you one hundred percent certain this order was legitimate?"

"Yes and yes. Stand down, Mr. Schmitz. Abort."

"But—"

"Stand down!"

Alexander didn't know what to say. "Very good. I will vacate these premises and evacuate the city, immediately."

"No rush. Stay if you like. Utilize your remaining gift cards. That's what I'm gonna do."

"What did you say?"

"I said I'm staying. For the parade."

"What?"

"Since we're not doing this other thing, looks like it won't be canceled."

"Mr. Brewster, I suggest that you pull out. Now."

"And, like I told you, I'm staying."

"You should leave!"

"Schmitz?"

"Yes?"

"Listen to me: do whatever the hell you want. But, before you leave the city, drop off your package here at the Novotel."

"My package?"

"The Stinger. Drop the bag with the concierge. Tell him you're returning the golf clubs I let you borrow over the weekend."

Schmitz depressed the *Off* button with a sharp jab of his thumb.

"Is everything okay, Alexander?" Anna asked.

"Fine."

"Who was on the phone?"

"Business associates."

"Do you need to go to work today?"

"No. In fact, I am free to leave New York City whenever I please. I plan to do so immediately."

Her eyes saddened. "Really? Where will you go?"

"Home."

"I see."

"I want you to come with me."

"To Buffalo?"

He smiled. "It's where my father lives. I'd like to have his blessing before we wed."

Anna blushed. "Do you mean that?"

"Yes. They have an Applebee's in Buffalo. You could easily find work."

"We could start a family."

"Right away."

"I want children. Lots and lots of children!"

"Me, too," said Alexander. "At least three. It's the only way to save our race."

Anna agreed. "Remember when white families had six, seven, and eight children?" she said. "Now it's the mongrel races who have large litters."

Alexander looked at her tenderly. What a wonderful woman.

"Be ready to leave in thirty minutes," he told her.

He went into the bathroom. Saw where Anna had written A L + A S with her finger on the fogged mirror. A big, loopy heart surrounded the initials.

It was forgivable that last night she had succumbed to the uncontrollable passions Schmitz aroused in her. It would not happen again, however, until their wedding night. Alexander understood these things better than she and must set the example.

In Buffalo, the two of them would do something to avenge Anna's little sister, the missionary who had been raped by a horde of filthy foreigners.

No way in hell was he giving the Stinger back to that moron Brewster.

And, if Dr. John Tilley had some kind of problem with that, too fucking bad. He could come to Buffalo and try to take it back.

What did that bumper sticker say on the back of his father's pickup?

THEY CAN HAVE MY GUN WHEN THEY PRY IT FROM MY COLD DEAD FINGERS.

He felt the same way about the Stinger.

66

Dr. Karin Ryan was the chief medical examiner for the Commonwealth of Kentucky.

It had taken her and her CSI team over a week to reach the site of the plane crash on the steep side of Little Black Mountain.

"Looks like another FWI," said a member of her team as he sniffed at the open neck of a flask found in the underbrush about fifty feet away from the twisted fuselage. They found some other items thrown from the plane as well. A toilet seat. Orange and white seat cushions. Scattered body parts.

"Flying While Intoxicated," said Dr. Ryan. She'd seen it before. Drunks smashing into mountains they couldn't see because of cloud cover. Hell, even if the clouds weren't there, some of these blitzed bozos still wouldn't see Everest.

She'd come slogging down the muddy track expecting to find the remains of Mr. Thomas Hancock, a wealthy businessman from Knoxville, Tennessee, whose plane had been reported missing. She didn't know that he had had a passenger until she examined the decomposing corpse of what used to be a pretty young girl. The worms had eaten away her face but her breasts still pointed to heaven. Silicone lasts longer than flesh. The young woman was probably a blonde. They'd have to do microscopic analysis of her charred scalp to be certain.

"Find any sort of ID on her?" she asked one of the state troopers.

"No, ma'am."

"Keep looking." She pointed to a rocky outcropping. "Seems to be the main trajectory path for the debris. Might be something over that way."

"Yes, ma'am." The trooper hiked toward the cliff, careful to brace himself along the way.

As she watched him make his way down the slope, something shiny caught Dr. Ryan's eye. Near the biggest clump of rocks. She hadn't seen it before. Clouds must've opened up. Let in the sun. Whatever it was, it glinted like a signal beacon.

Dr. Ryan took an angle toward the outcropping. Her boot slipped out from under her on a wet patch of leaves. Pebbles and dead branches skittered down the hill.

"Over there, Bill," she called out to the trooper. "See it?" Another silvery glint winked at her. "Something metal. Maybe aluminum. Could be a suitcase."

It was Thomas Hancock's briefcase.

There was a T on one lock, an H on the other.

"Want me to pop it open?" asked the trooper.

Dr. Ryan nodded.

The trooper pulled out a Swiss army knife, pried out the flathead screwdriver tip. He wedged it into the keyholes. Wiggled.

When that didn't work, he jammed the screwdriver into the tiny slit between the lock and the catch, tried to lever the two apart.

"Man. These suckers are pretty tight."

The trooper yanked down hard on the knife handle.

The lock popped.

"What've we got?" Dr. Ryan asked as she tugged on a pair of latex gloves.

"Looks like papers mostly."

Dr. Ryan sifted through the pile.

"Damn," muttered the trooper. "Didn't know the Klan still rode up here."

"Mr. Hancock wasn't from Kentucky," said Dr. Ryan. "He flew in from Tennessee. Besides, they don't call themselves the Klan anymore. They're just good ol' boys full of White Pride."

A few years earlier, Dr. Ryan had worked with the FBI Hate Crimes Working Group. She had helped uncover definitive proof that eight-year-old Shantelle Lewis had been shot to death before the fire engulfed the church where she and her sister had been rehearsing with the Mount Zion AME's children's choir. Dr. Ryan had helped put those particular villains away on murder charges.

Examining the contents of Thomas Hancock's aluminum attaché case, she had a pretty good idea what she was looking at.

White supremacist hate literature.

Antigovernment screeds.

And something that looked a lot more sinister.

"Jesus," she muttered.

"What is it?" asked the trooper.

"He might've been an arms smuggler." She used forceps to lift up the document. Beneath it was Hancock's "Month-At-A-Glance" daybook.

Inside were notations. She skimmed the squares that made up November. Some dates were circled with a red marker. Notes in those boxes were scribbled in red as well.

"Kentucky Game"

"Vanderbilt Game"

The entry for this coming Wednesday was the one that gave Dr. Ryan chills.

"D-Day."

Inside that calendar box, Hancock had doodled the kind of airplane boys in the fifth grade scribble on the covers of their notebooks: a jumbo jet tumbling out of the sky with thick plumes of black smoke billowing out both of its wings.

67

Alexander reached across the Toyota's armrest and took Anna's hand.

It felt warm.

"Do you need to call Applebee's?" he asked. "Let them know you won't be coming in to work today?"

"I suppose I should." She glanced at the dashboard clock. It was 11 A.M. "I'll call in a half hour. My manager gets in at eleven-thirty."

He nodded. "That would be wise."

"Yes. I'll need a good reference from him. There are two Applebee's in Buffalo. One in Cheektowaga."

He let go of her hand. "You know, Anna, I won't want you working long."

"Just until we're pregnant."

"I'll find a new job, too. I'll find two jobs if I have to."

"I know you'll be a good provider, Alexander. And an excellent father."

They were taking the New York State Thruway north. They had been out of the city for over an hour. Alexander enjoyed seeing trees again. Real trees. Not the ones New Yorkers held captive in their concrete sidewalks.

They passed minivans and station wagons loaded

down with luggage racks. Families getting an early start on Thanksgiving.

"I'm sorry you won't be home with your family for the holiday," Schmitz said.

"We don't celebrate Thanksgiving anymore," said Anna. "There's not much to be thankful for after your sister has been raped and killed."

Alexander glanced over at Anna. Her eyes were moist.

"I'm sorry," he said. "You'll have your revenge. I promise."

His words gave her hope. He could tell. He looked back to the road. He knew he would be the one to help heal her emotional scars. He had the power to do so. The weaponry. He could feel the rocket launcher bounce with a thud in the trunk every time the car hit a pothole.

He reached for a bottle of purified water in the cup holder.

"When I was a kid," Anna said, "my father used to bring us up this way every autumn."

"Really?"

"There was a farm. You could run through the fields and pick your own pumpkins. We'd come up right before Halloween."

"Do you remember where it was?"

"Certainly," she said. "It was my favorite thing to do. Better than Christmas."

"Picking pumpkins?"

"They had hot doughnuts and cold cider. The farm was right up here." She pointed to the approaching exit sign. "This exit."

"Would you like to see if they're still open?" He drained the water bottle.

"Could we?"

"Of course. I need a rest stop anyway."

He smiled. Flicked on his turn signal. Eased into the right-hand lane. They took the exit.

They drove about five miles east of the Thruway.

"You're sure that was the correct exit?"

"Yes. It's just a little further up this road. It's a farm so, unfortunately, it's in the middle of nowhere. My mother always thought my father was lost every time we came."

They were on a winding two-lane state road with a solid yellow line down the middle and a tangle of trees on either side. No farms or cow pastures.

"I'd like to be in Buffalo before dark," said Alexander.

"Have you called your father? Does he know we're coming?"

"No."

He didn't add that he couldn't risk it. The mission may have been called off, but the FBI was probably still snooping around his father's house, tapping his phone lines. It would be better if they just showed up in his driveway.

"There's a gas station," said Anna, pointing up the road. It was the only building visible. "They probably have a restroom."

"Thank you, dear."

He checked his rearview mirror. No traffic. No need for a turn signal. He pulled the Toyota off the road.

"Odd," said Alexander. "Looks like they're closed."

The place seemed abandoned. Brown weeds grew underneath big plate glass windows. Padlocked chains were wrapped around the rusty gas pumps.

He spied a sign taped to the door.

"I was correct. They're closed."

"I'm sorry. How badly do you need to go?"

Alexander pushed his sunglasses up the bridge of his nose. "I've been hydrating all morning."

"Well, maybe the men's room is open."

He nodded. "It's possible. If not, I'll use the woods around back." He opened the door.

"Hurry back!" Anna said sweetly.

The men's room was locked up tight: a hasp had been bolted into the door. A lock secured through its loop.

Alexander moved around to the back of the building. Unzipped his fly.

Stopped.

How would he be able to wash his hands without a sink?

He tugged the zipper back up.

He'd go get a bottle of water from the car. Before they left the Marriott, he'd sterilized tap water by heating it in the small hotel coffeemaker. Then, he'd poured it into plastic bottles.

He moved back around the left side of building.

He saw Anna standing outside the Toyota.

He dropped into a crouch beneath the window. He had an angled view through the building to the area near the gas pumps.

She was pacing back and forth, a cell phone glued to her ear.

No. The antenna was thick and stubby.

Anna was talking to someone on a secure satellite phone.

68

"I'm sending it to you in an e-mail," said Jackson.

Miller hung up the phone. Swiveled sideways in his chair. Clacked a couple keys on his computer.

The state of Kentucky's chief forensic expert and medical examiner, Dr. Karin Ryan, had just e-mailed her old pal Special Agent Andrew Jackson a thick stack of evidence she had recovered from the side of a mountain somewhere south of Lexington.

Laptops with cellular modems were a marvelous thing.

"This is it," Jackson had promised Miller. "Our big break."

"Whose briefcase was it?"

"Thomas Hancock. Millionaire from Tennessee. Major financial backer of Dr. John Tilley. Hancock paid for the Stinger, Chris. He kept the goddamn receipt."

The receipt. A goddamn receipt. All neat and typed up, probably in triplicate. Proof that Thomas C. Hancock had paid an Israeli arms merchant five hundred and fifty-five thousand dollars for one Stinger launcher and two ready-to-fire antipersonnel warheads.

The image now filled his screen.

How could anyone be so stupid? You don't document illegal arms sales. Unless, like Andy suggested, this good ol' boy from Tennessee was so vain he wanted some kind of trophy to show off to his friends: *You know that jet airplane that got blown out of the sky? I paid for that. Don't believe me? Look at this bill of sale from my Israeli arms dealer.*

Miller clicked open the second attachment.

Jackson was right.

This was their lucky day. A second document had also been recovered from Mr. Hancock's briefcase and it was the missing link.

A shipping manifest.

Documentation related to a cargo ship sailing from Japan to the port of New York. The Trans Future 7, a car carrier vessel, operated out of Nagoya Port by Toyofuji Shipping. Six automobiles on the boat were to be off-loaded at the Toyota Auto Processing Facility in Port Newark and immediately transported to Hancock Motors in Knoxville, Tennessee.

Scheduled arrival date at Port Newark: October 31.

Halloween.

69

Alexander could not believe his eyes.

Anna had an Iridium satellite phone.

She also had a pistol.

He saw her take it out of one of the gas pumps!

She raised its sheet-metal front like she was opening a breadbox, reached in, and came out with what looked like a Glock semiautomatic.

A cop pistol.

Anna tucked the weapon into the waistband of her skirt.

She was working for the government! Anna was an undercover FBI agent. A spy. A tool of the Zionist Occupation Government.

Alexander stayed low. Peered through the window at the woman who had betrayed him. No. The bitch who had entrapped him.

How could he have been so stupid?

She had used her body to get to him. Pretended to be pure and innocent when, in truth, she was a whore—just like his mother.

Anna stared at something. Gave a quick glance in both directions and started for the side of the building.

Moved like she was military. Swift. Light on her feet. Muscles tense. Body poised.

She was coming to arrest him. For what, Alexander wasn't certain. He had been sharp enough not to reveal his true reason for living at the Marriott for nearly a month.

Maybe somebody else had talked.

That idiot at the Novotel. His so-called Squad Leader.

Maybe some friends of that asshole he had blown into the lake with the test round.

She had something. Some trick up her sleeve.

Fine.

He assumed she would follow the same path he had taken. So he would circle the building, come out on the opposite side.

He moved along the rear wall. The hardpan was dimpled with a drip line from the clogged gutters overhead. The ground was wet.

He left an easy trail of footprints.

It didn't matter. He needed to move quickly. Make it to the trunk of the Toyota. Retrieve his weapon.

At the right rear corner of the building, the ground fell away, became a sharp cliff of eroded clay. He jumped down. Scrabbled along the right side of the building. Ran hunkered over. Kept below the window line. He slapped his pocket. Good. He had taken the keys with him when he left the vehicle.

"Alexander?"

She was behind the building now.

"Where are you, honey?"

The bitch was good. Still sounded sincere.

Bent at the waist, he dashed across the concrete, made his way toward the gas pumps. Pulled out the key fob. Thumbed the remote. The trunk flipped open with a chirp-chirp before he reached the rear bumper.

"Alexander?"

She had heard the chirping.

He reached into the trunk. Fumbled with the golf bag.

"What are you doing, honey?"

She was behind him.

"I need a towel to wipe my hands."

"A towel?"

His fingers fumbled for the Velcro flap on the golf bag's ball pouch.

"Yes. I like to cleanse myself after I urinate."

"We don't have any towels in the luggage, hon." She was moving closer. Slowly.

He opened the pouch. Felt inside.

"I stole some towels from the hotel," he said. "Hand towels. I figured they charged me so much for that room, the towels must be included in the price."

"I need you to step away from the vehicle, Alexander."

He didn't turn around.

"Say again?"

"I need you to show me your hands and step away from the vehicle."

She was a fucking Fed, all right. Had memorized their stupid songbook.

"Why?"

"Just do as I say, Alexander. Turn around and place your hands on top of your head."

"I can't."

"What?"

"I can't do it."

He heard her pull back the hammer on her weapon.

"Now, Alexander."

He glanced over his shoulder.

"Anna?"

"I have my orders, Mr. Schmitz." She motioned with the pistol. "Turn around."

"Okay."

He did.

He spun around and dropped to his knees and assumed his preferred firing stance, at the same time reducing his own presence as a target.

She seemed surprised. Her momentary hesitation gave him a slight advantage.

He took her down with five quick pops. Silent rounds no one would hear.

He worked the shots down the target. Head. Neck. Heart. Stomach. Cunt.

The Russian-made PSS silent pistol worked flawlessly. The bullets made no noise whatsoever.

Neither did Anna.

She died too quickly to scream.

70

"No problem, Saint Chris."

Miller had just asked his friend and neighbor, United States Customs Agent Freddy Acevedo, to help him track down the Vehicle Identification Numbers for the six Toyotas shipped to Thomas Hancock's Tennessee dealership on Halloween night. Freddy was at Port Newark. Miller was at his desk.

"This is why they kidnapped my Carlos? To move a couple Camrys off the dock?"

"We think there was something hidden inside one of the cars."

"Something bad?"

"Yeah."

"Drugs?"

"Something worse."

"Terrorist shit?"

"Yeah."

"Jesus."

"I need these VINs, Freddy. ASAP."

"I know the guys over at the Toyota processing facility. I'll get back to you within the hour."

Within two hours, Miller knew that three of the six Toyotas that came off the dock on Halloween night were still on the lot in Knoxville.

The local FBI office in Tennessee sent a team of agents over to Hancock Motors, talked to the sales manager. Some of the bunting and banners flapping in the breeze were now black instead of orange—a show of respect for the dealership's dearly departed boss. Businessman, loyal Vols fan, white supremacist, all-around solid citizen. The three remaining vehicles were impounded for further forensic examination.

Miller appreciated the Knoxville office's efforts, was grateful to have somebody (anybody) in the Bureau actually taking his requests and concerns seriously, but he didn't think the workups on the unsold vehicles would prove necessary.

According to the sales manager, two of the other three Toyotas that had been transported out of Newark that same night were almost immediately sold during what was called "The Tailgater's Toyotathon." One car went to a high school chemistry teacher in Oak Ridge. Another to a graduate student at the University of Tennessee.

The third car, according to the dealership's accountant, was given away "as part of a special sales promotion."

When pressed for details, the number cruncher produced a sheath of papers documenting the title transfer of the Toyota in question from Thomas Hancock Motors to Reverend John Tilley, spiritual leader of the American Christian Church, headquartered in Cody, Wyoming.

Miller hadn't realized that Dr. Tilley was an ordained minister.

Guess it helped him on his income taxes.

Especially when devoted followers like Thomas Hancock were showering Reverend Tilley with gifts like a fully loaded Toyota Sequoia fresh off the boat from Japan.

VIN: JT4RN5632F0139246

71

Tilley stared at the satellite phone resting on the end table.

He wondered why the unit had remained silent for nearly an hour.

The girl had called from the designated killing zone.

She had found the weapon in its prearranged hiding place.

She should have terminated Schmitz by now.

Maybe the battery on her portable SATCOM phone had died. Maybe she was in the Toyota right now, recharging it via the cigarette lighter.

Anna Lang had been a good and loyal soldier. A mercenary, technically, since she had been paid for services rendered. She'd taken the job at Applebee's to guarantee that Dr. Tilley always knew where "the Eagle" was, what he was doing. Anna was also an excellent actress. Tilley had enjoyed hearing some of the more salacious details of her relationship with Schmitz. How he practically scrubbed his penis raw with the scouring pad side of a nylon sponge following their single session of frigid sexual intercourse. He had used sterilized water for that purpose, too.

Tilley smiled.

Alexander Schmitz was a young warrior serving a higher calling, just not the one he imagined. *It's unlikely,* Tilley thought, *that the swelling of my bank balance would inspire him the same way it does me.* Unfortunately, the Trans African Airways people had made it known through their intermediary that they not only wanted proof of Schmitz's death, they also wanted the Stinger as a warranty against future blackmail schemes.

Anna Lang would provide both. The dead body. The missile launcher.

In return, she would receive two hundred thousand dollars for less than one month's work. This didn't bother Tilley. Expenses were to be expected. Besides, it was a mere pittance when your own payday was two hundred *million*.

The team in Buffalo that had eliminated Alexander Schmitz's father would receive slightly more. After all, there were two of them and they were both men.

Finally, the phone beeped.

Tilley put down his tumbler of Scotch.

"This is Tilley."

"Sir, I know I wasn't supposed to phone you again."

It was Schmitz.

"Alexander?"

"Yes, sir. I wanted to warn you. We have been infiltrated. Repeat: we have been infiltrated."

"What do you mean?"

"The FBI. One of their undercover agents, a female, just attempted to take me into custody."

"Really?" This wasn't going well.

"Not to worry, sir. I have eliminated said threat."

Not well at all.

"Is she . . . ?"

"Yes, sir. She no longer presents an obstacle to the completion of our ultimate agenda."

Not well at all. The boy had killed Anna.

"Listen, Alexander—"

"Sir, we need to terminate this call."

"What do you mean?"

"No doubt her backup is somewhere sweeping the radio spectrum and attempting to monitor all telecommunications in this grid. Cellular and satellite. She had an Iridium Secure SATCOM 9500. The model the army uses in Iraq. Government-issue matériel."

Tilley examined his own phone. Same make. Same model.

"Sir, I fear our ability to communicate may no longer be secure."

"Are you using her phone?"

"Negative. I destroyed her unit. I am currently employing the cellular telecommunications device your people provided me when I first reported for duty."

"What about the other, you know, high-tech item in your possession?"

"It is secure."

"Excellent. Here is what I want you to—"

"Good-bye, sir. Everything I now do, I do for you and our country. We built it. We will take it back."

"I know, Alexander, but—"

"I am going dark, sir. Repeat, I am going dark."

"Just a minute. Alexander? Alexander? Hello?"

The line was dead.

A quick scan of the hand unit's glowing green screen indicated that the phone was fully charged and uplinked.

Schmitz had hung up on him.

The Eagle had gone dark and he was taking the Stinger with him.

This could prove problematic.

There was a sharp knock on the front door.

Tilley didn't respond. He sat in his leather easy chair. Thought. The boy might go off on his own and take down the plane. Ruin everything.

Another knock. Rougher. Louder.

"Dr. Tilley?" A harsh voice echoed through the cavernous lodge. "This is the FBI."

The FBI. Excellent.

"Just a minute!" he called out.

He'd let the Federal agents into his home.

He'd point them in the right direction.

For the first time in decades, when questioned by the authorities, he would have something to say.

72

Alexander dragged Anna's body around to the rear of the gas station and tipped it into a ditch.

But first, he'd rifled through her pockets. Front and back. Nothing. He tore off her shoes. In her left sock, he found cash. Lots of it. A thick roll of hundred-dollar bills rubber-banded around her ankle.

She really *was* a slut.

He wished he could call his father.

No.

The Feds were close, he was sure. Anna probably had had a GPS device on her person. He pulled down her skirt. Tore at her panties. Examined every cold crevice. Nothing.

But, wait. They didn't need to track her. They knew she would bring him to this spot. They had planted the gun. Propped it inside the gas pump. Rigged up the false front. It was like that movie. *The Godfather.* Michael Corleone finds the gun on top of the toilet tank.

Shit.

It meant the Feds must know where he was. They were probably sending in a chopper right now.

Fine. Let them. The Stinger was created specifically to take down low-flying enemy aircraft. He'd use it now if he had to even though he'd rather save the weapon for some higher purpose. He'd show them. He'd do something bigger than Oklahoma. Maybe bigger than the World Trade Center.

Alexander checked his watch. He needed to move out.

The cash he'd just pilfered from Anna (if that was her name) made redeployment more manageable. He'd head back to the Thruway. Find a hotel.

Wait!

The car.

Would they know what kind of vehicle he was driving?

Negative.

Anna had never seen the Sequoia before this morning and she had been with him the entire time since it was retrieved from valet parking at the Marriott. She had not phoned in that information. Because she couldn't. He would've heard her.

Unless, of course, *that* was what she was phoning in when he saw her pacing around outside the car with her SATCOM unit.

Doubtful.

She had simply been letting her handlers know everything was on track. That she had duped her target. Thought she could handle him herself. Didn't call for backup. Stupid little girl.

She had no idea who she was up against.

Well, maybe now she did.

Because now she was dead.

Alexander drove south on the New York State Thruway, back toward the city. It was only Monday. The Trans

African Airlines jet wouldn't take off until first thing Wednesday morning.

He got off at Exit 20. Saugerties. Followed signs and found the Comfort Inn on Route 32. Check-in time was 2 P.M.

It was 1:45.

Fine.

He'd wait in the car. He'd park around back and wait. Maybe listen to the radio. Scan the news.

His cell phone rang. Not the secure unit. His personal cell phone, the one he hadn't used in over a week. He had just powered it up and connected it to the car's cigarette lighter to recharge the battery. He wanted it ready should his new plan require a secondary telecommunications device.

He checked the caller ID screen.

Uncle Bob. Cleveland.

Unexpected.

He opened the phone.

"Hello?"

"Alex! Where the hell are you? I've been trying to reach you!"

"I'm in the field."

"Jesus, Alex . . ."

"What's wrong?"

"They killed your father!"

"What?"

"The Feds! They killed him."

Alexander said nothing.

"The same bastards sent an undercover agent down here!" Uncle Bob continued.

"Come again?"

"The Feds sent a spy to our meetings! Called himself Tiny. Dressed like a biker. Fortunately, somebody nailed the fat bastard out near the Dumpster!"

He listened. Gripped the steering wheel.

He remembered his father saying the FBI had been tailing him. At the time, Alexander thought his old man was being paranoid. Now he could see the truth. Someone had talked. Alerted the Feds about what was about to go down at JFK. That's why Dr. Tilley had to abort the mission so abruptly.

"Alex? They'll come for you next!"

"They already tried. They failed."

"You gotta lie low."

"I know what to do, Uncle Bob."

He closed up his phone. Found the other one, the secure unit, and stepped out of the car.

He threw both of them as far as he could into a patch of trees fronting the parking lot.

Cell phones could be traced. If they tracked these two units, all they'd find with them was a heap of old tires and rusty beer cans.

He wouldn't be staying at the Comfort Inn.

He would head down the road.

He had work to do.

They would be watching the airports. They knew what was in the wind.

That is, they knew what *used* to be in the wind.

His plan now was to hit the Zionist Occupation Government with something new. Something totally unexpected so all the intelligence the ZOG had thus far gathered would be rendered meaningless. Alexander would improvise a fresh attack plan in no way connected to the previous plot at JFK.

Well, that wasn't completely true.

He'd probably still use the Stinger.

73

On Monday afternoon, Christopher Miller and a dozen agents gathered in the main conference room at the FBI field office in Newark, New Jersey.

"This is our primary suspect." He pointed to the photograph projected on the wall: Alexander Schmitz posed in his dress uniform in front of an American flag. "Alexander Schmitz. Also known as the Eagle." He clicked a remote. "This is the same man spotted at JFK Airport two weeks ago when he and his strike team did their initial reconnaissance. Apparently, they knew about the security cameras to their west and used their truck to block that line of sight. Fortunately, other cameras captured these images."

The picture changed. Schmitz in his Desert Storm camos, a sniper rifle resting against his hip. "Schmitz is the triggerman. This, we believe, will be the weapon employed in a terrorist operation scheduled for this coming Wednesday."

Miller's PowerPoint presentation launched into a short video clip: Two soldiers riding in a Humvee. They stop, jump out, and snap open a cargo hatch to remove what appears to be a five-foot length of olive drab pipe mounted to a handgrip. One soldier points. The other soldier elevates the tube and fires. The screen flashes. A plume of white smoke streaks across blue sky. The contrail corkscrews as the missile hesitates, turns, changes course. Seconds later, a target drone, flying several thousand feet up, erupts into a ball of fire.

"That's from a Marine Corps training video. The Eagle, we believe, is currently in possession of one of our own Stingers. A man-portable, shoulder-fired, guided missile system."

The short Marine Corps video looped and repeated. The agents in the room remained silent.

"Schmitz's Stinger was one we left behind in Afghanistan. We know this because a spent launch tube we recovered in upstate New York had a serial number etched into it that corresponded to one originally procured by the CIA for use by the Afghan mujahadeen against the Soviets."

Miller clicked through a few more photographs of Stingers in action. Afghan rebels firing one in the desert. Russian helicopters exploding.

"We know they test-fired the weapon at this remote training facility, on land owned by known white supremacists. We know they have a second round standing ready because, according to documents in our possession, the Stinger and two missiles were purchased on the black market from an Israeli arms merchant, by one Thomas C. Hancock, recently deceased. Hancock had been a major financial backer of an organization sometimes known as the Brotherhood. The man who runs that organization is Dr. John Tilley. Yesterday, two of our agents visited Dr. Tilley in Wyoming. He has proved uncharacteristically talkative."

Miller clicked the remote and Alexander Schmitz was back on the wall, his grim visage glaring down at everybody in the room.

"Dr. Tilley advised our agents that he had 'heard about' the Eagle but said he in no way sanctioned terrorist activities. Furthermore, according to what Tilley said he was able to ascertain from members of his movement, Schmitz is determined to bring down a Trans African Airliner scheduled to depart from JFK on Wednesday morning."

"Wait a minute," an agent interrupted. "How'd Schmitz get his hands on the Stinger?"

"Good question. We know Mr. Hancock gave it to Dr. Tilley after the Stinger was smuggled into the country via the Toyota processing facility at Port Newark on Halloween night."

"What?" cracked Agent Barb Szydlowski, the resident wiseass. "These boys don't like Humvees anymore? They want better gas mileage?"

"The weapon was hidden inside a Toyota Sequoia SUV," Miller explained, "which Hancock then presented to Tilley."

"So Tilley had the Stinger?" said Szydlowski. "And now he claims he knows nothing about what Schmitz is up to?"

"Exactly."

"Unbelievable."

Miller nodded. "That's why Dr. Tilley will remain our guest at a federal holding facility for the foreseeable future. At this point, his story is as follows: he gave the Toyota, without knowledge of its secret cargo, to Alexander Schmitz because he had heard that the young man was unemployed and needed a car."

"What?"

Miller shrugged. "Tilley insists he drove the car up to Buffalo simply to help a struggling Iraqi war veteran who needed a means of transportation to search for gainful civilian employment."

"What a crock."

"Agreed. But, since Mr. Hancock got drunk and crashed his airplane into the side of a mountain, there is no one alive to contradict Tilley's version of what went down."

"So this Schmitz finds the Stinger hidden in the backseat or whatever, puts together a strike team, and sets out on his own to bring down a transcontinental jetliner?"

"Such is the story Tilley would have us believe."

"Sounds like total bullshit."

"Which it no doubt is. However, his providing information to help us nail Schmitz fits with what we know about Tilley. That incident out in Illinois?" Miller glanced at Agent Dale Krishock. "Andy Jackson did a weapons check after Carl Krieger was put on the ground. No one on our team took the shot. We now suspect that Tilley ordered Krieger's assassination. Furthermore, we think he might be doing the same thing with Schmitz—only this time he wants us to do the job for him. Best guess? Schmitz has done something to upset Tilley so he's giving us everything he thinks we need to take the kid out for him."

Miller clicked one last time.

The agents were once more presented with an image they had already seen: Alexander Schmitz surrounded by his strike team in the parking lot of Cargo Area C at JFK Airport. "We need to locate Alexander Schmitz, his weapon, and his friends before that plane takes off on Wednesday morning. We have less than two days."

"Next steps?" asked Szydlowski.

"We've already issued an APB on the automobile and have shared Schmitz's mug shot with law enforcement agencies throughout the tri-state area. We'll keep working Tilley for more information. At the present time, we have no idea where Schmitz might be."

Miller moved to his left, hit the light switch. The overhead fluorescents flickered on in a row.

His boss, Charlie Lofgren, the man who'd spent most of the last month busting his chops and slowing him down, stood up at the opposite end of the long table.

"Whatever you need, Chris," he said. "You got it."

74

It was nearly 5 P.M.

Through the slats between the clapboards, Alexander could tell that it was dark outside. He had parked inside a barn on a farm he had discovered when he took Exit 16 off the New York State Thruway and headed west toward some place called Bear Mountain.

It was a good hiding spot.

He assumed the Feds were looking for him, that they had probably retrieved Anna's body by now.

When she didn't report in, they had to come looking for her.

Alexander had been conserving gasoline and battery power (even though that meant the Toyota was without heat) because he didn't want to be forced into a refueling situation should his new plan, whatever it might be, involve travel. He checked his watch. He would turn on the radio and listen to the news at the top of the hour for two minutes, see if there was a report about a dead woman matching Anna's description.

"All news all the time, this is ten-ten WINS. Official radio station of the Macy's Thanksgiving Day parade. You give us twenty-two minutes, we'll give you the world."

Alexander didn't have twenty-two minutes. That much time would run down his battery or drain his gas tank.

Two minutes.

The top stories.

Something about the Middle East.

Holiday sales forecasts.

More about the Macy's parade and search-and-rescue dogs from the NYPD's K9 Unit that would be marching in it this year.

Nothing about that other bitch.

Nothing about Anna.

He shut off the radio. He needed to think. He needed a plan to avenge his father's death.

And make his way into the history books.

75

The Federal agent rattled Dr. Tilley's cot.

"Wake up."

"What?"

"Wake up. We need to talk."

"What time is it?"

"We want to go over your story again."

"What? We've gone over it and over it! I have my constitutional rights."

"Sorry, sir. Not in this instance. I just reread the constitution and you know what? The right to a good night's sleep is never mentioned, not even once."

Tilley sipped coffee from a paper cup.

"You gave Schmitz a brand-new car?" the agent asked for the tenth time in the interrogation. The hundredth time in less than twenty-four hours.

"Yes. As I told you before, Mr. Schmitz is a veteran of the Global War on Terrorism. When he came home, he could not find work. He is also white, so the government would not help him the same way it would if he were black. There is no affirmative action for whites. No hiring quotas."

"Did you know that Schmitz was planning to shoot down an airliner?"

"Of course not."

"What about the Stinger? Where did you have your gunrunner hide it? Under the backseats?"

"As I stated previously, I never saw this weapon you speak of nor did I have any knowledge of its presence in the vehicle."

"And, as I indicated previously: I don't believe you."

Tilley smiled. "Believe what you will. However, do you have any evidence or testimony to the contrary?"

Tilley knew they didn't. He never touched the damn thing. Thomas Hancock was dead and, therefore, unable to save his own skin by handing Tilley over to the Feds.

These morons had nothing.

"Gentlemen, I suggest you concentrate your efforts on locating Alexander Schmitz. The boy is obviously troubled. Mentally unstable."

"Tell you what, Dr. Tilley: you help us locate Schmitz, I'll let you sleep."

Tilley realized he would need to spoon-feed these imbecilic investigators more information or Schmitz might not be apprehended in time to guarantee his payday.

"Fine. I'll need my notebook."

"Excuse me?"

"The notebook you gentlemen confiscated when you invited me to spend the night."

"Don't worry. It's with your other personal items."

"Kindly retrieve it."

"Why?"

Tilley sighed. "I remember now that I gave Mr. Schmitz certain other gifts."

"Such as?"

"I had heard that he was about to be evicted."

"He lived with his father."

"An unfortunate housing situation for a decorated veteran. I devised a scheme to further assist Mr. Schmitz and passed on to him what you might call 'temporary housing vouchers.'"

"How?"

"I gave him Marriott gift cards. Each one, of course, carries a distinctive serial number. Perhaps if you ask the good people at Marriott to check their computers they might be able to tell you if Mr. Schmitz has used any of those coded cards and, if so, where he might be sleeping. I also gave him similar gift cards, each with a nineteen-digit serial number, for a restaurant chain called Applebee's."

76

Miller led the team of agents that swept into the Marriott Marquis in Times Square at six on Tuesday morning.

Two other teams were making similar sweeps.

One would enter Applebee's when the restaurant on Forty-second Street opened. The second was already at the Courtyard Marriott on the corner of Sixth Avenue and Fortieth Street. The Bureau's early-morning computer searches, using the serial numbers provided by Tilley in Wyoming, indicated that Schmitz's gift cards had been used in all three locations.

The Marriott Marquis's manager met Miller and the agents in the lobby. The first-floor entrance wasn't very crowded even though Miller knew it soon would be. Tomorrow, tourists would begin descending on Times Square in anticipation of the holiday and the Macy's parade.

The hotel manager had a manila file folder tucked under his left arm. He extended his right hand to greet Miller.

"Special Agent Miller?"

"Yes, sir."

"Jim McNeely. Let's go up to my office." McNeely gestured toward the escalator.

"We'd rather go up to Alexander Schmitz's room."

"He's not here," the manager said.

Miller's eyes instinctively swept the lobby. "He may have registered under an alias."

McNeely shook his head. "He didn't. He checked in under his own name."

"You're certain?"

"Positive."

Okay, Miller thought, Alexander Schmitz must have missed a few special-ops training sessions. Like the one on how to remain undetected while operating undercover. Lesson one: never use your real name. Unless, of course, you think you're invincible, which, maybe Schmitz did.

"What's in the file?" Miller asked.

"You sure you want to do this here?"

"Yeah."

"Okay." McNeely led Miller and his team over to a marble security desk. "This is the picture you sent us." It was Schmitz's military mug shot. "When your people called at three A.M. . . ."

"Sorry about that."

"No problem. I figure that's when the information first became available."

Miller nodded.

"I had my security chief spend the intervening hours scouring our security tapes, looking for any visual matches. Now, he's only been at it three hours, but this looks to be your guy."

Miller studied the curled thermal printout. It was Schmitz all right. In a restaurant. There was a young woman sitting across from him.

"That was taken in our Broadway Lounge."

"Any idea who the girl is?"

The manager shook his head. "No. But, when the lounge staff gets in, we'll definitely show them this—and any others we dig up by then. My guys are still in the video room, running through tapes."

"Good. Agent Hargrove here will stay with you and your team. He'll coordinate communications and assist in any way possible."

"Great."

Miller looked at the next sheath of pages in the folder.

"That a copy of his itemized bill?"

"Yes. Nothing too interesting. He ordered room service quite often. Watched pay-per-view movies in his room on a regular basis. Mostly pornography."

"What about this?" Miller tapped a number on the printout.

"That's our daily garage charge. He must've parked a vehicle with us."

"Why does the charge start four days after he checked in?"

"Perhaps he rented a car later in his stay."

Perhaps. Or maybe that's when Dr. John Tilley gave Alexander Schmitz a brand-new Toyota Sequoia.

"Okay," Miller said. "Show his picture around. He's been in residence here for nearly a month. Folks will probably recognize him."

"Is he some kind of terrorist?" the manager asked.

"We're not sure," Miller said.

"Is he planning something here? If so, I'd like to take the necessary precautions."

"We don't think this building is at risk. This man is not a suicide bomber. I see no need to initiate evacuation protocols or to needlessly panic your guests."

"Good. We're completely booked."

"Yeah." Miller remembered the trouble his wife had had finding them a room on Broadway for Thanksgiving Eve. If Saint Chris could stop the evil Mr. Schmitz from shooting down a Trans African Airlines jet on Wednesday morning, the whole Miller family would be heading into the city on Wednesday night.

His cell phone chirped.

"This is Miller."

"Barb Szydlowski over on West Fortieth."

"What've you got?"

"Schmitz checked in late Sunday. Used gift cards to pay for dinner. Drinks. Dirty movies up in his room. He checked out yesterday. Took the Toyota with him."

"Damn."

"That's not all."

"What?"

"The bellman remembers he had a very unusual piece of luggage. It looked heavy but Schmitz wouldn't let him touch it."

"What kind of luggage was it?"

"A rolling golf bag. So, tell me this: who plays golf in New York City in November?"

77

"You're not coming home, Daddy?"

"No, Angel. They need me at work tonight."

Miller and his team had set up a base of operations inside an empty warehouse at JFK's Cargo Area C. They'd brought in phones, computers, weapons, and, of course, cots—not that Miller thought he'd get any sleep tonight.

It was 8 P.M. Tuesday. Still no sign of Alexander Schmitz or his Toyota. The people at Applebee's remembered him, said he came in for breakfast and lunch almost every day, always sat at the same table, always had the same waitress, but they hadn't seen him since Saturday. Miller asked to talk to the waitress who seemed to be Schmitz's favorite.

The manager hadn't heard from her since Saturday, either.

Her name was Anna Lang. Miller put Barb Szydlowski in charge of finding out who she was. An hour later, the Applebee's manager had identified Anna Lang as the girl sitting at the table with Schmitz in the security camera still from the Marriott Restaurant. Szydlowski also had another piece of evidence to report: while searching

Schmitz's vacated room at the West Fortieth Street location, they had discovered the ghost image of something scrawled with a fingertip across the bathroom mirror. By steaming the glass, they had been able to read it: A L + A S. They had also been able to lift Ms. Lang's right index fingerprint. She, too, was ex-military.

Miller figured his man was lying low, maybe even knew the Feds were on his trail. He also figured he had taken his girlfriend with him.

But this is where he planned to strike.

This is where Schmitz, the Eagle, would have a clean shot at Trans African Airlines Flight 1122 when it took off for Lagos, Nigeria, at 7:30 A.M. Dr. Tilley had provided his interrogators with very specific information about the plot, all of which he claimed to have "heard from reliable sources within the movement." For whatever reason, Tilley wanted Schmitz stopped. He also wanted the FBI to do the stopping for him.

"Are you at the No-hotel already?" his daughter asked over the phone.

"You mean the Novotel?"

"Is that where we're staying tomorrow night?"

"Like I said, honey, that's the plan."

"But first you have to stop the bad man?"

"Yeah."

"Daddy?"

"Yeah, Angel?"

"I really, really, really want to see the parade and Santa and the balloons. Blues Clues is a balloon this year."

"He's that big bear, right?"

"No, Daddy. Blues Clues is a dog. Remember? We see him on TV."

"Is that the blue dog or the red dog?"

"Blues Clues is blue. Clifford the Big Red Dog is red."

"Oh, right . . . I remember. . . ."

Miller saw some activity to his right. An agent had a phone cradled between her neck and ear so she could frantically jot something down. Miller caught her eye. Raised his eyebrows to ask, *"Got something?"* The agent shook her head and mouthed back, *"Ordering pizza."*

Hurry up and wait. Deploy the SWAT teams. Set up a perimeter, seal off Cargo Area C. Wait some more. Order dinner.

"Daddy?"

"Yes, Angel?"

"If you catch the bad man and we come into New York and see the parade, I'll let you have my sweet potato pie after Thanksgiving dinner."

"You don't have to do that."

"I know. But I will. Because I really, really, *really* want to see Blues Clues and the bands and Santa and the dogs. Did you know this year they're going to have police dogs in the parade?"

"With Santa?"

"No, Daddy. He has reindeer, not dogs. Remember? *Flying* reindeer."

"Oh, right."

"Okay," his daughter said. "You better get back to work."

"Yes, ma'am. I miss you, Angel."

"I miss you too, Daddy."
Miller closed up his cell, rubbed his eyes.
His daughter was right.
He had work to do.
And only a couple of hours more to catch the bad man.

78

Miller took up his position inside the command truck at 6 A.M. on Wednesday morning.

He had stretched out on one of the cots around 3 A.M. and had slept until approximately 3:15. He closed his eyes again at 4 and made it all the way to 4:30 before the dream about West Virginia woke him up. The one where he dropped the girl he was trying to rescue from the kidnappers. The one where she disappeared into a field of wind-whipped weeds and he was blown out of the sky by a rocket-propelled grenade.

The rocket was a new twist on an old nightmare.

At 4:35, he started drinking coffee. He wouldn't try to sleep again. He'd only end up sleepwalking into somebody's bedroom like his daughter. It was time to start the waiting, the vigil, in earnest.

Andy Jackson flew up from D.C. and arrived at JFK at 5 A.M. They were together now, huddled in the back of the command vehicle, staring at the racks of video monitors, searching all twenty screens for any sign of a dark-blue Toyota Sequoia. Both men wore full body armor, watch caps, and gloves. Still, the truck was chilly: its heater off, its engine shut down so it would look like an idle cargo hauler waiting for the day to start on the loading docks.

"He's coming, Saint Chris," Jackson said when he caught Miller rotating his wrist to check his watch. "We'll nail him."

"We better. I earn an extra piece of sweet potato pie when we do."

"What?"

"I'll tell you later." Miller tapped a screen. "That van. Was that there before?"

"No."

"We should—"

"I positioned him there. He's one of ours."

Miller nodded. Thought. "Schmitz might've switched vehicles."

"Yeah. He might've."

Miller eased back into his seat. He was a body at rest again. He hated it. He rocked his wrist. Checked his watch. 6:32. The sun would be up in another seventeen minutes. It was one of the things Miller had checked on the Internet when the nightmare woke him up and he needed something to do besides sit around and wait for Alexander Schmitz to show up.

He heard a dog barking. The command center was set up in the cargo hold of a panel truck parked in front of the Vet Port. It looked like the half dozen other white trucks parked in Cargo Area C, backed up to loading docks.

All six trucks carried the same cargo: heavily armed men in black body armor, goggles, and helmets. They all had ammunition packs and serious weaponry jangling off their utility belts. FBI SWAT teams had been called in from the New York and Newark field offices. The NYPD sent over members of their Hercules Team, the city's special counterterrorist unit. More ninjas in ski masks, armed with Colt M-4 Commando submachine guns.

The Port Authority Police, the law enforcement agency directly responsible for protecting JFK Airport, didn't have a SWAT team, so they sent ten guys with rifles. The FBI lent them body armor.

"What's that?" asked Miller.

"What?"

"There. Screen fifteen."

"Toyota."

"Sequoia?"

"Some kind of SUV."

"You think?"

"Maybe."

Miller brought his handy-talkie to his mouth.

"All units, stand by. We have a suspicious vehicle entering parking lot. Headed in my direction."

"We see it," a voice crackled back. "Target acquired."

"This is Roof One. We have the shot." A sniper team had the Toyota driver in its sights.

"Can you ID Schmitz?"

"Negative. Tinted windows. No visual available."

"Damn," Miller muttered. "Wait for my go."

"Roger that."

On video monitor #12, Miller saw the Toyota pull into the Vet Port parking lot, into the space behind the command truck. He felt for the Glock nestled in the small of his back.

"Looks like we're on," he said to Jackson.

"Yeah." Jackson already had his weapon out.

"When we roll up that rear door, we're gonna make all kinds of noise," Miller thought out loud. "Sniper One?" he said into his handy-talkie.

"This is Sniper One."

"Command team is preparing to initiate a dynamic exit from this truck. If it's Schmitz and he makes a play for us, take him down."

"Roger that."

"You ready?" Miller asked as he and Jackson took their positions at the rear of the cargo hold. A third agent knelt in the center, ready to grab the pull handle and fling up the rolling door.

"Ready," said Jackson.

"On me," said Miller. "One, two, three . . . now!"

The metal door clattered up in a flash.

Miller and Jackson jumped to the asphalt, rolled in opposite directions. Took up firing stances behind the Toyota's taillights just as the driver flicked them off.

"Freeze!" Miller shouted. His Glock was aimed at the silhouette of a head. He saw red dots glinting off the car's windows. Snipers had the driver lined up with laser sights.

The driver screamed. "Ohmigod!"

It wasn't Schmitz. It was a woman.

"Stand down," Miller yelled.

"Stand down!" He could hear the command being relayed on radios, shouted across rooftops.

The woman stepped out of the Toyota. She raised her hands over her head.

"I came to walk Maggie!"

Miller tore off his ski mask.

"Hello, Ms. Stevens," he said.

"Agent Miller? Do you need to ask me some more questions?"

Miller escorted the volunteer dog-walker into the rear of the command truck. It was 6:45. The TAA jet was still listed as on time for its scheduled 7:30 A.M. departure. With taxi time out to the runway, it probably wouldn't be airborne until 8:30.

Schmitz still had time.

Miller and his team had more waiting to do.

79

Alexander Schmitz turned the ignition key.

The SUV started up. He punched the power button on the radio.

"*. . . for more turkey roasting tips, visit our Web site or call the Butterball hotline,*" said the radio newscaster. "*Well, this Friday will be Black Friday, better known as the day after Thanksgiving, when many retailers see the red ink on their balance sheets soar into the black as hordes of holiday shoppers swarm to the mall. . . .*"

So that was that.

Nine A.M. Wednesday. What should have been his hour of glory. This newscaster should be broadcasting a breaking-news bulletin: "*A Trans African Airlines jet has crashed into the Atlantic Ocean. Witnesses say it was shot down with a rocket.*"

Instead, the Eagle was hiding in an abandoned barn doing nothing.

He switched off the engine. Needed to conserve gasoline.

For what?

His mind wandered.

To John Wilkes Booth.

That's right. Of course. Booth. The original plan had been to kidnap Lincoln and hold him for ransom, use him to negotiate the release of Confederate prisoners. Then the Civil War ended. No more prisoners. So what did Booth do? Did he quit? No. He conceived a new mission. Something deadlier. A mission with more meaning. He didn't kidnap Lincoln! He killed the bastard. Brilliant. Better.

When one door closes, another door opens.

Be an army of one.

It came to him.

The parade.

The Macy's Thanksgiving Day Parade.

The official start of the holiday season. The official start of the shopping season.

The stupid parade marched down Broadway.

It marched down Broadway and crossed Forty-second Street. Times Square.

If he took up an elevated firing position, similar to the view he had had out his window at the Marriott, he could target one of the big balloons or a band or a float.

A float.

They had SUVs to drag them down the street. Or they had some sort of gas-powered vehicle hidden underneath all the decorations to provide locomotion. Vehicles with internal combustion engines that gave off heat signatures—not that he would need the infrared tracking capabilities of the Stinger warhead but a little insurance never hurt.

Alexander smiled.

He'd wait till the tail end of the parade entered Times Square, the same spot where millions gathered every

December 31 to watch a ball drop down a pole and announce the arrival of the New Year. He'd wait for the final float and take his shot.

Because Santa's sleigh was always the tail end of the Macy's Thanksgiving Day Parade. There had to be a motorized vehicle of some sort hidden underneath the sled and animated reindeer. He'd lock on to that. The ensuing fuel tank explosion would be spectacular!

He'd do all this in front of millions of children and their horrified parents watching the parade at home on TV! He'd destroy Thanksgiving, Christmas, and even New Year's in one bold strike!

He would unleash hell for the holidays.

80

"Face it, Saint Chris: this time, we won."

It was noon on Wednesday. Four hours earlier, Miller and Jackson had stood outside their undercover cargo truck, craned their necks, and watched TAA Flight 1122 soar across the bright-blue sky to begin its transatlantic voyage to Nigeria.

Alexander Schmitz never showed up.

"He's still out there," Miller said to Jackson. "So is that damn army surplus Stinger."

"And we have his face plastered all over the Most Wanted List. Every police department in the country is on the lookout for him. He's being pinned up on bulletin boards in post offices. Hell, he and his girlfriend, Anna Lang, are going to be the next stars on *America's Most Wanted*. In other words, Chris—relax. We're going to catch him. It's just a question of when and where."

"What about that uncle in Cleveland? Schmitz might try to run there."

"His Uncle Bob is under surveillance twenty-four-seven. The bosses back in D.C. were suitably impressed with what we dug up. It's finally become a major manhunt. Bureau's top priority, right up there with Al Qaeda. Nobody wants another Timothy McVeigh, especially one with a rocket launcher instead of a rental truck. We did our job, Chris."

"You think Schmitz knows we're onto him?"

"Maybe. Maybe he heard what happened to his dad. Maybe he got word that Tilley was basically handing him over to us. You know what? Maybe it's payback time and he's on his way to Wyoming to blow up Tilley's log cabin. If so, he won't get far—especially if he's still driving that damn Toyota."

"So what're you telling me, Andy?"

Jackson smiled. "Happy Thanksgiving is what I'm telling you. Enjoy your day off. Spend some time with your family. Pig out on that sweet potato pie."

Miller grinned. "Is that an order?"

"I can't order you around, Agent Miller."

"Why not? You outrank me."

"True. But you're older than me, man. *Way* older."

"Thanks, Andy." Miller checked his watch. Time to call the ladies. Tell Natalie to pack the bags and bring Angela into the city.

He tossed his bullet-resistant vest into the back of the cargo truck.

"Andy, if somebody grabs this guy, I want to know."

"You will. And it's not a question of 'if,' Chris. It's 'when.' My guess? Before the Lions game kicks off in Detroit."

"Who are they playing this year?"

"I forget. But I'll watch it anyhow. Always have. Always will."

"Yeah. Me, too." Miller was actually relaxing. Feeling the tight coil in his stomach starting to unwind. "But I gotta tell you, man—I don't like that damn domed stadium. Roof keeps out the snow. I liked the snow."

Jackson nodded. "The Snow Bowl. Man, that used to be the best part of Thanksgiving. Sitting in the living room with my dad and uncles, watching grown men roll around in the mud. Mom and my aunts out in the kitchen roasting the turkey, baking pies. That's what it's all about."

Miller looked around the parking lot. SWAT teams were breaking down weapons, packing gear into vans. All the sniper teams were down off the roofs, sharing coffee, swapping war stories.

Schmitz was on the run. Probably long gone. Saint Christopher had earned his extra slice of sweet potato pie.

81

The traffic was unbelievable.

Alexander was crawling down the West Side Highway into Manhattan.

Driving the Toyota made him nervous.

Were the police looking for him?

Fortunately, the only cops he had seen since he evacuated the barn two hours earlier had been busy with a fender bender on the shoulder of the Thruway.

But he didn't like the way the guy in the tollbooth at the Henry Hudson Bridge looked at him when he crossed over the river from the Bronx into Manhattan.

How much did the FBI know?

Why was traffic moving so slowly? It was only 4:30 P.M.

Of course. The long holiday weekend.

Alexander's mind drifted to memories of the Macy's Parade. He used to watch it on television, but then one year they went too far and had some fat fag from a Broadway musical dressed up as Mrs. Claus. A drag queen.

There were usually children riding on the float with Santa—a politically correct mix of kids of all different races and, if they could find a drag queen to play Mrs.

Santa, probably a homo kid, too. Then they'd toss in a token White or two.

He saw the exit for West Seventy-ninth Street. He would continue on the West Side Highway all the way down to Forty-second Street, go to the hotel.

He glanced up to his rearview mirror.

There was a black sedan behind him. Following too close. Could be an airport limo service. Could be the Feds. The FBI loved black vehicles. Big black SUVs and sleek black sedans. Were they tailing him?

He took the exit. Followed it down to where it became a traffic circle. The black sedan kept close behind him. Alexander continued east on Seventy-ninth Street. So did the sedan. He slowed down. Fell in behind a bus. The black sedan jerked over to the left-hand lane and passed him.

Good.

It wasn't the FBI.

He stopped when the bus stopped. Pulled in right behind it near the corner of West End Avenue. When the bus driver opened his doors to pick up the waiting passengers, Alexander climbed out and walked around to the rear of the Toyota. He raised the cargo door and pulled out the rolling golf bag. The Stinger was packed snugly inside. The Russian-made pistol was packed inside his jeans.

His plan of attack was simple.

He would walk four blocks across Seventy-ninth until he reached Central Park West. He would follow that boulevard down to where it met Broadway at Fifty-ninth Street in Columbus Circle. At that point, he would continue down Broadway itself to the hotel. He would carry no other bags. He'd take fresh clothes and needed toiletries from the man already in the room. He smiled. He realized his planned route was the same one the Macy's Parade would take tomorrow morning when it stepped off at 9 A.M.

Of course, the parade would march down the middle of the streets. Alexander would stick to the sidewalks. He did not want to attract any additional scrutiny; dragging a golf bag around New York City in November would attract enough.

It was 4:45 P.M. Dark already.

In a little over sixteen hours, he would strike the blow that would make this Thanksgiving one to be remembered forever.

A very red and bloody Thursday.

82

The Millers checked into the Novotel at the corner of Broadway and Fifty-second Street.

They immediately found the uptown subway and headed north to the American Museum of Natural History to watch the big balloons being inflated with helium. They exited the train at Seventy-ninth Street and Broadway, climbed up the steep steps to the street, headed in the direction of Columbus Avenue, and were amazed at the mob of people packing the sidewalks in front of them.

"Where's everybody going?" Angela asked.

"Same place we are, I guess," said her father.

"Maybe this wasn't such a great idea," Natalie murmured.

"We're in no hurry," said Miller.

"You're right," said Natalie. "Let's just enjoy it."

Miller leaned in close to his wife. "And have a stiff drink later."

"Cocoa?" Angela, of course, heard him. "Are we going to drink cocoa later?"

"We sure are," said Natalie.

"With Kahlúa," Miller added.

"What's that?"

"Miniature marshmallows for adults."

Angela's eyes grew wide.

"Up there! See?"

She pointed up the street to a sidewalk bathed by portable floodlights. A sign indicated "Balloon Inflation" with an arrow pointing straight ahead.

There had to be ten or twenty thousand people, all bundled up in puffy coats and ski caps, squeezing their way onto the wide walkway ringing the American Museum of Natural History, all there to take an early glimpse at the amazing creatures rising from the asphalt.

When the Millers finally reached Columbus Avenue, it was as if they'd boarded the subway at rush hour. A throng of strangers jostled them along. Police barricades corralled the mob, shunted them like cattle into an organized stream headed downtown toward Seventy-seventh Street, where they could see the first balloons, already inflated, trapped under netting so they couldn't escape.

"That's Ronald McDonald!" Angela squealed.

The clown's head was visible, attached to a limp body lying wrinkled in the middle of the road.

They turned east. Moved along Seventy-seventh Street.

"Look! Blues Clues!" Angela jumped up and down and pointed at a flat sheet of rubber rolled out across the roadway. Men in mustard yellow jumpsuits with red Macy's stars plastered on their backs attached hoses from a helium tank into the flattened dog's side.

"You sure that's Blues?"

"Yes, Daddy! He's all blue!"

Miller could actually smell chestnuts roasting on an open fire. Well, he could smell the smoldering charcoal from a chestnut vendor's cart. It felt like the holidays had officially begun.

He bent down and scooped up his daughter. Hoisted her up over his head and brought her down on his shoulders. He was six-two. Angela had a great view.

"Thanks, Daddy! I can see everything from up here! Everything!"

She could not, however, see the man a block behind them, trying desperately to drag a rolling golf bag through the dense and exasperating crowd.

83

This wasn't in the plan.

Thousands and thousands of stupid people blocking his path.

"Watch it, pal," said some douchebag pushing a stroller.

"I need to go downtown," Alexander said.

"The subway's closed."

"What?"

"You can't get on the subway at Eighty-first and Central Park West. Not tonight. On account of the balloons."

Alexander needed to backtrack. Rethink his route. The subway was actually a good idea. They all went to Times Square—he remembered seeing the brightly colored sign at the Fory-second Street station when he walked from the Marriott to Applebee's.

"You should go back to Broadway," said the guy with the stroller. "Take the One train."

"Does it go to Times Square?"

"Yeah. Catch it at Seventy-ninth. Times Square is the fifth stop."

"You're certain?"

"Positive." His new friend started counting on the fingertips of his glove. "Seventy-second, Sixty-sixth, Fifty-ninth, Fiftieth, Forty-second."

"It stops at Fiftieth Street?"

"Yeah. Right near Seventh Avenue and Broadway."

Even better.

"Thank you."

He needed to be at Fifty-second and Broadway. He was going to "borrow" a hotel room from his so-called Squad Leader. The idiot who announced that he would stay in New York after the mission was aborted because he wanted to watch the stupid parade. Who had a superb view down Broadway—all the way to Times Square.

Alexander turned around, towed the golf bag behind him, pushed his way upstream through the teeming mob. He would do as suggested. He would take the subway down to Fiftieth and Broadway and walk up the two blocks to where William Brewster already had a room.

The Novotel.

84

The police cruiser twirled its red-and-white roof bar lights, gave the siren two short blasts.

It pulled in behind the blue SUV parked way too close to the bus stop, too far from the curb.

The two cops got out.

"You can't park there, pal," one officer shouted until the sweep of the roof bar lights revealed that the vehicle was empty.

"Great," muttered the cop. "Just what I need. Back on the street writing parking tickets."

His partner climbed out of the passenger seat. "That's a Toyota, right?"

"Yeah. I think." He glanced at the raised lettering on the trunk. "Sequoia."

"It's also blue," said his partner, who had been on the force ten years longer. "Makes it a blue Toyota Sequoia."

"No kidding. And I should care because?"

"Because we're supposed to be on the lookout for a blue Toyota Sequoia, especially one behaving in a suspicious manner."

"Says who?"

"The sergeant. During roll call. Drink more coffee, Foster. I'm calling this in. Get me the VIN."

"Where from?"

"Driver side dash. Front window. Should be a label there in the corner."

"Hold on. Here we go. JT4RN5632F0139246."

85

It was so easy to gain access to the Novotel.

Just like at any hotel, all you had to do was walk through the front door like you belonged there. Alexander headed toward the elevator that would whisk him up to the eighth-floor lobby.

"Need a hand with your bag, sir?" asked a bellman.

"No, thank you."

He pressed the call button.

"How'd you hit?" asked a man in a black woolen overcoat who had come in behind him and was, apparently, intent on making small talk while they waited for the elevator.

"Quite well," Alexander replied. He had no idea what the hell the man was talking about.

"Where'd you play?"

"Excuse me?"

"Where'd you hit your balls?" The man gestured toward the golf bag. "Chelsea Piers?"

Alexander nodded. "Yes."

"Is the driving range still open? In November?"

"Yes. I believe so."

That earned him a puzzled look but Alexander didn't care. The elevator dinged, doors slid open.

"You staying for the parade?" The guy wouldn't shut up.

"Yes."

"Me, too. Family's coming into town." The doors opened on eight. "Enjoy!"

Alexander smiled. He would. He would have a blast.

He strode across the lobby, heading toward the banks of elevators ferrying guests up to their rooms on the higher floors. The golf bag rolled smoothly behind him. He avoided making eye contact with the uniformed clerks stationed behind the four reception podiums. They had no time to notice him, anyway: they were far too busy dealing with long lines of eager holiday travelers.

Alexander stepped into an elevator. Pressed the button for the twenty-second floor. No one entered the car behind him. He glanced up at the sparkling ceiling of the ascending box. There was a security camera lens hidden discreetly amidst the rows of round halogen lamps.

He would have to wait until he reached the twenty-second floor before pulling out the Russian-made pistol.

"Schmitz! Hey! So you decided to stick around town, hunh? Come on in!"

Alexander smiled.

He stepped into the doorway and popped one silent round into Brewster's chest. One shot is all a shooter qualified as Expert ever needed. Yes, he had been extravagantly wasteful in bringing down Anna with five bullets but, in that situation, his anger had been squeezing the trigger.

Now he was back in full command of his faculties.

The team leader's eyes blew open wide with surprise. Alexander shoved him backward into the room, kicked the door shut behind him. Blood stained the tasteful tan carpet, made it more russet.

"Honey?"

A shapely woman wrapped in a towel, her flesh hot pink from her shower, stepped out of the bathroom.

"Who are you?" she asked.

In reply, Alexander shot her. One round to the chest. The white hotel towel blossomed with a crimson circle; terry cloth sponging up her blood. She collapsed in a heap.

He went to the window. Pulled open the blinds.

Perfect. A clear shot all the way to Times Square and that building with the steaming Cup o' Noodles sign up top, the NYPD station at street level. In between was the Panasonic Jumbotron.

It was 6:30 P.M. Time for Brian Williams and the NBC Nightly News. It filled the giant outdoor TV screen just like it would tomorrow night when they'd definitely have a big story to report.

"Terrorist Hits at the Heart of Thanksgiving!"

He wondered if the Jumbotron would survive the rocket blast. Doubtful. He figured anything within a fifty-foot radius of Santa's sled would become collateral damage—including however many of the parade's 2.5 million spectators were watching from the crowded sidewalks of Times Square.

86

The Miller family made its way back to Broadway for a quick stop at Starbucks for hot cocoa.

They were joined by about a million other shivering balloon-watchers. The quick cocoa stop took nearly an hour.

"Happy holidays," Natalie said when they finally picked up their drinks at the counter.

"We need to go to bed early tonight," Angela announced.

This was a new one. Usually, Angela, like most seven-year-olds, worked every angle she could think of to bargain for more time before going to bed.

"Can I finish my hot chocolate first?" Miller asked.

"Okay. But then we better go back to the hotel and go to bed. We need to get up real, real early to see the parade."

"But you just saw all the balloons, Angel."

"Daddy! Tomorrow will be better."

The Millers had booked a room in the Novotel with two double beds. One for mom and dad. One for Angela. If she was waking up early, nobody would be sleeping in.

"You want to eat dinner before we go to bed?" Natalie asked.

"Do we have to?"

"Honey, it's only seven o'clock. We'll eat dinner up here, then head downtown to the hotel."

"Okay," said Angela. "Look! There's a McDonald's across the street."

Great, Miller thought. *We're in New York City, home to world-renowned restaurants. And we're eating at Mickey D's.*

Miller could still taste the quarter-pounder rumbling in his stomach two hours later when they entered the eighth-floor lobby of the Novotel on Fifty-second Street.

"Time to go to sleep!" Angela announced.

Miller caught his wife's eye. They'd both been checking out the bar scene across the lobby. Imagining how good a nice glass of smooth red wine would taste right about now.

"I'll push the button for the elevator," Angela chirped.

There would be no romantic sipping of wine.

They stepped into the elevator.

"What floor are we on, Daddy?"

"Twenty-two."

Angela found the button with the two twos. Pressed it. "Got it."

Angela yawned dramatically, then jumped into her bed.

"Good night, everybody."

"Good night, Angel."

Miller snapped off the bedside lamp.

Natalie was soaking in the tub. If she couldn't enjoy a glass of wine, she figured she should at least take a bubble bath. The tub was free. Well, after you paid the three or four hundred dollars for the room.

Miller moved to the small desk and opened his briefcase.

Yes, he was on well-deserved, hard-earned holiday with his family, but one member was asleep, the other was enjoying the little bottle of foaming herbal soak.

So he slipped the Schmitz folder out of his bag. Switched on the desk lamp. Studied the man's photograph. Reread his bio. Pretty impressive military record. Qualified on MANPADS. Man-Portable Air Defense Systems. Stingers.

Jackson had called during dinner to let Miller know that the NYPD had located Schmitz's car. It had been abandoned near an entrance ramp to the West Side highway. One theory had it that someone, maybe his girlfriend Anna Lang, had picked Schmitz up and hauled him out of town. Miller wasn't so sure about that. The Toyota had been parked on the south side of Seventy-ninth. That meant it was headed east. If he wanted to get on the highway, he would've been going west. Jackson and the guys down in D.C. were working on it. Told Miller to enjoy his one and a half days off. They'd take care of finding the elusive Eagle.

He felt heat behind him. Smelled lavender. He turned around. Natalie swaddled in a hotel bathrobe. She looked all kinds of cuddly.

"Relax, old man," she whispered. "They'll catch this boy."

"What if they don't?"

"Then on Friday I'll pack you a leftover turkey sand-wich and send you out hunting for him. Let's let Angela have tomorrow, okay?"

"Yeah."

She leaned in. Kissed him. Her lips felt soft. So did her whole face. Soft and warm. Miller started feeling all warm and cozy, too.

"Who's he?" Angela was out of bed and staring at the photograph on the desk. "Is that a bad man?"

"Yes, honey," said Natalie. "But you don't need to worry about him. You need to go back to sleep."

Angela stared at the photograph.

"Come on, Angel," Miller said. "You heard your mother. Back to bed. Don't forget, we need to get up bright and early."

Angela went back to bed. Closed her eyes.

"Good night, everybody!"

"Good night, Angel."

Miller prayed the bad man wouldn't visit her in her dreams.

87

Alexander dragged the two bodies into the bathroom.

He dumped her in the tub, him across the toilet. He wanted to be able to get to the sink when he shaved his head as part of his final preparation for the attack. He wasn't some kind of crazy Arab, wouldn't shave his whole body, but the careful concentration required to closely razor one's scalp would force him to focus.

He'd found some underwear in the dresser. It was slightly baggy but clean. Found fresh socks, too.

"Thank you," he said to the dead body slumped over the toilet. Fortunately, the hotel provided guests with plenty of towels. Alexander mopped one around the floor with his foot to sop up the sticky blood.

It was nearly 3 A.M. Time to get ready. He knew it would take almost an hour for the parade to reach Times Square. Maybe two for Santa, the end of the line, to show up. He'd probably be taking his shot sometime between 10:30 and 11 A.M. He had seven, maybe eight hours to go.

But he couldn't sleep. He was too jazzed. Adrenaline was pumping.

He took off his sunglasses and inspected the razor sitting on the sink next to a crumpled toothpaste tube. A disposable Bic. Blunt to begin with. And, the blade was filthy. Caked with dry shaving cream and the dead man's stubble.

He needed a new razor. Something sterile and sharp. He'd risk a trip downstairs.

He put his sunglasses back on, grabbed the tube of toothpaste sitting next to the sink and stuffed it into his pocket.

He found a baseball cap in the bedroom closet. Apparently, the team leader had been an Atlanta Braves fan. He pulled the brim down to further shield his face and made his way to the elevator.

He was the only passenger.

He reached the eighth-floor lobby.

The sundries shop was closed.

He glanced over toward the bar. It was empty, except for a sleepy old man pushing a vacuum back and forth across the same patch of carpet.

Alexander took a deep breath. Steeled himself.

He moved to the concierge desk. No concierge.

He walked toward the reception area. No receptionists, either.

"May I help you, sir?"

Alexander spun around. Saw someone in a blazer. Had to be a hotel employee. The guy was sipping a cup of coffee from a blue paper cup.

"Uh, yes," he said. "I forgot to pack my razor. The shop is closed."

"Yes," the night clerk said, moving around to stand behind one of the reception podiums. "I'm sorry for any inconvenience. However, I do stock a small supply of essentials." The guy opened a drawer. Fished out a plastic-wrapped razor. "Do you require anything else? Toothpaste? Toothbrush? Shaving cream?" The clerk gestured toward Alexander's face. The sunglasses. "Eye drops?"

"Just a toothbrush."

"Very good, sir." The guy bent down again, came back with another plastic-wrapped essential.

"What about the morning newspaper?" Alexander asked. "I'd like to, you know, check out who's marching in the parade this year. Read about the balloons, what order they'll be appearing in."

"Sorry, sir. The morning papers haven't arrived yet. If you like, I could have one sent up to your room as soon as they're delivered." He took up a pen and prepared to jot down a room number.

Alexander shook his head. The last thing he needed was some bellman pounding on his door while he was setting up his rocket launcher—even though he really wanted a newspaper to find out if anybody had found that bitch Anna's body yet.

"Once again, I apologize for any inconvenience. If you like, we have a brochure listing all the participants in the parade."

The guy disappeared under the counter.

Alexander didn't wait for him to pop back up. He turned around and headed back to the elevators.

It was time to shave.

88

Just like she did at home, Angela slid out from underneath the covers, found the floor, and sleepwalked across the room.

Her parents, fast asleep in the other bed, didn't hear her. They were both too exhausted. Worn out from an extremely long day.

Angela's subconscious sent her on her usual path: she shuffled across the carpet, opened the bedroom door, and walked down the hall to her parents' room.

Only this wasn't her bedroom.

There was no parents' room down the hotel corridor.

Angela let the door glide shut behind her. She turned left, just like she would have done at home, and proceeded to walk down the long corridor.

She moved slowly. Silently.

Near the elevators, a cascade of ice cubes rattled down a plastic chute in the vending-machine room.

That woke her up.

The elevator bell pinged.

The doors slid open.

Angela's eyes went wide with terror.

89

"What are you staring at?"

The bad man stepped off the elevator in front of her.

Angela said nothing. She knew it had to be a nightmare. She wasn't really awake. She was still dreaming and that's why she was seeing the bad man whose picture her father had been looking at.

The bad man tried to smile. It was strange looking.

Angela stood frozen.

"Are you marching in the parade?" he asked her.

Angela didn't answer. She wanted this nightmare to be over. Now.

The bad man leaned in, whispered. "You better watch out."

Now he was grinning just like the horrible Santa did that other time when he'd bragged to Angela about all the horrible things he was going to do to her.

"I hear Times Square can be very dangerous."

The bad man laughed. Stepped away. Began walking down the hall.

Angela kept staring straight ahead, watched the elevator doors slide shut.

She felt a warm stream trickling down her thigh.

90

Christopher Miller woke up.

He glanced at the clock. It was in the wrong place. Had the wrong color digits. Then he remembered: he was in a hotel. It wasn't his alarm clock. It was some kind of Sony Dream Machine with too many damn buttons.

He was zonked. Wiped out.

No sleep last night. All the action out at JFK first thing in the morning. The balloon crowds. He wished he could be like that guy Jack on the TV show *24*. Go all day without ever needing a nap. Jack never even yawned or guzzled coffee. He just kept going like that battery bunny. Saved the world and maybe grew a little extra stubble on his chin.

Miller rubbed his eyes, looked over to the other bed.

It was empty.

"Angela?" he mumbled. "Angela."

He noticed light leaking in around the partially opened door.

He threw off the covers and headed into the hall.

91

"Angela!"

Her father's voice frightened her.

"Angela?"

He ran up the hall. Hugged her tight.

"Don't ever do that again! Please! You scared me!" He sounded mad.

"I'm sorry, Daddy."

He took her hand.

"Come on, Angel. Back to bed. This time, I'll put the chain on the door."

"Yes, Daddy."

She wouldn't tell her father anything. He'd probably only get madder if she told him about the bad man who told her to be careful in Times Square.

92

At 6 A.M. on Thanksgiving morning, the newspaper deliveryman rolled a luggage cart off the elevator coming up from the street.

It was stacked high with bundled copies of the *New York Times*, *USA Today*, the *New York Daily News*, the *Wall Street Journal*. He pushed the heavy cart into the empty lobby, paused near the reception kiosk, handed one copy of the *Times* to the night clerk.

"Thanks."

"Happy Thanksgiving."

"You, too."

The newspaperman grabbed a fistful of twine and unloaded the bundles. Bellmen would be clocking in soon. Their first task would be to take the newspapers upstairs, place them in front of doors.

The night clerk always liked to do a quick scan of the paper before his shift ended. He'd check out the front page, see if the world had blown up overnight, then he'd head off to the Sports section. After checking in on the Knicks, he'd move over to the Metro section and see if New York City had blown up overnight. Then he'd fold up the page with the crossword puzzle and work it on the subway ride home to Queens.

He never made it to the crossword page.

A picture in the metro section caught his eye.

FBI Seeks Terror Suspect read the headline next to it.

"Oh, shit."

He called 911.

93

Miller's cell phone started chirping at 6:33 A.M.

He looked at it with one eye open. The damn unprogrammable alarm clock was right behind it on the bedside table, big green letters letting him know just how early it was.

"Hello?"

"Chris? Charlie Lofgren."

Miller sat up. Swung his legs off the bed. Spoke softly so he wouldn't wake up Natalie or his Angel.

"What's up?"

"NYPD just called. Their 911 people have a lead on Schmitz."

"The car?"

"No. This is fresh intel. Somebody saw him."

"Where? In the city?"

"Yeah. Hotel clerk in midtown. Recognized the photograph in this morning's paper. Said Schmitz came down to his lobby early this morning for a toothbrush and a razor."

"Which hotel?"

"Place called the Novotel. Fifty-second and Broadway."

94

By 8:15 A.M., the Novotel lobby was swarming with NYPD and FBI.

Clumps of agents and officers pushed their way off the elevator coming up from the street while families pushed their way on for the quick ride down and an up-close view of the parade.

"Is anything wrong?" someone asked.

"Yeah!" answered a cop. "It's friggin' cold outside."

It was a decent cover story. All the cops were in the hotel to warm up. It seemed to work. Nobody wanted to panic the tourists.

Several agents, headed by the rookie Krishock, had set up a mobile communications center in an isolated conference room. The TV set in the wall unit was tuned to NBC, the network that would broadcast the Macy's Thanksgiving Day Parade live when it stepped off in less than an hour.

"I need some of your men stationed at both elevator banks," Miller said to an NYPD captain named Griffin. "You have his photograph?"

"Yeah. You sure he's still here?"

Miller nodded. "We checked the security tapes. He came down to the lobby a little after three A.M. Went back upstairs."

"What floor?"

"Couldn't tell."

"How long was the ride?"

Miller sighed. "We don't know. He covered the lens on the surveillance camera inside the elevator car."

"Spray paint?"

"No. Toothpaste. We did, however, check out the tapes from the lobby cameras from three A.M. on. He's only been down that one time."

"So he's up in his room. Which narrows it down to what?"

"Four hundred and eighty possibilities," said Miller. "Maybe we should lock this place down. No one in or out."

The New York cop grimaced. "You do that, you're gonna create a very ugly situation. Kids screaming. Parents yelling."

"They can watch the parade from the terrace," Miller suggested.

"Not all of 'em. Not enough room. Could be dangerous. Everybody pushing and shoving, leaning over the railing."

"Captain Griffin, we have reason to believe that Alexander Schmitz is armed with a military-issue Stinger missile. That could get dangerous, too."

"Yeah."

Both men remained silent for a moment. The captain said what they were both thinking.

"You want we should call off the parade?"

Miller rubbed his cheeks. Squeezed them hard. "Can that be done? Cancel the whole thing? Who would we need to talk to?"

The captain shrugged. "Not certain. I'll have my guys call the mayor's people. Talk to Macy's."

"Have them coordinate through Agent Krishock." Miller gestured toward the rookie, who was actually proving to be a valuable asset. Had all sorts of laptops, satellite phones, and field radios up and running in the conference room less than thirty minutes after he arrived on the scene. A real geek.

Krishock had even apologized to Miller.

"You were right to chase after this," he had said. For Krishock, that constituted an apology.

Miller's eyes darted to the TV set. Al Roker and the *Today* show were already broadcasting live from West Seventy-seventh Street and Central Park West, where the parade would begin.

"Have your people make the calls. Let's at least delay the start. If we take away his target, maybe Schmitz won't shoot. Might give us time to find him."

The captain motioned for a lieutenant. Gave him the unpleasant assignment.

"Get the mayor on the horn. We need to hold off on the parade. Maybe cancel the whole thing."

"You're kidding," said the lieutenant.

"Just do it."

The lieutenant shot instantly over to Krishock's communications command center.

"You want my guys to start going door to door upstairs?" the police captain asked Miller.

Miller checked his watch. "We're waiting on a warrant."

It was the police captain's turn to flick his wrist, check the time.

"No way a warrant's getting up here before nine. Not on a holiday."

"I know," said Miller.

"So what do we do?"

"What color is the Homeland Security Advisory right now?"

"In New York, it's always orange."

Miller nodded. "Okay. We should beef up security for the hotel chambermaids."

"You want my men going into rooms to make certain they're safe for the cleaning crew?"

"Yeah," said Miller. "Like I said, seems prudent. Seeing how we're at level Orange and all."

"Definitely," said Captain Griffin. "I'll have my SWAT guys take the steps up from the street. Don't want heavily armed ninjas in the lobby scaring people. They'll assemble one flight up on nine."

"Excellent. Once they're ready to roll, have them take the elevator to the top floor. Thirty-three. Sweep all the rooms with a view toward Broadway. Work their way down, floor by floor." Miller handed the captain a card key. "This will open any door in the building."

The cop took the card, shook his head. "I always figured it'd be the Arabs who hit us next. You know, Al Qaeda or whatever."

Miller nodded. Stopped. Something clicked.

"Al Qaeda," he mumbled.

The police captain saw the look on Miller's face. "What?"

"This guy's been following their playbook pretty tightly."

"How so?"

"It's like he read their manual."

"They have a manual?"

"More or less. British Intelligence found some of their documents on a computer in a London safe house. Had all sorts of guidelines on how to terrorize the West. Blast and destroy their places of amusement was one. They specifically mentioned parades."

"Jesus. So what else do you think he borrowed?"

"Their field-command structure. Al Qaeda operatives never work alone. They put together small teams of what they call brothers; each man is assigned a very specific task. Schmitz was the shooter but, most likely, he wasn't the field commander."

"You're telling me there're other terrorists running around town?"

Miller nodded. "At JFK, we know he had a backup crew of three."

"You know what these other guys look like?"

"Yeah. We picked them up on security cameras. The images are grainy."

"Any idea as to where these other brothers are currently located?"

"I'm guessing one of them has a room here," said Miller. "Schmitz was originally down the street at the Marriott Marquis. He checked out on Sunday, went to a different Marriott, left that one on Monday. Now he's here. How do you think he was able to find a room so close to the parade route on such short notice?"

"The other brother already had one booked! We need those photos."

"It'll take too long. Do any of your people draw?"

"What?"

"Can you find me a sketch artist?"

"Yeah. Sure. But you said you already got pictures of these other guys."

"We do. But I need the artist to draw something else. A woman on a horse. What they call a Valkyrie."

95

While the police artist worked up the sketch, Miller called Natalie on her cell.

She and Angela were down on the sidewalk, on Broadway between Fifty-second and Fifty-first. Angela wanted to be as close as possible to the parade. Wanted to shake hands with a clown, be right underneath the big balloons. Wanted to catch the real Santa's eye and blow him a kiss.

"Go back to the room," he told her.

"What's the matter, Chris?"

"We have reason to suspect that Schmitz is targeting the parade."

"Chris, I need to tell these other parents."

"Tell them the parade is being delayed."

"Is it?"

"Nobody's hauling a single balloon down Broadway until we have him in custody."

"Okay. I won't mention, you know, the threat. Just that I heard there were problems uptown."

"Good."

"Okay. We're heading in."

Miller closed up his phone.

"Captain Griffin?"

"Yeah?"

"How do we clear out those sidewalks downstairs?"

"Let's wait," the captain suggested. "We don't want to start a stampede."

"Captain?"

"It'll go much smoother when the parade is officially canceled. If nobody marches, your boy doesn't get his target and all those families go home—disappointed but alive. We try to move them out now, there'll be hell to pay. Panic. People crushing other people."

And if Schmitz didn't wait for the balloons and bands to strut their stuff down Broadway? If he just decided to take out a clump of spectators packed seven deep along the curb?

There'd be worse than hell to pay.

Miller had to find the Eagle. Now.

"This what you wanted?" The police sketch artist handed Miller his drawing of the Valkyrie.

"Perfect. Copy it. Give it to everybody who works here."

To find Schmitz, he had to find his pal who'd taken a room at the Novotel. Given all he had seen on this case so far, it was a pretty safe bet that the man would have a visible distinguishing mark.

A lady on a horse.

96

Alexander peered out the peephole in the hotel-room door.

It was fifteen minutes until 9 A.M. and the start of the parade. For over an hour, the hallway had echoed with the squeals of giddy children.

He went to the peephole to watch them.

"We're late!" said the mother. "Put on your mittens, Sam."

"It's too hot for mittens."

"It's cold out."

"I don't want to wear mittens."

"Put them on now," said the boy's father, "or none of us is watching the parade."

The kid pouted. Reluctantly pulled on his mittens.

Alexander smiled. They were a good white family. The mother was correct. The boy should put on his mittens. It was 28 degrees outside. The television said so.

Of course, when he was that age, no mother had ever reminded him to put on his mittens.

He felt his bald head go hot. He picked up a wet towel off the floor and used it to dab away the sweat. His head always perspired much more profusely immediately after shaving. A few beads trickled down his brow, straight between his eyes and down to his nose. His aviator glasses slipped slightly. He pushed the bridge with his forefinger and slid them back into place.

A black maid pushed a cart up the hall. It was loaded down with fresh linens, little soaps, and tiny shampoo bottles. The rolls of toilet paper stacked on top wobbled.

"You can clean our room now," said the little boy's mother. The maid nodded.

"All right," she said to the family. "Have fun now, hear?"

The kids giggled in excitement. They went to the elevator.

The maid went to their room.

Schmitz watched her pull out a card key. It was attached to the waist tie of her uniform with a coiled cord. She propped the door open with a rubber wedge. Went in to make the beds.

Schmitz grabbed his rolling golf bag. Pulled it down the hall.

Why not take the corner room with the even better view of Times Square? The family would be gone for the duration of the parade and the maid wouldn't pose any problem.

After all, Schmitz still had his pistol.

97

At 9 A.M., Al Roker of the *Today* show gave America the bad news.

"*Well, Matt—we've just received word that, because of heavy air traffic in and out of New York City, Santa's sleigh landing will be delayed this morning. And you really can't start the Macy's Parade without Santa Claus.*"

Angela sat on the edge of the bed watching the men on television explain why the parade wasn't starting when it was supposed to. Her mother had been sitting beside her. Now she was pacing over near the window.

"Don't worry, Mom," said Angela. "Santa's just running a little late."

"I know, honey. I know."

"*Meanwhile,*" said the television man named Matt, "*let's go down to Herald Square where the Broadway cast of the new Joseph Thalken musical is all set to do a number from their smash hit show!*"

Angela closed her eyes and said two prayers.

One for Santa, that he'd have a safe landing.

Another for her daddy. He had to go to work today. He never worked on Thanksgiving. But today he had to.

Somebody must be in trouble.

Angela prayed it wasn't her father.

98

"Room twenty-two eleven," said the bellman named Reggie.

"You sure?" asked Miller.

"Damn straight I am. I seen that tattoo on his arm when I took a tray of breakfast up there this one time."

The cops who had been showing the Valkyrie drawing to the staff had hustled Reggie into the conference room to speak directly with Special Agent Miller and Captain Griffin. Reggie was black. Looking at the drawing made him mad.

"Cracker had his head all shaved off bald and all. Came to his door in his boxer shorts. Had a good build. Cut, you know what I'm saying? That damn fat lady riding the pony was up on his guns." He tapped his biceps. "Room twenty-two eleven."

"You sure about the room number?"

"Hell, yeah. I memorized it on account of all the attitude he be giving me which I couldn't do nothing about at the time on account of I was wearing my uniform. Hoped to hook up with Mr. Twenty-two Eleven one day when I wasn't working."

Miller turned to Krishock.

"Where's the NYPD SWAT Team?"

Krishock glanced at a computer screen. "Thirty-second floor."

"Send them down to twenty-two eleven," said Captain Griffin. "Now. We've got the bastard."

"Roger that." Krishock relayed the orders to the SWAT Team Leader.

"Twenty-two eleven. Copy that," came the crisp response.

Miller stood up from his stool.

"I need to be upstairs."

Captain Griffin raised a hand. "Let the SWAT guys handle this."

"No. I need to be upstairs. My family is in room twenty-two-oh-two."

99

Dale Krishock could tell from the tracking program on his laptop that the SWAT units were in place.

They had Schmitz trapped in Room 2211.

"Dale?" one of the other agents called out, cupping his hand over a satellite phone mouthpiece. "It's the mayor."

"His office?"

"No. Him."

Krishock motioned for the agent to bring him the phone.

The other agent looked relieved.

"Mister Mayor? This is Special Agent Dale Krishock."

He let the mayor rant for a few seconds.

"Sir?" he interrupted. "We are confident we have our man. That's right. Sorry for the temporary delay, but, trust me, it was a necessary precaution. What? Yes, I believe so. You're good to go. Yes, sir. Happy Thanksgiving to you, too."

100

"Let's have a parade!"

The words echoed from the television set. Crowds cheered. Somebody in a top hat cut a ribbon. The black weatherman stepped aside.

The big turkey started rumbling down Broadway.

Finally, Alexander thought.

They were twelve minutes behind schedule.

He looked out the windows, down to Times Square. Whirlwinds of trash were swirling at the street corners. Of course. Wind delays. The gusts were too strong for some of the balloons. That explained it.

He looked over to the bed. The maid looked like she was kneeling beside it praying—only she had flopped forward and currently had her face buried in the bedspread. Blood seeped out of the single hole in her back. Every now and then, she whimpered or moaned a little. She wasn't dead, just dying. Fast. Alexander wouldn't waste another bullet on her sorry black ass. He'd just let the life slowly dribble out of her.

He turned back to survey his target and realized he would need to punch a hole through the window facing Times Square just prior to launch. He didn't want to do it too soon: a shower of glass sprinkling down on the sidewalk below might attract unwanted attention. Raise curious eyes.

He'd wait.

As soon as Santa appeared in Times Square, he'd smash out enough glass to create a firing port in the windowpane. He'd assume a kneeling position, take aim, fire, and forget.

He might linger at the window to admire the fireball ten blocks south. Then he would head to the fire exit. Make his way down the stairs to the street and flee the hotel by becoming just another scared tourist in the mob thrown into a frenzy by the horrible tragedy.

"And here's our live camera view from Times Square," he heard the TV say.

Wonderful.

His moment of ultimate glory would not go unnoticed.

It would go out live to millions.

101

"Natalie, I need you both to wait inside the bathroom until I call you on your cell."

"Where is he, Chris?"

"This floor."

"Come on, Angela." She prodded her daughter toward the bathroom door.

Angela pouted. Pointed toward the muted television glowing in the credenza. "The parade just started!"

"What?" Miller spun around, stared at the TV. Clowns on roller skates were zooming down the empty boulevard. The first big balloon made its way down Central Park West. A squad of police dogs followed it.

Miller yanked the handy-talkie off his belt.

"Agent Krishock?"

"This is Krishock. Go ahead."

"What the hell is going on?"

"The SWAT team is assembled on twenty-two, sir."

"No. The parade."

"The mayor insisted that since we have the suspect in custody—"

"We don't have anybody in custody!"

"Just a matter of time, sir. Not worth ruining everyone's holiday."

Miller realized he'd been wrong.

Krishock *was* an idiot.

He'd deal with it later.

Now, he hustled up the hall.

The SWAT team stood poised at the door.

The two men up front held riot shields. Eight more men were splayed out in symmetrical clusters on either side of the door. They had visors down, weapons drawn.

Miller reached around and pulled out his Glock.

The team leader looked to Miller.

Miller nodded.

The passkey went into the lock.

"Go!" the team leader screamed.

The ten men stormed into the room. One of the guys carrying a riot shield almost slipped when his boot hit a wet towel.

"Clear!" someone shouted.

Miller checked out the window. Nothing. Nobody.

The television was blaring from the credenza facing the bed.

"*. . . the NYPD search and rescue dogs. They look ready to take a bite out of crime. And here comes McGruff the Crime Dog—*"

"We have bodies," a SWAT cop yelled from the bathroom. "Two down. Male and female."

Miller peered over the shoulders of the men crowded in front of him. He could see the tattoo on the dead guy's upper arm quite clearly. It seemed brighter, more vivid than any of the others he'd seen so far.

Probably because the dead guy's skin was so white, drained of color.

Most of his blood was congealed in a thick pool on the floor.

102

Shit.

Alexander heard the commotion down the hall.

He switched off the TV. Tried not to breathe.

He tiptoed to the door, peeked through the peephole.

Jesus.

There had to be a dozen storm troopers in the corridor. Half were black, of course. Including the nigger who seemed to be in charge. Guy in casual clothes, like he'd had the day off but got called in to work at the last second.

They'd just raided the team leader's room.

Why? Security cameras out at JFK? Did somebody on the hotel staff ID the asshole team leader?

"He's changed locations," he heard the big black man say. "We need to resume our search upstairs. Go room to room, work your way down. Use extreme caution. Schmitz is heavily armed, gentlemen."

Shit. They know my name!

"Move fast, move smart. We only have ten minutes till the parade's right outside."

Alexander watched them tromp up the hall to the elevators and fire exits.

They were going upstairs to search the top floors while the head darkie stayed with a small team in Room 2211 to deal with the bodies.

Okay. Fine.

Ten minutes.

He could wait ten minutes. He would adjust his plan of attack. He could no longer wait for the tail end of the parade to reach Times Square.

He'd take out the first float to make it to Forty-second Street. The Stinger's infrared tracking could lock on the engine of the vehicle dragging it down the street. Times Square would become a sea of raging flames.

It would be spectacular.

Of course Alexander needed to accept the fact that this had, most likely, now become a suicide mission.

He'd get the shot off, blow up the float, score a thousand or more casualties, maybe top the World Trade Center death numbers, but the government goons down the hall would hear the weapon recoil, receive intel as to its point of origin, and, in a matter of seconds, burst through his door and take him out.

Fine.

Everybody had to die sometime. This was as glorious a way to go as any he could imagine. He would join his father in Valhalla.

It would be a good death.

And he had an advantage over the fools down on the street.

He knew his life would end in ten minutes. They did not.

He pulled the Stinger out of the case.

103

Natalie's phone chirped.

She snapped it open.

"Chris?"

"Stay where you are. We have not apprehended our suspect. We are now going room to room."

Natalie slumped down on the closed toilet seat.

"You starting on the top floor?" she asked. That's what she'd do.

"Right. We've already checked thirty-three and thirty-two. We'll fan out. Send two-man teams into every room with an easterly view toward Broadway. We need to get him before the parade gets here."

Natalie knew her husband didn't have much time. There was a radio in the bathroom. She and Angela had been listening to the parade simulcast.

"Radio said the first balloon just stepped off at Seventy-seventh Street."

"It's Blues Clues!" Angela shouted, trying to help out.

"I gotta run."

"Okay. Be careful, old man. Let the guys in riot gear take the point on this one."

"I love you."

"I love you, too."

Natalie closed up the phone.

"Is Daddy in danger?"

"Yes, honey. We all are."

"Tell him to stay out of Times Square."

"Why?"

"The bad man said Times Square can be very dangerous."

"What bad man?"

"The one in Daddy's briefcase. I saw him last night."

"Where?"

"On the elevator."

104

Miller closed up his cell, practically ripped the handy-talky off his belt.

Natalie had just relayed the news: their daughter had seen Schmitz!

"All units, concentrate on rooms at the southeast corner of the building. Repeat—suspect is most likely in a room facing south to Times Square."

If Angela had really seen "the bad man" during her sleepwalk, they were in luck: she had narrowed the search parameters considerably.

Tomorrow he'd have a word with Angela about not telling her parents important stuff—like when she saw a bad man lurking in her dreams.

Today, he'd just hope she'd been right.

One of the cops snapped on the TV.

"The Turkey just passed through Columbus Circle," he reported. "Looks like it's at Fifty-seventh Street."

The Turkey was always the first float in the parade. A celebrity sat on its back and waved to the crowds.

"Coming up," said the TV announcer, *"McGruff the Crime Dog. Plus the NYPD Canine Corps . . ."*

"We need one of those dogs!" said Miller. "Now!"

105

*"McGruff the Crime Dog. Plus the NYPD Canine Corps
. . ."*

Alexander had the television volume set to "1"—
nearly silent.

*"And making his way down Broadway to Times Square,
Tom Turkey!"*

He glanced at the screen. The Turkey was at least two
stories tall. A black couple, sacrilegiously dressed up like
Pilgrims, sat atop it. The giant gobbler's head bobbed.
Its wings flapped.

He mopped the sweat off the top of his head.

Nudged the tip of his rocket launcher against the
glass. Tapped it. Heard the ting.

When the time came, the firing tube would first serve
as a battering ram. He'd knock a hole through the
window. Take aim. Fire.

That made him smile.

Fire.

There'd be a lot of it when his warhead pierced the
gas tank of whatever vehicle was hidden underneath the
tail feathers.

Roast turkey.

106

Miller watched the NYPD dog handler wiggle the crumpled bath towel in front of the German Shepherd's nose.

The wet one they found on the floor when they first entered 2211.

The SWAT Team members were still working their way down the thirty-three-story hotel and had reached the twenty-seventh floor. No sign of Schmitz in any of the corner rooms.

"This is good," said the K9 Unit cop as he rubbed the towel around the dog's snout. "It's like your guy rubbed his scent all over this thing."

The German Shepherd wagged its tail. Stepped back from the towel. Started sniffing the floor.

"Can he track this guy?" asked Miller.

"Otto can track anything. Right, boy?"

The dog barked.

"We should take him up to the SWAT guys on twenty-seven," said Miller. "Have him sniff doorways. Might speed up our search."

The dog barked again. Louder. It wanted to go to work. Now.

"Come on," said Miller. "We'll take the elevator up to twenty-seven."

The dog handler clutched the towel, brought it with him, just in case they needed to remind Otto what smell he was searching for.

Miller and the Canine Unit cop hit the hall, turned left.

The dog turned right.

107

Alexander heard a dog barking outside his door.

Shit.

No time to wait.

Now he heard someone slamming against the door. Trying to break it down with their shoulder.

He automatically turned to look at the source of the sound. The sunglasses made it difficult to see inside the dim room after staring at the sunlit sidewalks.

He squinted.

Scanned the shadows.

Couldn't see the maid sprawled across the bed. She must've slid off. Probably dead on the floor.

"Schmitz!" someone yelled. "This is the FBI!"

Shit.

Time to rock and roll. Fuck the Turkey. Aim for the crowd.

He rammed the nose of the missile launcher against the glass.

It bounced off.

Another thud pounded against the door.

Alexander stood and took the Stinger off his shoulder. He gripped it at his hip with both hands, swung it like a battering ram.

Another bounce off the glass.

Damn.

Now he cradled the heavy steel pipe against his gut, wrapped both arms around it, reared back, and flung it forward with everything he had.

Glass shattered.

108

The damn door wouldn't budge.

Miller threw his body against it one more time.

The knob turned.

Somebody inside was letting him in.

He kicked at the door, held his Glock with both hands in front of his chest.

A scared hotel maid stared up at him from the carpeted floor, then tumbled sideways.

The snarling dog leaped over her body, charged into the room, went for the man standing near the window.

Miller aimed his Glock.

Schmitz spun around and aimed the Stinger at Miller's heart.

"Fucking nig—"

He didn't get to finish that thought.

Miller took him down with two pops to the chest.

109

Alexander Schmitz died.

The cleaning lady lived.

Sometimes things just worked out the way they should.

The paramedics already in the hotel with the SWAT Team were able to stabilize the hotel housekeeper, Stephanie Wilson. Before they rushed her off to the emergency room, she had regained enough strength to squeeze Miller's hand softly and whispered two words: "Thank you."

Three hours later, a little after noon, Miller joined his family down in the eighth-floor lobby. The parade was over at Fifty-second Street. Had been for almost an hour.

His two girls sat sipping hot cocoa in overstuffed chairs. The mobile command center had been dismantled in the conference room. Krishock had left the building.

Miller decided to worry about that one on Monday. Today was Thanksgiving and he had a whole lot to be thankful for.

"You missed the whole thing, Daddy!" said Angela when she finished hugging him.

Miller squeezed back hard.

"Did you see Santa?"

"We sure did," said Natalie. "We didn't miss much of the parade at all."

When Schmitz went down, Miller had phoned in an "all clear" to his family. Natalie and Angela had watched the parade from the Novotel's eighth-floor patio.

"Did you like the balloons?"

"Yep!" said Angela. "Blues Clues was the best. He was right at the beginning and we saw him!"

"And how about Santa?"

"He waved at me."

"Really? Right at you?"

Natalie nodded. "He did, indeed."

"He recognized me because he's the real Santa."

"I know."

"The reindeer pulling his sleigh were fake, though."

"Is that so?"

"Yep. But that's okay. Mommy said it was too warm for real reindeer to march in the parade so they stayed home at the North Pole where it's even colder than it is here."

"Makes sense," Miller said. He rubbed his shoulder. It hurt. Fifty-one was probably too old to be slamming his body up against steel. The steel always won.

"And you know what?" said Angela, hopped up on cocoa and sheer joy.

"What?" Miller creaked down into a squat so he could look his daughter in the eye.

"I'm not scared of that other Santa anymore. The mean one. He was just a bad man pretending to be something he really wasn't."

"That's right, Angel."

"Besides, if another bad man comes along, you'll always catch him like you did today, right, Daddy?"

"I'll try, Angel," he said. "I promise. I'll try real hard."

GIVING THANKS . . .

To Michele Slung, editor extraordinaire.

Eric Myers, super agent.

Tricia Clark and all the experts who so generously help authors get the details right through their online Yahoo group: weapons_info.

Fellow writer and former FBI Special Agent Rae Monet for helping me get that part right.

Don Weise, Wendie Carr, Sarah Coglianese, Will Balliett, Karen Auerbach, Shaun Dillon, Shana Smith, Linda Kosarin, Michele Martin, Lynn Mazur, Jamie McNeely Quirk, Lisa Roe, Ann Kirschner, and everyone at Avalon and Carroll & Graf who have been so supportive of my work.

Kathy, Dave, Herndon, Susan, Jennifer, Ronny, Lianne, Buffy, and all my "first draft" readers.

The Mercantile Library in midtown Manhattan for letting me borrow a writing desk and power outlet from time to time.

And J.J. Thanks to her, there's no place like home for the holidays.